B

ALSO BY MICHAEL HAMBLING

THE SOPHIE ALLEN BOOKS
Book 1: Dark Crimes
Book 2: Deadly Crimes
Book 3: Secret Crimes
Book 4: Buried Crimes
Book 5: Twisted Crimes
Book 6: Evil Crimes
Book 7: Shadow Crimes
Book 8: Silent Crimes
Book 9: Ruthless Crimes
Book 10: Brutal Crimes
Book 11: Hidden Crimes
Book 12: Vicious Crimes

Michael Hambling

BRUTAL CRIMES

Detective Sophie Allen Book 10

JOFFE BOOKS

Revised edition 2024
Joffe Books, London
www.joffebooks.com

First published in Great Britain in 2021

Cover art by Nick Castle

ISBN: 978-1-83526-897-1

FOREWORD

This is a work of fiction, and none of the characters and situations described herein bear any resemblance to real persons or events. Many of the locations do exist, however, and off the page, provide the bases for some first-rate walking breaks. Some parts of the Purbeck Hills are owned by the National Trust. Corfe Castle is at the centre of a network of footpaths and tracks in the area.

The reader may find the short glossary at the end of this book useful. It also lists the main ranks within the UK Police Force. You'll also find a brief introduction to some of the local food and drink.

CHARACTER LIST

Dorset Police Violent Crime Unit (VCU):
Detective Superintendent Sophie Allen
Detective Inspector Barry Marsh
Detective Sergeant Rae Gregson
Detective Constable Tommy Carter

Dorset Police uniformed officers:
Sergeant Rose Simons
Constable George Warrander

From Bournemouth CID:
Detective Sergeant Lydia Pillay
Detective Constable Jimmy Melsom

Other Dorset personnel:
Detective Sergeant Stu Blackman
Sergeant Greg Buller (in charge of the Fast Response Unit)
Dave Nash (County Forensic Chief)

Home Secretary in the UK government:
Yauvani Anand

The Birkbeck family (living on Woodside Farm near Norden)

To Margaret

PROLOGUE

The distant hoot of an owl, the flap of a wing and a sudden shaft of bright moonlight. The cloud cover seemed to be breaking up.

'Get a move on, Crustie. We ain't got all night.'

His companion continued to busy himself with the body that lay prone at their feet, poised at the top of a steep slope.

'I hate bent cops, Crustie,' the man went on. 'I mean, can you really trust 'em? Can anyone? Why become a cop in the first place if what you fancy's the high life? Know what I mean? There's always a bit of doubt in my mind when we use one of them fellas. What do they want? Why are they doin' it?' He prodded the corpse with the toe of his boot. 'Just like this 'un. What was going through 'is bonce? What made 'im turn on you-know-who and start making demands? What did he think would 'appen?'

Crustie, the taller of the two, stood up. The moonlight glinted silver on his bald head. 'Dunno. Never thought about it.'

'You sure he'll sink?'

Crustie scowled. 'Yeah. Them stones in all his pockets, those chains around his middle. He'll go down like he was made of lead.'

The first man nodded with satisfaction. 'Okay, then. Do it.'

He watched without much interest as his colleague put a foot onto the body and pushed. It rolled and slid quickly down the steep slope and out of view, entering the water with a satisfyingly loud splash.

'These old clay pits are deep,' Crustie said. 'He'll stay there at the bottom till the earth freezes over, like the other one. You can be sure o' that.'

'Couldn't give a toss, Crustie. Six months, that's all we need. C'mon, let's get moving.'

They walked away from the slope towards a narrow track through the woods. A third shadowy figure, tall and heavily built, emerged from a dark copse and joined them. The trio made their way along the muddy path that led back to the road and soon faded from view.

Ten long, silent minutes passed. With the merest rustle, a young girl slowly emerged from behind a dense clump of holly bushes. She looked about eleven or twelve and was short and slight. A shadow in the flickering moonlight, she crept forward to the crest of the slope, her wide eyes darting about her watchfully. She stood at the top of the slope, looking down, her limbs occasionally convulsing in nervous spasms. Then the moon went behind a cloud and she slipped back into the gloom, still shivering.

CHAPTER 1: LOST

Monday morning

Three of the four permanent members of Dorset's Violent Crime Unit were deep in conversation in their office at the county's police headquarters.

'It's decision time,' Superintendent Sophie Allen said. 'Tommy's completed his three-month trial period with us. So, do we make him permanent, or do we end it now and look for someone else?'

She looked at the other two and cocked her head to one side. Her short blonde hair glinted in a sudden ray of sunlight that burst in through the window. She was middle-aged and middling in height, with a slight West Country accent that had been blunted by spells in London and the Midlands.

'Who would we get if we decided not to keep him?' tall, dark-haired Detective Sergeant Rae Gregson asked. 'That has to have a bearing on our decision, surely, ma'am?'

Sophie shrugged. 'I don't know. That's assuming we get anyone. The bottom line is this. If we decide we don't want to retain him, we could end up with no one.'

Detective Inspector Barry Marsh frowned. 'Look, surely there are positive reasons for keeping Tommy on? I know we had our doubts at first but as far as I'm concerned, he's turned out better than I expected. And he's keen to learn.'

'I agree,' Rae said. 'He may be a bit slower than I'd like, but he's willing to get stuck in. He's come on no end in the past three months. Personally, I've no wish to dump him and then find his replacement is lazy or inept. Or we can't find anyone. That would put me back at the bottom of the pecking order, and I don't like being the tea-girl.' She smiled.

'Well then, that settles it. But it has to be your decision, not mine. You're the ones working with him on a day-to-day basis. If you're happy, then I'm happy. Off the record, I wasn't sure at first, but I have to say he's impressed me more as time's gone on. I think he's shaping up well.' She looked around the office. 'Where is he, by the way? Isn't he usually in by now?'

Rae shrugged. 'You're right. Maybe the traffic's bad on the road from Bere Regis.'

They went through the rest of the agenda items and settled down to work. The county had seen a significant upsurge in the theft of expensive cars, and the police were struggling to cope. Detective Constable Tommy Carter, the Violent Crime Unit's junior officer, had been lending a hand at the Stolen Vehicle Unit in Poole. He was a car enthusiast and had been enjoying his Wednesdays and Thursdays there. But today was Monday.

Rae and Barry were tidying up the paperwork from their last major case and reviewing the evidence needed in court. Mid-morning came and went, and still no Tommy. Rae became fidgety. She kept glancing at the clock. 'I'll phone again,' she said.

The call went to voicemail.

She frowned. 'Where can he be? This is so unlike him.'

Barry checked with the traffic division. There were no reported incidents or delays on any of the county's roads. He too was perplexed. He ran his fingers through his ginger hair, a sure sign that he was worried. Then Sophie reappeared.

'There's a missing person report out,' she said. 'And it's an unusual one. A twelve-year-old girl went missing last night. The family live on a farm near Stoborough, just outside Wareham, so I feel a bit of a personal connection since I live in the area. Apparently, she's deaf, so she's classified as vulnerable. I'm heading off to get the details. Any word from Tommy?'

Barry shook his head. 'Nothing. We were just wondering whether to contact his girlfriend.'

'Good idea. Her name's Olivia, isn't it? Do you have her number?'

'No, but she's a nurse in Poole. She shouldn't be difficult to find.'

'Okay. I'll be back around midday. Let's hope he appears before then.'

Rae phoned Poole hospital to contact Tommy's partner but found that Olivia was unable to take the call because of a ward emergency. The receptionist took a message and said he'd pass it on to her. Nearly twenty minutes passed before Rae's phone rang. She explained the reason for her concern to Olivia.

'I'm a bit worried, to be honest,' Tommy's girlfriend said. 'He didn't phone last night, so I assumed he'd been called out on an emergency. But if that's not the case, then where is he?'

'We don't know. When did you see him last?' Rae asked.

'Saturday night. I've been on early shifts since then and I was really tired yesterday, so I didn't see him. He's meant to be coming to mine this evening. I'm getting anxious.'

Rae could hear Olivia's voice start to quaver.

'Listen, I'm sure there's no need to worry, Olivia. There'll be a logical explanation. Did he say what he intended to do yesterday? He wasn't on duty.'

'He just said he'd see how the weather turned out.'

'Leave it with us. I'll get back to you, I promise.'

'Please tell me when you find where he is. I've got a key to his place in Bere if you need one.'

Rae turned to face Barry, a troubled look on her face. 'This is so unlike Tommy. Is there anything we can do?'

Barry frowned. 'Look, this stuff we're working on can wait. Let's drive over and have a look. Maybe we can pick up that key from Olivia. But we'll keep it quiet for now.'

'Thanks, boss. I'm worried about him. I never thought I'd feel maternal about one of my work colleagues, but in Tommy's case, I do.'

Barry gave her a sidelong glance. 'Maternal? Someone of his age? You're not going middle-aged on me, are you, Rae?'

'Well, you know what I mean. It's that "little boy lost" look he has.'

* * *

Sophie walked into Wareham's small police station and waved to the receptionist, a fellow member of the local keep-fit club.

'I thought I'd just check up on this missing person case, Jill.'

'They're up in the office. Shall I call to let them know you're here?'

Sophie hesitated. This was an entirely unofficial visit on her part. But she didn't want to cause any friction by deliberately ignoring protocol. 'Okay. But tell them it's only for a quick chat, nothing heavy.'

She climbed the stairs to the small CID room, taking her time. She knew the small local squad well, having chipped in a significant amount towards the purchase of their coffee machine the previous year. Pete Saunders, the local detective sergeant, was deep in conversation with his DC, Laura O'Connell. He looked up as Sophie came in.

'Morning, ma'am,' he said. 'You're here about the missing girl, Jill said. Drink?'

'Coffee, if you're making. I just want to check on the details. Any news?'

He shook his head. 'Amy Birkbeck. She's twelve and suffers from complete hearing loss, though she has implants. That makes it difficult for the search teams because, according to her parents, she sometimes switches them off. They also told us she's keen on wild animals. She keeps bat boxes in the woods and sometimes goes off at night to watch for bats and owls. She did that yesterday but never came back. We're just here to pick up a few extra bits and pieces.'

Sophie walked across to the map that was spread out on the table. It was divided into search zones, with a letter code allocated to each area.

'Norden Woods?' she asked.

Pete nodded. 'The parents have a small farm just outside Stoborough, butting up against the woods. Nice family. There's a young boy as well as Amy. He's still a toddler, though. We've talked to them, and the family life seems above board. No one raised any suspicions.'

'I don't want to get officially involved, Pete. Leastways, not at this stage. I only came across to make sure you've got access to everything you need.'

'Yes. It helps that she's classified as vulnerable. It speeds up the process.'

Sophie walked across to the incident board and examined the details. The girl might be twelve, but she certainly didn't look it. She was thin and wan, and looked two years younger.

'The parents say she's tougher than she looks,' Laura said. 'She spends a lot of her free time outside, wandering about in the great outdoors, come rain or shine. Apparently, she knows everything there is to know about those woods, all the paths and tracks, and also the dangerous spots.'

'You mean the old, flooded clay pits?' Sophie asked.

'That's right. Some of her bat boxes are nearby apparently.'

Sophie frowned. 'Let's hope it doesn't come to dredging them.'

'I want to give it the rest of the day before we escalate it to that level,' Pete said. 'The parents said she's often off all day, though she's not stayed out at night before.'

Sophie took a sip from her mug. 'Good stuff.'

Pete smiled. 'Of course it is, ma'am. You more or less paid for the machine. One visitor said it was the best office coffee they'd ever tasted.'

Sophie laughed. 'I'm on a one-woman crusade to improve the palates of Dorset police personnel. I had to make a start somewhere, and why not at my local nick? Just in case I'm ever incarcerated here.'

'Oh, we don't give it to anyone in the cells,' Laura said. 'They just get the usual rubbish.'

'You're a cruel lot. Listen, are you just about to head back to the search? If so, could I tag along?'

* * *

Barry slotted the key into the lock and opened the door to Tommy's compact flat in the small village of Bere Regis. It was surprisingly tidy, with all his books, magazines and similar items put away neatly on shelves.

'Have you been to his place before, Rae?' Barry asked.

She shook her head. 'We had him and Olivia across at mine for a meal a few weeks ago on a weekend when Craig was staying over. We hadn't got around to organising a return visit, but Olivia said one was in the offing, though it wasn't clear whether it'd be here or at her place in Poole. She sounded really worried just now, didn't she?'

'I'm not surprised,' Barry said. 'To be honest, I am too. It's so unlike him. If he doesn't appear soon, we'll have to start an official search.'

They looked through the flat but could find nothing amiss. Tommy's car was still outside, parked in its designated spot. Barry scratched his head, causing a few tufts of ginger hair to stick up.

'I'm really not happy with the situation,' he finally said. 'Do you have any idea of his hobbies? Could he be off somewhere with a football team or anything?'

Rae shrugged. 'He doesn't say much about himself, to be honest. When they came over that evening, it was Olivia who did most of the talking. She's a lovely person. I think he idolises her. They've only been going out for a month or two. As for being away on some trip or other, the answer's no. Not Tommy. He wouldn't do that without telling me in advance and asking for time off. Anyway, he doesn't seem remotely interested in team sports of any kind.'

'Okay. I think we need to escalate our search. We can start with his family and see if they know anything. The chances are he was off somewhere for the weekend and forgot to tell anyone, and he's just got delayed on a late train. Let's see if his family know — if we can find a phone number for them.'

Like most people these days, Tommy didn't seem to have an address book. Presumably he kept a note of all his contacts on his mobile phone. Barry shook his head in frustration.

They drove back to Poole hospital and managed to catch Olivia as she came off shift. She was clearly even more troubled now than when they'd seen her in the middle of the morning, so they agreed to call Tommy's mother in Weymouth.

The phone call yielded little, other than causing his mother, Victoria, to start worrying too. She hadn't heard from her son since the middle of the previous week and had no idea where he could be.

Olivia told the two detectives that she'd only met Victoria once but that she'd be happy to call on her that afternoon if necessary. The two detectives left, promising to keep Olivia informed of any progress.

Rae was frowning as they made their way to the car. 'I'm not sure this has been one of our most successful trips, boss. All we've done is make two people anxious.'

'That was bound to happen, Rae. We did what had to be done. To be honest, they're not the only ones. Where could he have got to?'

* * *

Woodside Farm occupied an idyllic spot between the village of Stoborough and the hamlet of Norden. Sophie climbed out of her car and joined the two local detectives. She looked at her surroundings. The wooded slopes of the western Purbeck Hills loomed on one side, with the ruins of Corfe Castle on the other. In summer, the area would be crawling with tourists, but in mid-January, a week after the New Year celebrations had died down, it was an entirely different matter. January was the only month when the nearby steam railway was silent, while maintenance work was carried out on the most picturesque heritage line in the country. The farm buildings were set out around a central courtyard with the house occupying the north-facing side. This meant that the rooms on the other side of the house faced south, overlooking a sunny garden.

The three of them walked towards the door. It was opened before they reached it, and an obviously anxious couple stood on the doorstep. Geraldine Birkbeck was wringing her hands. She looked haggard. Andy Birkbeck had his arm around her waist. He looked rigid and under strain. His face was even more pinched than that of his wife. Both looked pleadingly at Pete as he approached.

He shook his head. 'Still no news. But the search teams haven't finished the first sweep of the woods yet. We're just about to re-join them. This is Superintendent Allen, by the way.'

Sophie shook their hands. 'We're doing all we can. Search and Rescue teams from Wiltshire and Hampshire have just arrived, so things should speed up now we've got all the personnel we need. DS Saunders here has told me you've already searched the farm. Are there any places you could have missed, do you think?'

Both parents shook their heads. 'We knew how thorough we had to be,' Geraldine said. 'And she wouldn't hear us calling out. No, we've triple-checked all her possible hidey-holes.'

'Does Amy have many hiding places, then?' Sophie asked.

'Only a couple on the farm, but she might have some in the woods that we don't know about. She uses hides when she's on the lookout for owls and things,' Geraldine said.

'Does that mean she could avoid discovery if she wasn't sure who was out there? Deliberately, I mean?' Sophie asked.

'It's possible.' Addressing the two local detectives, Geraldine said, 'There is something I spotted since you were here earlier. Yesterday, I baked a batch of buns and there are two missing. Amy must have taken them before she went out last night. The thing is, she's never left the farm before, not at night. Our boundary butts up against the woods and she's been told not to go any further after it gets dark. Amy's fiercely independent though. She's always been the same, ever since she was little. She sees her deafness as a challenge.'

'She sounds a lovely kid.' Sophie looked at her watch. 'I'll go and speak to the search leader, Greg Buller. He'll be co-ordinating things. I've known him a long time, and if anyone can find her, he can. Then I'll need to go to HQ for a short while, but I'll be back this afternoon.'

* * *

'Is something else going on, ma'am?' Pete asked as they went back to the cars.

'Unfortunately, yes. One of our officers has vanished.'

Pete looked at her. 'Bloody hell. Two mispers at the same time.'

'We haven't started an official search yet. I just hope it doesn't come to that and he turns up. We've got to be prepared though.'

'I don't envy you.'

'You're not the only one, Pete. I don't envy myself either.'

CHAPTER 2: FOUND

'We need to go back, Rae — to Tommy's flat, I mean. I've been on the phone to one of his neighbours and she told me there's a row of sheds out the back. You can't see them from the flat.' Barry and Rae had eaten a hurried lunch of sandwiches at the local police station. It was a tense time. Barry had yet to declare their colleague Tommy Carter an official missing person. Consequently, there was still no formal search in progress, although most of the local police personnel not on other duties or involved in the search for Amy Birkbeck were out looking for the young detective. If there was no information by mid-evening then the declaration would be made, and the current low-key enquiries would be ramped up.

'So, does Tommy have a shed?' Rae said.

'Apparently, yes. Even Olivia was barely aware of it, but they've only been going out for a month. She hasn't been to his flat more than a few times, and I imagine that when she was there, the existence or not of sheds and outhouses wouldn't have been at the forefront of their minds.'

Rae managed a smile, the first for an hour. 'I did say he seemed besotted with her, didn't I? He's landed on his feet there, boss. She seems like such a lovely person.'

It only took a few minutes to reach the small block of flats and find the neighbour. She told them that she'd seen Tommy with an off-road bicycle on two or three occasions.

Rae hurried back into Tommy's flat and sorted through the keys hanging on a row of hooks under one of the kitchen cupboards. 'I think this must be it. It's got that clunky outhouse look to it.'

She followed Barry out of the back door. A row of small sheds sat alongside the communal drying green, each bearing the number of a flat on its door. Rae opened the door of Tommy's. It was empty, apart from a small rotary lawn mower and what looked to be several boxes of assorted junk.

'His bike's not here,' Rae said. 'Maybe he goes cycling in his spare time.'

'Why didn't we know this?' Barry said. 'Why didn't Olivia, come to that?'

'Maybe he never talked about it. Let's face it, boss, Tommy can be really shy at times. He doesn't ever talk much about himself.'

Barry was frowning. 'I spotted a local trail guide on a shelf in his living room when we were here earlier. I didn't think much of it at the time. Maybe we should take another look.'

The trail guide covered the whole of the county and listed the best cycling routes. The booklet didn't look as though it had been heavily used, except for one page that was somewhat dog-eared. It had a map of the area around Bere and southwards towards Bovington Heath, along with information about a network of country lanes, bridleways and tracks.

It only took Barry a second or two to decide. 'Let's go. I'll inform the local uniformed bods what we're up to since they've already started some discreet enquiries. We'll tell the local CID later, and only if we need to. They'll all be involved in the other search — the missing girl — and that takes priority. There'll only be one or two people spare if we do need to organise something a bit more formal.'

'Not Stu Blackman, please. He might have missing person experience — if you can call it that, considering the disaster he nearly created a couple of years back — but you know what I think about him.' She rolled her eyes.

Barry grimaced. 'Yes, well, we all have our feelings about Stu, Rae. You've just got to lower your expectations when working with him. Anyway, let's hope it doesn't come to a formal search.'

Rae refrained from mentioning the way Stu still leered at her whenever they met. He'd made her feel nauseous on numerous occasions when she'd still been a lowly DC. He'd never made any overt comment about her being trans, but he hadn't needed to. His face said it all. Thank God he no longer outranked her. Now she could needle him in her turn, paying him back for all those times when she'd been forced to bite her lip at both his creepy attitude and his lazy incompetence.

* * *

They made their way around the country lanes south of Bere Regis in a police Land Rover, which they'd taken in case they needed to check some of the bridleways and off-road farm tracks. Both detectives had binoculars, and they scanned every path and track that a cyclist might use, all to no avail.

Rae consulted the map. 'If he was out this way, he might have used the track north of Cloud's Hill to get back.'

Barry took the Land Rover in another sweep, this time past a heavily wooded area. The bridleway reached a narrow lane that curved tightly away down a slope near a rough entry point to the woods. Suddenly, Barry drew to a halt. He'd spotted skid marks on the road surface.

The two detectives climbed out and looked at the tarmac, then at the low bank at the edge of the track. Rae hurried across.

'Boss, he's here!' she shouted.

Tommy was lying on his side in an overgrown, shallow ditch. His eyes were closed, his face deathly pale. A badly damaged bicycle could be seen a few yards further on, bits of it poking out of a patch of scrawny brambles. They crouched down beside Tommy and Rae felt for a pulse.

'It's there, but very weak,' she yelled to Barry, who was already running back to the Land Rover to use its radio. Precious minutes might be saved by using the on-alert police system rather than a mobile phone. When he'd logged the emergency call, he looked again at the marks on the road. They bore all the signs of a sudden collision on the tight bend. If that was the case, had it been a hit and run? It had to be. No driver could possibly be unaware that they'd hit a cyclist on that road.

An ambulance was with them within ten minutes, along with several more police vehicles.

'What do you think?' Barry asked the senior paramedic as Tommy was stretchered into the back of the ambulance.

She pursed her lips. 'I'm not committing myself. It'll be touch and go, I can say that. Just keep your fingers and toes crossed.'

Barry phoned Sophie with the news, then waited until the RTA forensic specialists arrived. He and Rae then drove west to the county hospital at Dorchester. They were soon joined by Olivia, who looked desperately unnerved.

'You say it was a hit and run?' she said.

'Looks like it,' Barry replied. 'I've checked the log of emergency calls and there's been nothing about a collision with a cyclist. Whoever hit him must have known they had. The lane's narrow and twisty at that point, so the bike would have directly impacted the front of the vehicle. But we'll wait and see what the experts have to say. You haven't contacted his mum yet, have you?'

Olivia shook her head. 'I don't know what to say to her. Everything's happening so fast. My head's reeling.'

'That's fine, Olivia. Better you leave it with us. I'll phone with the news and Rae can stay here with you. I'll offer to collect her and bring her back here.'

* * *

Sophie, Barry and Rae were all present in the waiting area, along with Olivia and Tommy's mother, when a doctor appeared.

'He's stable,' she said. 'He was lucky. Or maybe it wasn't luck, but rather how fit he was. Anyway, whatever the reason, he didn't suffer as much in the way of internal injuries as we feared. He's got a couple of broken ribs and a fracture of his right tibia, but it was clean, so it should mend well. Concussion, but we think it's not too serious. No significant organ damage.'

'Thank God,' Tommy's mother said. Olivia squeezed her hand.

All three of the detectives visibly relaxed.

'How long do you think he'll be kept in?' Olivia asked.

The doctor shrugged. 'Difficult to say at the moment. We'll keep him in intensive care for a couple of days just as a precaution. Then, if all's well, we'll shift him to a general ward.' She left the room.

'I'm just so relieved,' Olivia said. She sat down suddenly. 'I feel faint and all mixed-up.'

'Tea or coffee all round, I think,' Sophie said. 'And just to help you feel more positive, you probably know that Tommy's probationary period with us is up soon. We've decided to keep him on permanently but haven't had a chance to tell him yet. We wouldn't normally inform you first, but in the circumstances . . . well.'

'Oh, wow, thank you. I know he was worried about it. He was sure he wasn't good enough. He'll be over the moon.' Olivia looked momentarily thrilled.

'Please don't mention it to him when he comes round or spread it further. We'll be back in a couple of days to let him know officially.'

Sophie made her goodbyes and walked out into the corridor, followed by her two juniors.

'They'll be sending us photos of his injuries,' Barry said. 'And the doctor will talk us through the likely scenarios once she's had time to gather her thoughts. What now, ma'am?'

Sophie thought for a moment. 'Maybe Rae can drive Tommy's mother home, then meet us over at Norden. You and I, Barry, are going to join the search team for the missing girl. Something about it is making me uneasy, but I can't put my finger on it.'

* * *

It was late afternoon. Geraldine Birkbeck had been out with the search teams along with her husband, Andy. They had brought their young son, Alex, who had been sitting on his father's shoulders for much of the time. He'd grown tired and restless, understandable in a four-year-old who had no idea what was going on. The family were now back at the farm. Andy needed to get their small herd of cows milked. The interruption to their normal routine had already caused obvious discomfort to the beasts, judging by the loud bellows that had echoed across the woods. While Andy had headed for the pasture to move the impatient cows into the milking shed, Geraldine had taken Alex into the kitchen for a glass of milk and a biscuit. She was just putting the milk back in the fridge when she spotted something odd.

Geraldine stood stock still. She looked at the plate of chicken legs again, counting them carefully. There were only six. She'd cooked eight of the things that morning, allowed them to cool and then popped them into the fridge, ready for a quick cold meal that evening. Chicken drumsticks were Amy's favourite, especially when cooked in barbecue sauce, even if it was the middle of winter. And two were gone.

Geraldine ran upstairs to Amy's bedroom, but there was no one there. Every other room was empty, with no sign of anything out of place. She returned to Amy's room and opened the top drawer of the dressing table. A thick pink jumper was missing. Geraldine rushed back to the kitchen and looked in the cake tin. Several more buns had gone.

Had Amy been back? She must have been. Sneaked in, taken the food and the clean sweater, and then crept out again. But why? Part of Geraldine's problem was that she had never formed the sort of understanding with her daughter that Andy had. The two of them were often to be seen marching round the farm, Amy trotting happily alongside her father. Amy never followed her. Geraldine felt much closer to Alex. Was it Amy's deafness? It certainly created a communications barrier between them, although Andy didn't appear to have any trouble. He and his daughter seemed to have an instinctive understanding.

Amy's severe deafness had resulted from an attack of meningitis when she was still a baby. Cochlear implants had meant that she had gained a basic level of hearing and had learned to listen carefully and speak, but she'd always known she was different to everyone else at school, particularly since the age of seven, when children start to notice individual traits. Not that any of Amy's close friends had ever made an issue of her hearing difficulties or the small units tucked behind her ears. In any case, they were mostly hidden by her long, fair hair. And the encouragement she'd received both from other children and from the county support team had been second to none. But Amy was fiercely independent and often deliberately switched her implants off. 'I like the quiet,' she sometimes said.

After checking through the house again, Geraldine ran to the milking shed to give her husband the news. He sank to his knees, his head in his hands.

'Thank God,' he said. 'But why? Why sneak in, take food and go away again? What's going on in her head?'

'I don't know. I just don't know,' Geraldine said. She threw her arms around her husband and burst into tears.

She left Alex with Andy in the milking shed and hurried across to the police search team van parked, along with a cluster of other vehicles, in the driveway. A few police personnel were gathered around a map, though most were away in the woods, searching for Amy. Geraldine noticed that the senior detective was back, talking to the search co-ordinator. What had she said his name was? Greg? They looked up as she approached. How could she best explain this to them?

'Has something happened, Geraldine? You look a bit flustered,' the detective said.

'Umm, well, yes. Sort of.' She explained her discovery of the missing food and the sweater.

'Was the house securely locked?' Greg asked.

'Yes, absolutely. I had to unlock the door to get in just now.'

'You don't keep a spare hidden somewhere that someone else might know about?'

'We have a key-safe, as you've already spotted. The thing is, Amy has her own key. She got one when she started at secondary school. Anyway, it has to be her. Nothing else is missing, just the chicken from the fridge, two more buns and the sweater.'

'Why would she do this? Could there be a possible problem at home that has upset her?' the detective asked.

Geraldine shook her head vigorously. 'No, honestly. Amy was as happy as Larry yesterday evening when she went out to check the bat boxes and do some owl spotting. Something must have happened, but I can't think what.'

'And we won't know till we find her,' the detective said. She sounded authoritative. 'In a way, this does alter the approach we need to take. Greg's been looking for a missing child, but from what you say, we're really looking for a child who's hiding. Greg? Any thoughts?'

The tall, burly search leader frowned. 'So far, we've been looking at ground level, searching in bushes and hollows, that kind of stuff. What if she's up a tree?'

'That wouldn't surprise me at all,' Geraldine said. 'She climbs like a monkey.'

CHAPTER 3: AMY

Amy had known the woods all her life and had always thought of them as her friend. She had started by exploring the copses close up to the farm boundary when she was still small. Later, she found the denser areas deep in the interior — the dark, cool, dank places that people rarely visited. And those still, inky black pools of water. Her parents told her to stay away from them, that they were dangerous, but they held a strange fascination for her. Their steep, muddy slopes led down to water that looked as though evil monsters might lurk beneath the surface. According to her dad, they were old clay workings of unknown depth. The trouble was, the area near the pools was the best place for watching woodpeckers during the daytime. They could be heard hammering away at half-rotten bark, trying to dislodge insects and grubs. And then there were the owls at night. They liked to perch on a couple of long bare branches that reached out across the water. It had always been a magical place — until yesterday evening. Now it was tainted. Amy was petrified by what she'd seen. But what had she seen? Had it really happened? Could she have imagined it? Remembering it still made her shudder.

She'd spent the rest of the night curled up in one of her little dens, and the day hidden in a fork in a tall beech tree. She'd discovered it three years ago and it was one of her favourite places in the woods. It was such a huge tree that the fork was big enough to make a great den that was just about invisible from the ground. She'd made a small shelter out of branches and a few small planks to keep the worst of the rain off, not that it was raining today. As the day wore on, she heard more voices and whistles. She'd peeped out and spotted groups of people with long sticks, probing the undergrowth. They were looking for her, she knew. But she wasn't ready, not yet. How could she explain it? They'd laugh at her, at her odd way of talking. Her dad would be fine, but Mum would be angry with her for staying out this long. She'd be told to stay in her room and not go out, even though it wasn't her fault. It's not your fault when you see something wrong going on, is it? Something horrible that makes you hide.

She'd turned off her hearing implants for much of the time. The sounds of all those people down below, calling, frightened her. The silence was better. The food had helped too. She'd slipped back through the trees after the search party had passed by and crept into the house when no one was looking. She was sure it was going to be colder tonight, the sky was clear. That's why she'd taken another jumper as well as the food. She ought to be warm enough now, with the jumper and her thick parka on.

She saw movement in the distance, shrank back and switched her implants back on. Voices. Her mum's voice, her dad's, both calling her name. Other voices. She saw her parents. Alex was with them. Amy started to cry. It was all too much. She didn't want to stretch her arm out and wave, but she did want to as well, both at the same time. Why was she so confused? She leaned out for a closer look and dislodged a dead branch. It fell to the ground, landing with a crash in a patch of dry bracken.

* * *

Amy refused to talk. Her dad asked her gently, her mum less so. But Amy said nothing. She was hot with embarrassment.

All these people watching her, wondering about her, talking about her. She just wanted to slip away and disappear again. She sipped at her cup of warm cocoa, nibbled another fruit bun, stared at the floor in front of her and swung her legs. Her favourite chair in the kitchen was just a little too high to allow her feet to touch the floor, but it had her own cushion to sit on, the one she'd made in class when she was back in primary school.

The police people finally left, saying they'd be back tomorrow. She had a warm bath, another bun. She still didn't speak.

She went to bed, snuggled down and finally fell asleep. She slept soundly for several hours then woke up with a start. She'd dreamed of a body being rolled down a steep slope into deep water. Sobbing again, she went into to her parents' room and slid into their bed beside them. Her mum opened her eyes and put her arm around her. Amy finally started to talk.

* * *

Back at county headquarters the three detectives were tidying up their office before heading home for the evening. They were all tired, barely suppressing their yawns, when a call came though. Sophie listened and jerked upright.

'You're joking,' she said.

The call continued for a few more seconds, and then she replaced the receiver. She looked at the other two, who were both ready to leave, and shook her head in exasperation.

'That was Matt Silver. Apparently, Stu Blackman has gone missing. He was meant to be with Blandford CID today but never turned up.'

'Are we needed?' Barry asked.

'Not yet. Let's go home, get ourselves fed, watered and rested and be ready for whatever tomorrow throws at us.'

CHAPTER 4: THE BODY IN THE POOL

Tuesday morning

Theresa Jackson was a sergeant now, with a wide range of responsibilities. But she was still the best family liaison officer in Dorset police. Sophie found the way Theresa managed to strike up a relationship of trust so easily, particularly with youngsters, quite uncanny. She'd spotted it years ago when Theresa had managed to win over a traumatised girl who'd discovered a child's body buried in her garden. Young people could just relate to Theresa and form a bond with her. Why? How? It was impossible to say. But it looked effortless.

Here Theresa was, sitting in the kitchen of the Birkbecks' farmhouse, sipping at a cup of tea, nibbling at a currant bun and talking calmly to Amy. It was like watching a magician's stage show — so smooth, so unforced.

'Was there anything else, Amy? Anything you think we should know? It's our job to catch these criminals, remember.'

The girl was swinging her legs again. 'No. That's all.'

Sophie smiled at the girl and went outside into the chilly farmyard. Greg Buller had just arrived, complete with search personnel and several vanloads of kit.

‘A body,’ Sophie said. ‘In the nearest of the pools. Weighted down with rocks and chains. That’s what she says. Two men arrived, carrying a body-shaped object, then dumped it in the water. Then they left, along with a third man who must have been keeping watch. We need to retrieve the body but try to maintain the location’s integrity for a forensic sweep. Though God knows how many pairs of feet trampled across the area yesterday during the search for her.’ She rolled her eyes.

Greg looked at her, eyebrows raised. ‘Do you think . . . ?’

She sighed. ‘Yes. Possibly. Probably. Almost definitely, in fact. The girl thinks she caught the words “bent cop,” or so she says. Let’s assume she heard right, though we need to remember her poor hearing. Who else could it be? I thought he was just lazy and inefficient. We all did. I also thought there was a chance he’d turn out all right once he got out from under the shadow of the late and odious Phil McCluskie.’ She paused. ‘Maybe it’s better not to speculate at this stage. It’s always possible that just as you’re pulling the body out of that stinking pool of watery sludge, the handsome and fragrant Stu Blackman will wander into Blandford nick and cheerfully report for duty a day late. And I’ll be left with egg on my face.’

Greg laughed. ‘That ain’t gonna happen, is it?’

‘No. I’m too much of a bloody pessimist, that’s my trouble. Optimism just doesn’t work for me. Like taking him seriously a couple of years ago when he said he’d turned over a new leaf. Rae, on the other hand, was never convinced. She says he had a way of looking at her that made her flesh crawl. She felt she had to stay quiet about it because he was a senior officer. Barry was going to have a word with him. Too late now, eh?’

They consulted the map, climbed aboard the vehicles and headed off towards the site. A track branched off some two miles further on that looped around and approached the pool from the far side. Greg wanted to get the vans as close to the scene as possible — underwater retrieval gear was too heavy to lug for miles along narrow woodland paths. But first, they'd need to check that particular track for signs of recent use. There was no other way that a body as heavy as Stu Blackman's could have been brought to the pool.

It took less than an hour for the forensic squad to examine and record the damp surface. A set of tyre tracks was clearly visible. Sophie and Greg watched as the experts crouched down and peered at the evidence, then moved on to allow the photographers in. The vehicle had managed to get within two hundred yards of the pool and had left fairly prominent marks where it had turned. Several sets of footprints had been found in the damp ground. Dave Nash, the county forensic chief, gave them the all-clear to proceed.

'Probably a four-by-four,' he said. 'Might be a Range Rover.'

'You can't give us the registration number?' Greg said, sardonically.

'Almost,' Dave said. 'We'll have the make of tyre confirmed within a few hours. If they're Firestone, which is what we think, all you need to do is phone around the local dealers and find who's had a set fitted recently. You guys have it easy nowadays.' He laughed. 'Forensics is the future of crime fighting, you know. You can't do without us.'

Sophie shook her head, smiling. 'You two. Whenever you get together it's like being back at school watching two boys joshing with each other. Get a grip, please. I need to know how you plan to set about getting that body out. If there actually is a body, of course.'

They approached the edge of the pool and stood looking down. The stagnant water was the colour of strong tea and covered with a scummy film. An odour reminiscent of drains or sewers rose up from its surface.

'We'll only use the underwater squad as a last resort,' Dave said. 'With water that colour they'd be working blind. Grappling hooks first, I think. How deep are these pools? Do either of you know?'

Sophie shrugged. 'They vary. The Blue Pool, the big tourist attraction further up the road, is in a disused quarry.

It's forbidden to swim even in that one. You never know what toxins are left from the old clay workings. As for this one, your guess is as good as mine. How will you go about it? These slopes are really steep.' She peered down over the rim.

Dave pointed to a spot a few yards to their left. 'It's a shallower gradient there. We'll begin by roping up a couple of the guys and sending them down. The body can't have gone very far, not if it went in at this point. People look at the slope and the speed at which something rolls into the water and assume it'll sink at the same speed. But once it's in the water it slows very quickly because of the resistance. Unless the slope is nearly vertical — and we have no reason to think that — it'll have stopped pretty quickly.'

They watched the two members of the underwater team, suitably clad and with looped ropes around their shoulders, lower themselves down the slope, turn to face the water and throw their grappling hooks out into the pool. Sophie shook her head at the pile of debris that began to accumulate. An old bicycle, bits of fencing wire, an ancient water cistern that needed both men to haul it out.

'Why do people chuck stuff in places like this?' she asked. 'A lot of this junk is metal. It has a value, surely? Why not take it to the tip?'

'I expect it's been there for years,' Greg speculated. 'Maybe decades. If it was abandoned fifty years ago or more, before there were household recycling centres. This pool would have been a useful junk disposal site for people from miles around. Out of sight, out of mind.'

'Got something,' came a call from below. He was joined by his colleague, who helped him slowly haul the object out.

Dave frowned. 'A body shouldn't be that hard to pull out. If it is what we're looking for, they made a good job of weighing it down.'

They stood and watched a soggy mass being laboriously hauled up from the water. There was no question as to what it was, the shape being all too familiar to any police or forensic officer who'd seen a body being pulled from the depths of a river, pond or lake. Streams of muddy water gushed out from sleeves, trouser-legs and neckline. Several of the people waiting at the waterline made a lunge and caught hold of some item of clothing. Sophie, Greg and Dave waited in silence at the top of the slope. They didn't really want the body to be Stu Blackman. But they didn't really want it to be anyone else either, because that would mean starting up yet another investigation from scratch.

* * *

'Doesn't look well, does he?'

'Christ, Greg, your sense of humour badly needs a remake,' Sophie said. 'Not that I intend to make an issue of it. But he was one of us, don't forget.'

Staring up at them was the discoloured, misshapen face of Stu Blackman. He'd been in the mucky water for hours, and it showed.

Greg turned to face her. 'Yes, in one way he was, and we'll act accordingly. But I know, and you know and Dave knows that he wasn't one of us, not really. He was a lazy, self-centred piece of shit who was always on the make. There. I've said it. Now we can move on and do our jobs in the professional and meticulous way expected of us. Not, by the way, as he would have done in our place.'

The other two said nothing. What was there to say? Greg had merely voiced what they all knew to be true.

Dave had a closer look at the body. 'The back of his head's caved in. He's been hit hard. And it looks like it happened before he went into the water.'

Sophie made a couple of quick calls. The first was to Benny Goodall, the senior county pathologist, the second to Barry, who was at Blandford police station, helping to coordinate the search for the missing Stu Blackman.

'We'll have to release something to the press,' Barry reminded her.

'I know. Let me think about it. I want to buy us as much time as possible. The people who pushed his body into that pool will assume he won't be found for a long time. Young Amy Birkbeck thinks she overheard them say something like that. I might just say that a body's been found in Norden Woods and leave it at that.'

'I reckon that'll give the game away,' he said. 'As soon as you mention Norden Woods.'

'Well, what else can we do? Who's his next of kin? I can't remember him ever talking about any family.'

'Me neither. He lived in Blandford, that's all I know. I kind of assumed he lived by himself because he didn't wear a wedding ring. Leave it with me. It's bound to be on file somewhere,' Barry said.

She ended the call and turned to Dave. 'Benny Goodall should be here within the hour. Let's get a tent up over the body.'

CHAPTER 5: MAPS AND PHOTOS

Barry slid his phone back into his pocket and sighed.

Rae had been watching his face. 'So, it was Stu Blackman? What now, boss?'

He put his hand to his forehead as if to wipe away a troublesome insect. He remained silent for several moments. 'We find out what he was working on, but we keep quiet about our suspicions of what he was up to while we're here at Blandford nick. We don't even breathe a word of what that girl overheard — not to anyone, even people in the force. As far as the public are concerned, he was a police officer killed in the line of duty. That's what the boss will want, and she'll be backed up by Matt Silver and the rest of them up at HQ. He may not have been the only one, Rae, that's the problem.'

'It's gonna be hard trying to pin down who he might have been involved with, boss. He was a loner. Everyone says so.'

'I know. He didn't fit in anywhere. No one really wanted him. He got shunted around from one unit to another, from one investigation to another, from one station to another. We know why, but it didn't help his self-confidence, did it? Maybe that was the problem. Maybe that's why he was an easy target.'

Rae grimaced. 'And maybe you're being too soft-hearted, boss. You get out what you put in, that's my experience. Be honest, he put zilch in, and he was always unreliable, without exception. Even in the days when he partnered Phil McCluskie, it was always Phil, nasty-minded slug as he was, who came up with the ideas. Stu just wasn't cut out to be in the force. God knows how he made it to DS, considering how lazy and inept he was.' She paused and looked more closely at Barry. 'Ah, I see your point. Sorry it took me so long. You think he was being protected by someone on high? That might make it tough for us.'

Barry shook his head. 'It's a possibility, but I don't think it's the case, to be honest. The boss once told me that Stu's uncle was a superintendent a couple of decades ago and he swung the job for him. But he's long gone. Anyway, enough of this speculation. We're a member down, remember, with Tommy still recuperating. We can make a start by trying to find out what Stu's been working on recently. And we've got to contact his next of kin. Better get busy.'

At various times Stu had been attached to Blandford CID, Weymouth CID, the county force's Missing Persons Unit and the Stolen Vehicle Unit. Thank God he'd never been foisted on their unit. Maybe the powers that be up at HQ had more sense than he'd given them credit for.

From what they learned after talking to the local CID officers, Stu had kept his head down and got on with things, albeit at his own unhurried pace.

Later that morning, Barry received a call from Sophie. 'Once you've finished there, Barry, can you and Rae get yourselves across to Bournemouth? Kevin McGreedie called me. He wouldn't say on the phone, but I think he's got something to tell us about Blackman.'

'Will do,' Barry said. 'We're not making a lot of progress here. No one is. Could you sanction Ameera to come down from HQ? I was wondering if we might get something if we take his network account apart and see if he was up to anything suspicious. You know, logins to dodgy sites, suspect database searches, that kind of thing.'

'Good idea, Barry. I'll arrange it for tomorrow. Come back here once you've finished with Kevin. There's something I want to discuss with you — might turn out to be nothing. But I want your and Rae's opinion on it.'

'By the way,' Barry said, 'he didn't have any close family apart from his mother. She's in an old folks home here in Blandford. He was married, but they divorced some ten years ago. No children.'

'Okay. Message me with the details. I'll visit his mother later today.' The phone went dead.

'Hmm. Sounds like she's had one of her *ideas*.'

Rae laughed. 'She often comes up trumps though, doesn't she? It's all that ale she drinks. It gives her weird thoughts. That's what I reckon, anyway.'

* * *

DCI Kevin McGreedie had been in charge of Bournemouth CID for more than a decade. Calm, shrewd and reliable, he was one of the most respected detectives in the Dorset police. He greeted Barry like the old friend he was.

'Good to see you, Barry. And Rae, of course.'

'The super said you might have something for us, sir. It's a tricky business, and if you've got anything that might get us off the starting grid, we'd be eternally grateful.'

'Let's go through to my office. I want Lydia in on it too. She may have something to say.'

They crowded into Kevin's small room. DS Lydia Pillay, Kevin's second in command, was already present, and she grinned at her erstwhile colleague. Barry had been one of her first bosses.

He returned the smile. 'Glad to see you off those crutches, Lydia. Are you fit again now?' Lydia had sustained serious injuries a year earlier when she'd been assaulted by a psychopath wielding a heavy crowbar.

'Well, I still hurt sometimes, though maybe that's age catching up with me. On the whole, I'm pretty good.'

'So, what do you have for us?' Barry asked.

'We all understand the sensitivity of this case,' Kevin began. 'Sophie told me this is purely on a need-to-know basis. We had Stu here recently because we've been involved with the Stolen Vehicle Unit on some recent criminal activity, and he came across to see if it linked in with what he was working on. He was here a couple of days a week or thereabouts. The thing is, he seemed very guarded. He got a lot of information from us, but we never seemed to get much in return. It wasn't a real dialogue, if you get my meaning.'

Lydia took up the story. 'You know what Stu was usually like. He never seemed to have much discretion. He'd blab to anyone about anything, which is why we were all cautious around him.'

'Not the only reason,' Rae added, raising her eyebrows.

Lydia laughed. 'Yes, well, he was a wanker of the first order, I know, but let's not get into that right now. It's just that I noticed a couple of times how tight he was being. I might not have seen it in anyone else, but with him, he couldn't even be guarded without making it obvious.'

'What were you working on?' Barry asked.

'The theft of high-end vehicles. The speciality models, probably stolen to order,' Lydia said. 'There's a ready market for them, not just in this country but across the world.'

'Anything else, other than your feeling that he wasn't being open?' Barry said.

'Well, yes. It was all a bit peculiar. He'd be on the system, but he'd close it down quickly if he saw me approaching. He was on the vehicle database. He had a legitimate reason to be on it, so why close it when he thought I could see? If he'd kept on working, I wouldn't have thought anything of it. It was his behaviour that was suspicious, not what he was looking at. To be honest, I hadn't thought much about it until Kevin mentioned it to me on the quiet this morning. It was all a bit weird, really.'

'That sums up Stu Blackman,' Rae added.

Barry cast her an irritated look. 'Don't go on about it, Rae. We know how you felt about him. It's time to move on.'

'Sorry, boss.' Rae looked at Lydia, who winked at her, and stared hard at the tabletop to stop herself giggling.

'It might be worth checking out his log record here, to see what systems he was accessing and what he was doing on them,' Barry said. 'I'll add it to the list. Ameera's going to Blandford tomorrow, but she might be able to move here next.'

'What about the Stolen Vehicle Unit, boss? If he was working for them, he'd have used their systems too,' Rae said.

'We'll let the super deal with that. She seems to like trampling on their toes. You know what she says about them — investigating stolen toys for naughty boys. It all stems from that row a couple of years ago when they were first set up and were all ready to call themselves the Vehicle Crime Unit. She spotted that the name would produce the same initials as us — VCU. Apparently, they had the cheek to suggest that we should change our name, even though we'd already been in existence for three years. There's still a bit of residual friction about it.'

'Oh, I'd forgotten about that,' Lydia exclaimed. 'I was still with you then. Those were the days!'

* * *

The incident room had been set up at Wareham, the nearest police station to where Blackman's body had been found, and convenient for a very simple reason. They merely had to move into the room set up for the investigation into Amy Birkbeck's disappearance, which was already stocked with maps, photos and snippets of local knowledge.

When Barry and Rae arrived, they found Sophie staring at a high-resolution aerial photograph of the area around the abandoned clay pits. She turned to them.

'That pit, the one we found Blackman's body in.' She pointed to it on the photo. 'It's by far the most accessible from the main road. The others would be a lot trickier to get close to.'

Barry looked at the photo, then at the Ordnance Survey map beside it. He nodded and waited.

'We found a few bits of rusty junk, then his body. We knew roughly where he'd be because of what young Amy Birkbeck told us, so it didn't take long to find him.'

Barry still couldn't see where this was going, so he stayed quiet.

'Why there? Why did they dump his body in that particular pool?' she asked.

'You've already explained that,' Barry said. 'It was the easiest place to get to.'

'Exactly. A convenient spot to get rid of junk. So, my question is this. What if they've used it to dump other stuff? And you can guess what I mean by "stuff," can't you?'

'Oh no, not more,' Barry said at once.

'Ma'am,' Rae said, 'with respect, you have the most macabre imagination. Having dragged a body out of a smelly pool, my first thought would be "glad that's over." I would have switched my attention to other things, happy to say goodbye to the place. I'm guessing Barry thinks the same. And everyone else.'

Sophie frowned. 'It's something young Amy thought she heard said on Sunday night: "Like the other one." Maybe she misheard, given her hearing problems, but we need to check.'

Barry was still deep in thought. 'But you're right, though. They knew exactly where they were going and what they were going to do when they got there. I hate to say it, but chances are it wasn't the first time they'd been there.'

'Glad you agree. I'll get on the blower to Matt Silver right away. I've no idea what the best approach might be, but I'm sure Dave Nash will. Dragging the whole pool with grappling hooks or just draining the whole thing.'

'He's not going to like this.'

Sophie looked at him, a mischievous twinkle in her eye. 'I'll use my seductive charm on him. It never fails.'

'It might this time,' Rae said. 'By all accounts, that place is foul.'

* * *

Sophie re-joined the team at the poolside, this time with Barry and Rae in tow. Dave Nash wasn't looking pleased.

'We were just about packed up,' he grumbled.

Sophie caught the smirk on Greg Buller's face. 'Look, Dave. I really don't know what we've got here. It might be a wild goose chase, but I can't afford to ignore it. We need to find out what else is in there. We all agree, right to the top. We need your advice about how to go about it, though.'

Dave walked back to the edge and peered over. He beckoned to Greg. 'What do you think? It was your guys on the grappling hooks. What do they reckon?'

Greg shook his head. 'They stir everything up too much, so they'd probably miss half of what's there.'

'So you're with Sophie? Drain it completely. You're not just saying that to wind me up?'

Greg grimaced. 'Would I ever? No, she's right. Too much uncertainty with the hooks. If it needs doing, we've got to do it properly.'

'You mean *I've* got to do it properly. Your mob can go back to HQ and put their feet up. We don't need you if it's being drained.'

'You never know. A lot of my lads have fishing waders. They'll be needed if the muck at the bottom is as deep as I think it is. No, we'll be back if you need us.'

Dave glowered at everyone. 'Okay,' he finally said. 'It'll be tomorrow before I can get all the kit organised and across here. Eight o'clock sharp. Anyone who's late is first into the muck.'

Sophie turned to her two VCU colleagues. 'Old clothes and wellies, I think. Might prove to be a bit of a mud bath.'

CHAPTER 6: MUDDY CORPSE

Wednesday morning

The day dawned bright and sparkling, with a crispness to the air. It was the kind of day to go for a long country walk, followed by a pub meal or a drink beside a log fire — a good wine or a glass of fine ale. None of that was on offer today, though. All Sophie had to look forward to was an extremely messy job. Not that she intended to get unnecessarily mucky. She'd never been attracted to activities such as bog-snorkelling or ditch-clearing that involved any kind of mud. Mud was for mudlarks, and she most certainly wasn't of that species.

Dave Nash was already there with his team, talking to Greg Buller, when she arrived. They both eyed her pink floral wellington boots but made no comment.

'I contacted the landowner,' Dave said. 'He'd prefer it if we pumped the water into the next pool. It's larger, and he reckons there's plenty of capacity because of the dry weather we've had. Water levels are down a bit compared to last year. Then we pump it all back once we've finished. I've got some of the team laying the connecting pipes. We should be ready to start by nine or thereabouts. Greg here managed to borrow a second pump from the local fire service, so we should get it cleared out at a fair speed. When's Blackman's post-mortem, by the way?'

'This afternoon. The preliminaries suggest he was hit over the head with the all-too-familiar blunt object, but we'll see what turns up. How long do you think it'll take to get this emptied?'

Dave shrugged. 'Maybe an hour and a half? We've done the calculations, but they're only approximate. We don't know the exact volume because we don't know what the pit's like below the waterline. It's all guesswork.'

They watched as the pumps started up. The plastic pipes jerked like injured snakes as water began to move through them on its short journey to the next pool, hidden from view some four hundred yards away. At first it was difficult to believe that anything was happening, other than the discordant sound of the generators. It was ten minutes before Sophie could spot any sign of a drop in the water level. She walked away to make a quick phone call to Matt Silver, her boss at headquarters. He'd been less than pleased about the cost of the operation and was obviously still jittery about it. By the time Sophie returned, the level had dropped a foot. As time slowly wore on, a few scattered bits of junk started to appear, dripping with muddy liquid. Some were unrecognisable, thickly coated in an orange-brown layer of muck. Bits of piping, tin buckets and an old set of bed springs. Sophie looked at Greg and shrugged.

By mid-morning, the pool had shrunk to half its original volume and more objects were beginning to appear, all coated in slime. It looked like something from a ghastly horror movie or art tableau. The macabre scene wasn't helped by the stink of decay. Several suspiciously lumpy shapes appeared, impossible to identify from the bank. All were coated in a brown slimy ooze.

'I don't like the look of them,' Sophie said to Barry and Rae, both of whom had just arrived from the incident room.

The onlookers ranged around the rim of the pit watched in silence as the water level fell to a few inches and more grotesque shapes appeared in the sticky ooze. Greg Buller gave a thumbs up and several of his team, clad in chest-high waders, moved into the remaining puddles, each roped for safety to a colleague on the bank above. They carried hoses and sprayed water over the lumpy shapes as they advanced, revealing their original form. An ancient bicycle. Several half-rotted tree stumps. A couple of sheets of corrugated iron. An old mattress near to another set of bedsprings. A hose was played onto a lumpy shape that could have been another tree trunk. It wasn't. A body was revealed, tightly trussed in a half-rotted mackintosh, its features misshapen, a dull grey.

'Stop there!' Dave called. He indicated to some other team members, who started to lay a duckboard pathway to the corpse. 'Time for my people to get to work. I don't want it disturbed.'

One of the wader team remained, moving beyond the body to continue hosing down the other objects lying in the mud. They were all bits of filthy wooden or metallic junk, except for a small, stained suitcase, which she picked up and carried to the bank.

Sophie looked at her watch and sighed. 'We need Benny here. I hate to call him, what with Blackman's post-mortem due in an hour. I'll have to ask him to reschedule it, and he won't be best pleased. What's the weather forecast?'

'Staying dry for a few more days,' Barry said. 'Rae, let's have a look round and decide the best way of securing the site. We can't afford to have people wandering around here at night.'

Sophie saw Dave and Greg deep in conversation and went across to speak to them.

'Can you pump the water back in once the body's been taken away?'

'That's what we were wondering. Why do you ask?' Greg said.

‘Well, whoever did this will probably be along for a quick look-see once they learn that Stu’s body’s been found. I know I would in their position. But we’ll make the announcement vague, so they don’t realise we’ve got the second body as well. If you can return the place to as near normal as possible so it isn’t obvious that we’ve emptied the pool, it will help a lot. It buys us some time, even if only a day or two.’

’Okay. You’re the boss. It won’t be hard. The piping’s in place, so all we need to do is reverse the pumps,’ Dave said.

‘Is there any way you can disguise the fact that those heavy trucks have been here?’ Sophie asked.

Greg raised his eyebrows. ‘You don’t want much, do you?’

She laughed. ‘You know, Greg, anyone listening to us would never guess I outrank you.’

‘Yeah, but I’m twice your size. And you like my lasagne too much to ever consider getting rid of me,’ Greg said, straight-faced.

Sophie rolled her eyes at him and turned away to phone the pathologist. Greg Buller, the sergeant in charge of the force’s so-called Snatch Squad, was right. Not only was he almost indispensable to Dorset police, he was also an amazingly good cook and always happy to share his recipes. Added to which, Sophie had absolute trust in him.

* * *

Benny Goodall arrived, tight-lipped. Sophie returned his hard stare.

‘Look, Benny, I had no alternative. We have no idea how long that body has been in there, we don’t know what state it’s in and we didn’t want it touched until you’d had a look. You’d have hit the bloody roof if we’d moved it before you had a chance to see it in situ, wouldn’t you? For all we know, it’ll fall apart as soon as anyone tries to shift it.’

The pathologist merely grunted. He stared at the rough planks that led across the surface of the mud to the corpse.

'So you want me to walk across those rickety bits of timber, do you?'

'I did tell you to wear old clothes and wellies. Come on, show a bit of pluck.'

'It's moments like this that make me wonder if I did the right thing in sticking with medicine as a career.'

Sophie laughed. 'Oh, no, not that old chestnut. Benny, you'd have been rubbish as a rock star, you care about things too much. You know what musicians are like — self-centred, egotistical and venal. You're none of those things.' She suddenly realised that he was grinning at her. 'You cheek. You really had me there for a while. I must be getting old.'

'Both of us,' he said. 'Okey-dokey. Let's get on with it.'

He masked and gloved up, walked gingerly across the duck boards and spent a good twenty minutes examining the body with Dave Nash at his side. They both looked pensive when they returned to the bank.

'Woman,' he said. 'Maybe late twenties or thirties. She's been in there for months, maybe years. Dave can move her now, then you can clear this place up.'

Sophie flashed him a smile. 'Thanks, Benny. When have you rearranged Stu Blackman's post-mortem for? This afternoon?'

'About three? That'll give me time to get back to Dorchester and have some lunch. Okay for you?'

'I guess so. And that one — whoever she is?'

He shrugged. 'I'll have to shift a few things to fit it in, but would late tomorrow morning be any good?'

'Yes, fine. I'll be across this afternoon. Maybe Barry can take the one tomorrow morning. Any sign of how she died?'

He pursed his lips. 'Not sure. But her skull is partly caved in on the left side.'

'Blunt object?'

'Possibly. We might know more when I get her on the bench.'

Sophie and Rae took a walk around the immediate area, looking for other entry points to the woods around the pool.

There were several footpaths, but just the single vehicle track, now blocked by a row of police vehicles.

'I'll take a spell here tonight if you like,' Rae said. 'But do you really think anyone will come nosing around?'

Sophie shrugged. 'The press release about Blackman is going out about now, for the midday news. I'm guessing that someone might try to slip in quietly to check the lie of the land either tonight or tomorrow night. There'll be a couple of uniformed people from Greg's squad here for the next couple of nights to keep the place secure, but I'd really like one of us keeping a sharper watch on things. I'd normally put Tommy with you, because under no circumstances do I want you keeping watch alone. Who else is there? I wonder if one of the local CID might do it. Do you know anyone?'

'Ma'am, I've got an idea. Craig's got a few days off at the moment. He's a bit of a camping fanatic, so why don't we keep it unofficial? If anyone asks, we'll be bat watching.'

Sophie thought it over. 'Okay. I'll go and have a chat with the farmer, Andy Birkbeck, just to let him know. Maybe I can check up on young Amy at the same time.'

Andy was coming out of the milking shed as she arrived. 'I was just about to have a cup of tea,' he said. 'Geraldine went in to put the kettle on a few minutes ago. You'd be welcome to join us.'

'That would be lovely, thanks. It's been a bit of a chilly morning.'

Andy stopped in the farmhouse doorway. 'Did you find anything?'

'That's what I want to talk to you about. Can we go in? It would be better if I explained to you both. How's Amy, by the way?'

'She's back at school today. But there is something you need to know. She's still trying to make sense of some of the words she thinks she heard on Sunday night. But it's hard for her, even when she has her implants turned up.'

Sophie followed him into the kitchen. 'Okay. Maybe Theresa can follow it up when Amy gets in from school. It'll need careful checking because of her hearing problem. But everything helps. You haven't seen anyone acting suspiciously recently? No strangers in the woods or anything like that?'

He shook his head. 'Nothing out of the ordinary. It's always quiet around here in winter. A few ramblers if the sun shines, but it's a different place to the summer months. There's all kinds of people then, and I have to keep my eyes peeled. Gates left open, litter, fires, all the usual problems. The latest one is those pesky disposable barbecues. People just up and leave them. It's ridiculous. The number of fires we've had in the area caused by those things. It drives me mental.'

'You're the closest farm to those flooded pits in the woods, aren't you?'

Andy nodded. 'We don't own the woods, mind. Our boundary stops at the field fence. The land beyond is part of an estate, managed by a wildlife trust. That's why it's been left uncultivated. Amy loves it, of course.'

Geraldine came in from the hallway. 'I heard your voices. Have you got time for a piece of cake?'

'Thank you, that would be very welcome. There's something I need to tell you, but please keep it to yourselves. We've drained the pool and found a second body. It's obviously been there for some time, though we need the post-mortem results before we can be sure.'

Geraldine put her hand to her mouth and sat down heavily.

Andy shook his head in disbelief. 'I just can't take it all in. What is going on in the world?'

'I don't think it's anything new, Andy. People have been bumping off their enemies since time immemorial. The murder rate in Victorian times was far higher than it is now,' Sophie said.

'I think Andy means here, in Purbeck. It's such a peaceful backwater,' Geraldine said.

'My guess is that the people involved don't come from around here. It's just a convenient dumping ground, chosen for the very reasons you mentioned. Something could lie undisturbed in that pool for decades. Amy's done us all a big favour. If it wasn't for her, two murders might well have gone undiscovered.'

'The first body was the missing policeman, then. I've just heard it on the local news.'

'Sadly, yes. One of my colleagues. So you'll understand when I say we'll leave no stone unturned. I'm afraid you'll be seeing a lot of us during the coming weeks. We'll get to the bottom of it, have no doubt.'

CHAPTER 7: OFF-PISTE

Attending post-mortems was one of the worst parts of a detective's job, and possibly the very worst was watching one carried out on a colleague. The sight of a fellow officer's pale, clammy body lying spread out and naked on a lab bench aroused all sorts of emotions. This was the second one for Sophie, following Andrea Ford's autopsy a year earlier. She now only attended post-mortems when the victim was a serving police officer. She left the others to Barry and Rae — a benefit of her rank.

Benny Goodall refrained from his usual humorous commentary and Sophie was grateful for her friend's sensitivity. There were times when black humour could lift a mood, but this wasn't one of them.

'Crushed skull,' he said. 'Look.' He showed her the wound, then the X-ray.

'Any idea what caused it?'

He shrugged. 'Something very hard, probably metal, like a rod or a heavy wrench. It's at the rear, but to the right side, as you see.'

'Someone hit him from behind?'

He nodded. 'Death was probably instantaneous. I'd guess that the killer was taller than Blackman.'

'But Stu was quite short, so maybe someone more than five ten or so?'

Benny agreed. 'There's nothing much else to tell. No other injuries. He didn't suffer a beating.'

Sophie thought for a while. 'Well, that fits with the footprint pattern. It looks as though three people climbed out of the vehicle and moved a few yards away. Then there's a muddle, and only two sets went on to the pool. They must have dragged him the rest of the way — there were score marks in the mud from his feet. Then the same sets returning to the vehicle.'

'So he was taken there after being killed?' Benny said.

'Looks like it. Our first job is to find out why, what he was up to. He obviously trod on the wrong toes.' She turned to face Benny. 'Stu had really poor judgement. My guess is that he found himself in too deep and wanted out. You came across him, Benny, you know what he was like. We're keeping quiet about it, but that's the line we're following.'

Benny frowned. 'That means tomorrow's examination of the other body could be key?'

'Yes, absolutely. Whatever you find then could be vital for us.'

After the examination was over, they returned to Benny's office and slumped into a couple of chairs.

'How's the big plan going? Any progress?' he asked.

Sophie pursed her lips. 'Closer than I'd like. I haven't confirmed it with Barry and Rae yet. I was about to a couple of days ago, but Tommy's disappearance got in the way.'

'It's going ahead then?'

Sophie nodded. 'It makes sense. Three counties, all rural, with relatively small police forces. Having one VCU spread across the region is an economic no-brainer. It makes policing sense too. In recent years we've spent more and more time linking up with Somerset and Wiltshire. Modern crime doesn't respect county boundaries, Benny. And it's come together so fortuitously. Polly Nelson is happy to join us. Steve Gulliver has been in Wiltshire for more than a year now, and he's positive too. It's a novel idea, because they won't need to move. He'll still be based in Devizes and Polly in Taunton. We keep the unit HQ based here at Winfrith, and only be physically together a couple of days each week or when there's a big investigation on. We'll be using videoconferencing and other communications media to keep in touch. There's not much point in trying to move to a central location, not with the populations of the three counties spread the way they are. Or should I say *not* spread? The bigger towns are all around the edges, so that's where most of the crime will be. It's a bit of an experiment, but it'll make things so much easier. Greg Buller's coming in on it too, with a couple of his team. He's been in the job too long. He's getting bored, although he doesn't realise it.'

'A sort of cross-county task force then?'

'Exactly.'

He raised an eyebrow. 'Do you get another promotion out of it?'

'Um, yes. Chief super. It wasn't the driving force, Benny. Or I wasn't, I should say. It came from the Home Office. They're really keen on cross-county initiatives. It was Yauvani Anand, the new Home Secretary.'

'I heard she was hot on making changes.'

'She's an innovator. I got to know her during that big case with the migrant smugglers. The thing is, Benny, when Dorset set up the VCU all those years ago, it was very much an experiment. I always knew that. It's worked really well, but we're underused here. Half the time, we're filling in for CID and other units, not using our expertise. This merger or expansion, whatever you want to call it, will suit us down to the ground. Three counties like ours will be just about right. The key to it will be getting the correct personnel, and I think we've managed that okay. Yauvani's got us official Home Office funding for the first year or so and merging the three counties will save some money. It's a win–win.'

'Sophie, be honest with me. I'm probably your oldest friend. Is it what you want?'

She looked at him and smiled. 'Yes, absolutely. It makes sense. And Polly in Somerset thinks so too.'

'I've worried about you, you know. We've been close friends for so long, you and Martin and me.'

'What do you mean?' She frowned, puzzled.

'Well, coming here to Dorset after the Met and the West Midlands. Those are big places with millions of people. And I always thought you had such a great career in front of you. I hoped you wouldn't suddenly find yourself trapped in a quiet backwater, unable to get back into the mainstream again. I did try to warn you way back, when you were first thinking of transferring here.'

'Yes, I remember. But Martin is a Dorset person, just like you. Jobs opened up for us both here, and at the same time. With you already in the place, it seemed the obvious thing to do.' Sophie put her hand on top of Benny's and squeezed his fingers gently. 'I'm touched, Benny. I always knew you had a good heart, but even so, you've surprised me. Anyway, it was a great move for the two girls. I know Hannah didn't spend long at school here, but Jade just loved it. And remember, I'm a Bristolian. The West Country is deep in my heart as well.'

'So, what comes next?'

'Well, this case takes priority. But the planning will still go ahead. Jim Metcalfe, the ACC, is in the driving seat here in Dorset. He has weekly meetings with his counterparts, and I sit in occasionally. I just hope that we won't need to move somewhere further north. I just love our place so much. Jade says she'll never speak to us again if we sell our home in Wareham.'

Benny laughed. 'That doesn't surprise me. To be honest, I don't think I'd speak to you again either. It's been great for the past six years with you both here. It's helped keep me sane.'

Sophie laughed. 'I wish I could say the same. I'm a good bit nuttier than when I first took up the reins here. Hannah thinks it's the beer. I'm sure at least one of my team puts it down to that as well.'

'Oh, who's that?'

'I'm not willing to say. I can't blame that on you, Benny, not with you being a wine person.'

'I have my pride, you know. Stumbling about with a pint glass in my hand is not the image I want to create for myself.'

She looked at him in surprise. 'Do I do that? Is that what you think?'

'No, of course not. I was trying to be light-hearted. I obviously failed.'

She glanced at the covered shape that one of the technicians was sliding into a chiller cabinet. 'Anything on that other body yet? I know I shouldn't ask, but you might already have a morsel for me.'

'Well, it looks as though she was in that pool for somewhere between three and six months. And she was weighted down in a similar way to your Stu Blackman.'

'That's useful to know. So probably the same people?'

He shrugged. 'I'm not committing myself. That's your job. The rest will come out tomorrow when we look at her more carefully.'

* * *

By the time Sophie arrived back at the crime scene, it was almost deserted. A police van and a squad car were still parked in the approach track, along with Barry's car. The van, packed with the uniformed officers who'd carried out the search, drove off as she opened the door of her own car.

She walked along the now silent path to the pool. There were few signs of the furious activity of the past two days. The water level in the pool was little different from before and the muddy banks had somehow been brushed and rinsed to restore their previous appearance and were devoid of footprints and noticeable marks. There was no sign that heavy pumps and pipework had been lying on the ground for hours.

Sophie stood looking at the scene, turning over the thoughts in her head. She was still thinking about her conversation with Benny about the unit's expansion plans. The problem with it lay in her own personality. People saw her confident, outgoing exterior and made assumptions. Few were aware, even Martin, that underneath lay a deep anxiety, a fundamental self-doubt. It had been with her since childhood, carefully hidden from the external world. People assumed that a successful, well-educated, seemingly confident woman in a responsible job couldn't possibly be riddled with constant uncertainty and unease. Ha! If only they knew.

She heard footsteps behind her. It was Barry.

'We've finished walking the perimeter,' he said. 'I've sent Rae home to get herself kitted up for her night out camping. I'm still not sure about that.'

Sophie looked at him. 'What's the problem?'

'It's just a bit . . . *off-piste*.'

'Exactly. Which is why it's such a good idea. You've got to give it to Rae, she has a real flair for originality. A couple of bored detectives slumped inside a car would stick out like a sore thumb. Plus, Rae and Craig get to do something they clearly enjoy. And we're one person down, remember, until Tommy's declared fit enough to come back.'

'Craig's not police, though, is he? What happens if something goes wrong?'

'How likely is that? Remember that there'll be two uniformed cops in a squad car further back up the main road. Rae's a big girl, Barry. She can look after herself. And I trust her judgement. I think you're worrying needlessly. Come on, let's visit the farmhouse and see young Amy. She cheers me up.'

She looked up at the sky, which was darkening. Twilight was already settling in.

* * *

Amy hadn't long been home from school when the two detectives arrived at the farmhouse. She was sitting at the kitchen table, still in her school uniform, eating a mince pie. Theresa, the police family liaison officer, was sipping a cup of tea.

'The mince pies are left over from Christmas,' Geraldine explained. 'I always buy too many. Feel free to have one. They're past their best before date, though. I'll make some tea.'

'How are you getting on, Amy?' Sophie asked.

'Okay,' the girl replied. 'I'm doing what you asked, I'm not telling anyone what I saw. They all know what's happened, though. It was on the news. Still, they don't bother me much. I just pretend I can't hear them.'

'Probably the best plan,' Sophie said.

'I was telling Amy that she's been very helpful,' Theresa said. 'She's managed to remember a bit more about the men she saw on Sunday night. Every little bit of information helps, doesn't it?'

'Absolutely. We rely on that kind of information to help us catch criminals. Thank you, Amy.'

Sophie thought the girl looked much more relaxed today. It was probably time for Theresa to return to her normal duties, with only an occasional visit. As long as the family knew she was quickly contactable by phone.

Andy arrived, having finished the milking. He looked worn out. Sophie guessed that the strain of the last few days was catching up on him.

'We're leaving a squad car parked overnight at the end of the track, near the main road. The officers will take an occasional walk towards the pool. It's for show really, just for reassurance. But we have something else up our sleeve. One of my team has volunteered to camp out in your top field, near the woods. She and her partner will pretend to be watching for bats. Is that okay with you? Her real purpose is to keep a close watch on the area around the pool in case anyone decides to slip back for a look. If they did, they'd find it all too easy to avoid the squad car. Several footpaths approach that pool from the back.'

'Of course,' Geraldine said. 'Tell them all that we'll do them a hot breakfast tomorrow morning. Is there anything else they'll need?'

'That's kind of you. No, they'll be fine, I'm sure. We're a rural county. Most of the uniformed officers are used to an occasional overnight stake-out.'

Andy's head was beginning to droop. He clearly needed a nap.

'We'll be off,' Sophie said.

CHAPTER 8: INFRARED

The early hours of Thursday morning

It was one o'clock in the morning. There was a pronounced January chill to the air, and Rae gave thanks for the invention of thermal underclothes. Sexy it was not, but it certainly did the trick in situations like this. She and her partner, Craig, were on their second circuit of the area, moving stealthily along the narrow footpaths that meandered through the trees. Rae held a sensitive night scope at the ready, Craig an infrared camera. Despite the underwear, Rae shivered. She was full of admiration for young Amy Birkbeck. How had she managed to survive a whole night out in the woods at this time of year?

An owl hooted in the distance and a fox slipped across the path ahead of them, its tail bushed up to give the illusion of size. All the foxes that Rae had ever seen were skinny, scrawny things that looked as if they hadn't had any decent food in weeks. This one was no different. It turned its head to look at them, then vanished as suddenly as it had appeared.

They moved slowly on, picking their way carefully and stopping every so often for Rae to scan the area ahead with her scope. She knew what she was looking for now. The fox had shown up through the scope as an eerily glowing shape, leaking heat into the air despite its furry coat. They were approaching the pool at its far side, away from the track, when Rae touched Craig's arm. There was something in the distance, a mere spot of colour in the coated lenses.

'Something's coming,' she whispered. 'Let's get behind these bushes.'

They moved off the path and waited. Through the scope, she watched the red glow slowly expand as it drew nearer, moving forward for a short while then seeming to wait. It took on more of an upright shape, walking on two legs, not four. It was definitely a person, moving forward with extreme caution. Craig readied his camera. Rae tried to decipher the image in the scope. It looked like it was wearing a parka with its hood up. The figure reached the edge of the pool and spent some time looking around, poking the ground. A dim torch beam could be seen now, directed at the ground around the edge, then at the pool itself. From Craig's movements at her side, Rae could tell that he was taking photos — the electronic shutter was set to silent. She lifted her own ordinary camera, already on a night-time setting and resting on a monopod, peered through the viewfinder and took some shots. They might show nothing of any use, but it was worth a try.

The figure turned and headed back the way it had come.

'Do we follow?' Craig whispered.

'We can try,' Rae replied. 'But I need to use the scope to check ahead. It would be too easy to blunder on and be spotted if he decides to stop suddenly. I think this track loops round the back of the woods and comes out on the road further along.' She paused, thinking, then pulled out her radio. Keeping her voice low, she asked the uniformed officers in the squad car to pull out onto the main road and head half a mile further north. 'Let's follow as best we can,' she said to Craig.

No more traces showed up on the infrared scope. They reached the end of the path in fifteen minutes, at a point where it joined a short farm track. They followed it out onto the main road, where the squad car was waiting.

'Anything?' she said, anxiously.

The driver nodded. 'A dark-coloured Land Rover passed by a few minutes ago. We waited further up the road, like you asked. The registration plate was a bit muddy, but we think we got it. It looked like it came out of this track. I don't think we raised any suspicion, though they must have spotted us.'

'They? There was more than one person?' she asked.

'Sorry. Figure of speech. We only spotted the one occupant.'

'Okay. Thanks. You've done a good job. Can you give us a lift back to our tent? We could do with some shuteye and a bit of warmth.'

The second squad car officer raised her eyebrows. 'In these temperatures and in a tent? You're hopeful, aren't you?'

'Flask of tea,' Rae replied, 'and a few of those chemical heat packs that warm up your sleeping bag. We came prepared. You're invited to breakfast in the farmhouse, by the way. They've promised us sausages, bacon and eggs. Seven thirty, when the farmer's finished the milking.'

'It sounds tempting, but we might just clock off and go home to bed. We don't have the option of kipping down for the next couple of hours.'

Rae laughed. 'My heart bleeds. Are you trying to tell me that you'll both sit here, wide awake, for the next five hours?'

* * *

They all turned up for breakfast in the farmhouse the next morning, including the two uniformed officers. It was as Rae thought — no cop can ever turn down the chance of free hot food after a long, cold night on duty, particularly if it was a cooked breakfast.

'How did you sleep in that tent?' asked the woman officer, halfway through her second sausage.

'Like I said, we came prepared,' Rae said. 'Sorry you were stuck in the car. Did anything else happen?'

'Of course not,' she said. 'Does it ever? We took it in turns to snooze, had a couple of walks up and down the track, saw some deer and a fox. I'd like to say I found it interesting, but all I wanted to do was to climb into a warm bed. Will you be on duty today?'

'Yes,' Rae said, 'but just for a couple of hours this morning. First, though, we pop back to my flat in Wool, have a hot shower and get a change of clothes. We're visiting a colleague in hospital. I'll be free this afternoon, so I'll catch up on my lost sleep then.' She turned to Geraldine. 'This is just great. It's the best camping breakfast I've ever had.' She slid another egg onto her plate.

'It's lovely to have some company, particularly in winter. We're a bit out in the sticks here. You like it too, don't you, Amy?'

Amy gave a shy smile. 'Yes.'

'Anything special on at school today?' Rae asked.

'We've got a cross-country race this afternoon. I always like that.'

Craig pulled a face. 'I hated sport of any kind when I was at school. Eugh.'

Amy giggled.

'Amy's really good at cross-country,' Geraldine said. 'You usually win, don't you?'

Amy nodded, still smiling.

'Can I watch? Would you like that?' Rae asked. 'I'll be back in the area by then. Do they allow spectators?'

'Not normally, they don't. But I don't mind people I know watching.'

'Okay, it's a deal. I'll tell the school I'm there for extra security. That should fool them.' She rolled her eyes.

Amy giggled again, slipped off her stool and went to get ready for school.

'Did anything happen last night?' Andy asked, stifling a yawn.

'Yes, but I can't tell you exactly what,' Rae replied. 'The boss may have told you that that the squad worked hard on the area immediately around the pool, trying to return it to its normal appearance. She has this canny sixth sense, I'm sure. She wondered if someone might return to check on the place after it went out on the news yesterday. That's why I was there, watching. Anyway, the guys did a really good job. You wouldn't have known that the pool had been emptied, searched and then refilled. It would have fooled anybody. We'll be keeping an eye on the area for a while longer, so if you see or hear anything suspicious, you must phone 999 immediately.'

* * *

Tommy Carter was sitting up in bed when the three detectives arrived. He still had bandages around his head, though fewer than when he'd been admitted. He looked up as they approached, wearing his normal pained expression.

'Relax, Tommy, we haven't come to arrest you,' Sophie joked.

He smiled weakly. 'I feel so stupid,' he said. 'A bike accident. I've always told everyone I was good on a bike.'

'We don't think it was your fault at all,' Sophie said. 'It was a hit and run. We've had the RTA experts poring over the road where it happened, and they say it's clear the car was speeding. We haven't traced them yet, but the boys are still hopeful.'

'You're a person down, though. And I've heard the news about what's been going on. I should be there,' Tommy said.

'Listen, Tommy, we can cope,' Barry said. 'We have people we can call on.'

'I can't believe Stu's been murdered. I was only talking to him last week,' Tommy said.

Sophie looked at him sharply. 'Really? What about?'

'Stolen vehicles.'

'Maybe we need to ask you about it once you've recovered. Anyway, we have some good news for you,' Sophie said.

'Oh?' He looked anxious again.

'Congratulations, Detective Constable Tommy Carter. You are now a permanent member of the Violent Crime Unit. You've passed your probationary period.' She gave him a beaming smile.

'I really thought I wasn't good enough. And I never thought you'd keep me on after this.'

Rae laughed. 'What, a handsome young man like you? No chance.'

'Can I tell my girlfriend?' Tommy asked.

'Of course,' Sophie said, 'though she already knows, Tommy. So does your mum. They were so worried about you on Monday, we broke the news to them to cheer them up. But we told them to keep it to themselves.'

Tommy's face cleared. 'No wonder Olivia's been so upbeat. I thought she'd found someone else.'

'You're such a pessimist, Tommy,' said Rae, helping herself to some grapes.

CHAPTER 9: A NEW JOB

'What does it look like, Crustie?'

In the small office of Sunnyside Cars, the company he owned in the outskirts of Poole, Mickie Rollins looked up from his computer screen. His senior mechanic and business partner lounged against the front of his desk. Crustie was a scruffy sod, always leaning on something, always causing other people to curl their lips in disgust. Like now, picking his nose and examining the little lumps of dried snot on the end of his grubby index finger. Please God, don't let him nibble them, Mickie thought. I'll have to kill him if he does.

Tall, bony Crustie wiped his finger on a torn tissue that he pulled from his pocket. 'Looks okay to me.'

Mickie idly wondered if he was referring to the bogey or the pool they'd dumped that cop's body in. *Don't be stupid*, he told himself.

'It's like we left it. There's nuthin' lyin' about, no marks on the banks.' Crustie gave a catarrhal sniff.

'So they found the cop's body but left it at that? Is that what you're saying?'

'What I'm sayin', Mickie, is that's how it looks. That's all I'm sayin'.'

'Okay. Point taken. So how did they find the cop's body so soon? Are you sure you weighted the body down good and proper? I asked you before you rolled it in, remember?' Mickie stared pointedly at his assistant.

'Course it was weighted down. You saw what I did. You 'eard the splash. You saw it go down. Something else must've 'appened.'

'Did he have a bleeper or something?' Mickie asked.

'I dunno. You searched 'im, didn't you? What you gettin' at?'

'How did they know he was there? That's what I'm getting at. It just don't make any sense.' He looked at Crustie's blank face. Better not push him too hard — not yet. He still needed his help in sorting out this mess and running the business. Maybe in a few months' time he could jettison the man and seek a replacement mechanic, but not yet. 'Could we have been spotted somehow? Or did we leave evidence? It's keeping me up at night, Crustie. We need to keep quiet about it. Don't mention it to no one unless we're asked. The other one in there, that woman, she bothers me. Though from what you say, it don't look as though the cops found her. We'll be in deep shit from you-know-who if that gets out.' He paused. 'Have you got Vinny's Jeep sorted yet?'

Crustie looked blankly at him for a few seconds. 'Oh, you mean the one that needs a touch up on the front end?'

'That's the one. We need to get on with it, Crustie. Vinny didn't say much when he came in with it, but it looks like he hit summat. Probably a bike, 'cause there's been nothing on the news about anyone being hit, and if it was a pedestrian they'd be dead and it would be splashed all over. You know how fast he drives. The scratches look about right for a bike. I don't understand why none of the local papers or radio stations have said anything about it. You'd think it would've been reported to the cops, wouldn't you?'

Crustie shrugged. 'Mebbe the cyclist wasn't 'urt. You can never tell.'

'In that case, why was Vinny so quick getting it in to us? And he wanted it inside, not on the forecourt where it could be seen. Odd, isn't it?'

'I'll get on wiv it now, if you like.'

'Yeah. And do a good job.'

'Course. I always do a good job, Mickie. You know that.'

'All right. Let's have a look at it then.'

The two men left the smart car showroom office and made their way to the rather less salubrious workshop. The three indoor areas that made up the company premises reflected the attitudes of the two men: the office and showroom, under the care of Mickie himself, were scrupulously neat, whereas the workshop sometimes looked as though a bomb had hit it, despite Mickie's complaints. The workshop was the domain of Mickie's senior mechanic, Christie Valentine, known to all and sundry as Crustie. It had room for two vehicles. Currently, a black Mercedes saloon was up on one ramp, a gleaming Jeep four-by-four on the other. They moved to the front end and Crustie ran his hand over the slight damage to the front nearside wing. 'I thought it was just scratches at first, but there's a couple of small dents. Maybe just a bit of filler paste, then a respray?'

'Yeah,' Mickie said, 'that should do fine. Let's say a couple of days. I'll get on the blower to Vinny later and say he can have it by the end of the week. Like I said, he's nervous about it.'

Crustie got to work, and Mickie returned to his office. Despite the economic slowdown, the market for luxury used cars was still pretty buoyant, particularly in Poole, with its so-called "Millionaires' Row" on the Sandbanks peninsula. He had quite a few orders to fulfil during the week ahead, so life was good and the money was coming in regularly.

* * *

Vincent Foster was feeling grumpy this morning, though he couldn't put his finger on why. Was it his long-time girlfriend,

Maddie Brooks, and the way she kept wittering on about getting married? Was it his lover, Bren Docherty, who just the previous evening had told him she had crabs and that he'd need to get treated? Was it his mother, constantly whining about her aches and pains when all she needed to do was lose some weight and exercise a bit more? Fucking women. Why did they create so many problems and then expect him to be all understanding? Surely, they knew Vinny wasn't that kind of guy.

His phone rang and he glanced at the caller display. Suleiman. It didn't make him feel any better.

'Hello, Suleiman. What can I do for you?' He listened, scratching his greying hair. 'Sure. No problem. Leave it with me.'

He held his head in his hands. Sodding Arab zillionaires and their sodding ridiculous expectations. More and more of them were buying up luxury properties in Sandbanks, using him to find them domestic staff, then complaining to him when the they walked out. What did the bastards expect? Well, he knew the answer to that. What they wanted was slaves, not paid housekeeping staff, and "slaves" wasn't an exaggeration either. A high proportion of the people he found for them couldn't handle the insults and the occasional blow, even though the money was good. Try explaining to these oil-rich gulf-based people that they couldn't treat house staff like they did back home, and they just stared blankly at you. To them, if the dusting hadn't been done to a high enough standard, a slap around the head was a perfectly acceptable way of bringing the point home.

He already knew that Mia, the chambermaid in Suleiman's house, had walked out. She'd contacted him the day before, in a rage. She was a young woman from Bristol, taking a year out to earn some money after completing a journalism degree at Bournemouth University. Someone like that clearly wasn't about to put up with being bullied. He had already explained this to Suleiman, hoping that the message would be passed on to his family members. Obviously, this had been too much to hope for. Suleiman's elder daughter, Shazia, had been staying in the house in recent weeks and was plainly unwilling to control her temper. Mia had shown him the marks on her forehead. God. The earlier bruises from before Christmas had only just faded. He'd slipped her some extra cash to persuade her not to report the assault to the police and was just waiting for Suleiman to request a replacement. The trouble was the time of year. Most people looking for a year's temping were students on a year out who wanted a position to fit in with the start and end of the academic year.

Vinny closed his mind to some of the more serious 'accidents' that he'd had to cover up on behalf of the Sandbanks' so-called 'oil sheikh' set, though Suleiman hadn't made his money through oil. Vinny was aware that there was far shadier activity behind his seemingly overloaded bank balance, involving gun running back in the Middle East. Suleiman wasn't someone to be treated lightly. He had a way of looking at people that made Vinny's blood run cold. Some of his family members weren't much better either. But Suleiman paid better than all the others in the group that employed Vinny as their go-to organiser for staff, and that wasn't to be sniffed at. He'd more than compensated Vinny for the sweetener he'd given Mia, so the situation had been resolved. Vinny now found himself in a position of trust where Suleiman and his elder daughter were concerned. Suleiman was increasingly coming to him for advice on other issues besides the hiring of staff and was willing to pay eye-watering sums for the help he gave. Vinny was gradually dropping most of his other clients in favour of this single source of wealth.

He phoned round the east Dorset employment agencies, asking if they had any chambermaids on their books. Luckily, he found one after only a couple of calls, so another wad of cash would soon be coming his way. The money had to be good for him to put up with a man who in his opinion was an out and out psychopath.

Cheered at the prospect of more money, he decided to pay a quick visit to Mickie Rollins. Vinny wanted his Jeep back and bearing no sign of his early-morning encounter with the cyclist. Stupid moron. What kind of idiot decides to ride his bike around there at that god-awful time in the morning? Whoever found him would probably have needed a shovel to scoop him up. Serves him right, cycling with earphones in. Another time he might have stopped to call the cops, but not on Monday, not with what he had hidden in the back of the Jeep. The cops would have had a field day if they'd decided to give it a once over.

Before he could call Mickie, his mobile phone rang. He glanced at the caller display. Well, would you believe it? Mickie.

'Hi there,' he said. 'I was just gonna call you about the Jeep. Is it ready yet?'

He listened to what Mickie had to say, then sat frowning. His bad mood was back.

* * *

Mia Lockhart had already deposited the cash sweetener in her rather minimal bank account. It would see her through another few weeks while she hunted for a job. The problem was, she was searching on two fronts and wondered if that meant she wasn't doing a good enough job with either. Ideally, she wanted a job in journalism, one that utilised her recently acquired degree, but such jobs were hard to come by, so she was also looking for another temping job. Maybe she'd be better off working in an office instead of hotels or homes, although the latter did include free accommodation.

Mia was a short, curvy young woman with long, dark-brown hair, a friendly personality and a winning smile. Despite the smile, she wasn't a soft touch, however. She'd grown up in an unhappy family and had learned early on how to look after herself. Her open, independent nature had led her to journalism, but jobs in the traditional type of investigative reporting that she hankered after seemed to be dying out. She was hoping that some freelance work might make her name. She wondered if her spell with Suleiman Hamdi's family could provide the story she needed. There were rich pickings to be had there, for sure. Hypocrisy, cruelty, double-dealing and possibly extreme violence. She'd only picked up hints of the latter during her spell in the household, but something had gone on before she joined the staff, she was sure of it.

The problem was that she had now accepted money from Suleiman in return for keeping quiet about his daughter's assaults on her. So how could she publish an article on what she suspected about the other goings-on? Would he come after her? She couldn't dismiss the possibility. She knew how vindictive he and his friends could be if they thought their 'honour' was being called into question. It was a scary thought. She decided to pay another visit to one of the temping agencies she was registered with. Maybe something new had cropped up.

She was in luck. By mid-afternoon she had a replacement job, albeit one that depended on a successful probationary period.

* * *

'Welcome to Bateson's.'

Mia was having a post-interview chat with her new boss in the plush interview room of a local solicitors.

Jane Trilsbech, the office manager, looked, in her tight-fitting, charcoal-grey business suit, to be a dragon of a woman. 'Your interview went well. You seem to have exactly the skills we're looking for, so the placement is yours, subject to a three-month trial. That's if you want it?'

She raised her eyebrows and stared at Mia as if daring her to turn the offer down. How likely was that? For once, Mia seemed to have landed on her feet. A law practice, situated on the west side of Poole, a job with a variety of office duties that she knew she could cope with. And the pay was good.

Mia gave the woman her brightest smile. 'I'd love to join you. It looks right up my street.'

'Well, we'll see how you get on. I can't emphasise enough that you must show some initiative. There's a lot to sort out and it needs to be done quickly and efficiently. The move from the town centre to new offices out here has got to work. The partners have sunk a lot of money into these premises, and a big part of your job will be to help me manage the settling-in process for the office staff. Rosie, from our permanent staff, should have been doing it, but her skiing accident has put paid to that. Broken leg, ruptured shoulder. I don't know . . .' She tutted, sounding more irritated than sympathetic. 'You can start tomorrow. The sooner the better, as far as we're concerned.'

Mia shook her hand for a second time and headed for the door. This was more like it. A job in a modern office with up-to-date technology. And a legal environment would do her no harm at all in view of her long-term plan of a career in journalism. It might even give her some ideas. The day had turned out well after all. Who'd have guessed it?

CHAPTER 10: CROSS-COUNTRY

Barry and Rae drove to Dorchester County hospital in near silence, both dreading the impending post-mortem. These were never pleasant, but having to witness one on a significantly decomposed corpse that had been lying at the bottom of a muddy pool for an unknown length of time was an appalling prospect.

The mood in the pathology theatre was sombre. Even the cheery Benny Goodall was restrained as he began his commentary.

'She's middle-aged,' he said, 'and much shorter than average. Small boned. Her facial bone structure appears to be Asian. I'll push the DNA analysis through as urgent because it could yield some important clues.'

He continued his probing. 'Death was probably caused by severe bleeding on the brain, judging by the severity of the damage to the skull. She was hit very hard. And look at the position of the fracture.'

'On the front, you mean?' Barry shook his head slowly.

'Exactly. And I can't feel any bits of grit or debris embedded in the wound, so it was probably something metallic.'

He continued his examination of the rest of the body. 'She has three broken toes on her left foot,' Benny said. 'The bones haven't even begun to heal, so the injuries occurred not long before death. Toes one, two and three.'

'How could that have been done?' Barry asked.

Benny shrugged. 'Your guess is as good as mine. Something heavy dropped onto her toes? Someone standing on them? I really don't know.'

They learned nothing else from the whole-body examination, so the two detectives left Benny to do what he could with the internal organs. They made their way to the hospital café and sat in silence, each nursing a strong coffee.

'Why would someone do all that?' Rae finally said. 'When you put everything together, it just doesn't make any sense.'

Barry shrugged. 'I know. The toe injuries could either be accidental or intentional, some kind of domestic abuse. But from what Benny said, the head wound was probably caused by a single powerful blow. And then the way her body was weighted down and dumped in that pool. It's so cold, so . . . efficient.'

'Have you come across anything like this before, boss?' Rae asked.

He stared into his coffee. 'I remember a case from way back, a psychopath called Andy Renshaw. If his girlfriends caused him any grief, he killed them. Dumped them in a pool up in Wareham Forest.'

'But this one has got to be linked to Stu Blackman, hasn't it? I mean, they were the only two bodies found in that pool, both weighted down in the same way. Surely the same person did both?'

'Well, we're all thinking that, I expect. But let's wait for this afternoon's meeting. The chief has a lot more experience of this kind of thing than either of us.' He looked at his watch. 'I guess we should be getting back. Are you feeling okay now?'

Rae was still pale but she gave him a weak smile. 'Yeah. I'll be fine.'

* * *

The meeting back in the incident room was muted and brief. Sophie seemed troubled.

'These two bodies were found in the same pool, and the MO was similar in both cases, although Stu seems to have been clobbered on the back of the head, whereas the unknown woman was hit from the front. But both were struck with a blunt object that caved their skulls in. It looks very much as though Stu was killed at the scene, so we'll need to make a stab at building up a timeframe of what might have gone on. We don't know about the woman. She was short and slim, so she could have been killed elsewhere, then carried to the pool and thrown in.'

'They could have been killed by the same person,' Barry said. 'The nature of the head injuries makes it a distinct possibility, don't you think?'

'It makes sense,' Sophie said. 'It means we concentrate our resources. But we need to be prepared to find separate killers if future evidence points that way. Remember our watchword: no lazy assumptions.'

Barry was tempted to state the obvious, that the phrase was three words long and didn't qualify as a watchword, but he thought better of it. The chief clearly wasn't herself today. She looked distracted and tired.

'Are you okay, ma'am?' he asked.

She shook her head. 'Not really, no. My gran Florence, the one in Gloucester, is terminally ill. I feel really frustrated, but there's not much I can do, is there? She and James have deliberately kept me in the dark about how unwell she really is. I'm going to have to visit, and I think it needs to be this evening. Trouble is, we're a person down already, and we've all this going on.'

'We can cope,' Barry said. 'We could draft someone in to help out.'

'I was thinking about that when I found out about Florence. It's even more important now,' Sophie said.

'I'll need to be back at HQ for five,' Rae said. 'I meant to say, I've been elected chair of the minorities support group and we have a meeting this afternoon. I think I mentioned it last week. Is it still okay for me to go? I also told Amy I'd watch her run in a cross-country race at about four.'

'Of course it's okay,' Sophie said. 'It's important you keep that going. Our personnel are the most important resource we have. We need to look after everyone. The other thing is young Amy Birkbeck. She's going to have to get used to us being around and keeping an eye on her and her family.'

'Really?' Rae sounded surprised.

'Think about it, Rae. Blackman's body was dropped into that pool late at night. They'd have been careful to check the area out. But we pulled the body out within a couple of days and plastered it across the news. They'll be asking themselves how we found it so soon. There are only a couple of possible explanations — either they left an obvious clue or they were spotted. So they'll be wondering who could have spotted them, and Amy and her family will pop up. They're the closest farm to the scene. I know there are a couple of cottages on the main road and a few industrial premises, but even so, we have to recognise that they could be under threat.'

'That reminds me,' Barry said. 'We need to get in touch with those industrial units to see if they have any CCTV. There's not much chance that they picked up anything useful, but you never know.'

Sophie agreed. 'This is why we need extra people. It's so time-consuming wading through hours of images. Who can we bring in to bolster our numbers for a while?'

'How about Rose Simons and George Warrander?' Barry suggested. 'They're uniform, but they know how we work, and they're very reliable.'

Sophie looked concerned. 'You're right, of course. They're good people. I'd be fine with it if it wasn't for George's relationship with Jade. You know why I'm edgy about it, Barry, don't you? What happens if someone accuses me of favouritism? The other option is to use the local Wareham CID people, but they've not got much experience of cases like this. You'll know what I mean, Barry, having joined us from another local CID unit all those years ago. It's all small seaside town stuff.'

He smiled as he reminisced. 'Ah, those were the days. Shoplifting and petty theft. A few drunken brawls.'

'Exactly. The search for Amy was the most serious thing they've been involved with for years. I know we use local cops for house-to-house work, but being closely involved in our end of things will be something new. Still, they'd do until we get Tommy back.'

'Rose and George would be better though. And I really don't see the problem. I think you're being too sensitive about it. Plus, if you really want to get George into the VCU in the long term, this is exactly the kind of experience he'll need. They get my vote. What about you, Rae?'

Rae was having trouble keeping her eyes open. 'Yeah, of course,' she mumbled.

'I'll think about it this evening.' Sophie glanced at her watch. 'God, is that the time? I need to be off if I'm to get to Gloucester in time for visiting hour.' She left the room.

Rae watched her go, looking puzzled. She yawned. 'Is she alright, boss?'

Barry sighed. 'Your guess is as good as mine. What I can tell you is that she's unusually close to her grandparents. She only discovered them four years ago, and she's their nearest relative. I've met them a couple of times, and they fret about her as much as she does about them, maybe more so. That's why they won't have told her.'

Rae still looked puzzled. 'What? She only found them four years ago? How did that happen?'

'It's too complicated to tell you the complete story, Rae, not just now. It's a bit tragic. Their son was a student in Bristol, and while he was there, he got a sixteen-year-old girl pregnant. He was murdered before he found out. He was in the wrong place at the wrong time. The girl was the boss's mum, and she's the result. They didn't know she existed, and she didn't know they did. They had no other children, so you can imagine how they felt when they discovered her. It's the oddest thing. I get the feeling they kind of cherish her and idolise her at the same time. You'd pick up on it of you met them, even more than me. You've got those emotional antennae.'

Rae laughed. 'Emotional antennae? You're imagining things, boss. But that's one helluva story.'

'Weren't you planning to get home for some sleep this afternoon?'

She shrugged. 'Ever hopeful, that's me. I'll watch this race at Amy's school, go to the meeting at HQ, pick up a take-away and then collapse into bed. I'll be okay. I'll be as breezy as a lark tomorrow.'

'Well, technically you've been off duty for a couple of hours now. The real work starts tomorrow. So, get that sleep while you can.'

* * *

For Rae, the rest of the afternoon was a welcome relief from the daily grind. Amy won her race, no surprise to Rae, once she had seen the effortlessly graceful way in which the slim girl moved along the muddy tracks. Amy was thrilled that someone other than her family had come to watch her run and beamed at Rae when she spotted her beyond the finish line.

The meeting of the Dorset Police Minorities Group also went well, although there were several issues to address, including their representation at that summer's forthcoming Pride event. Of more serious concern, though, was the fact that there was still a small group of serving personnel who seemed hostile to officers from ethnic minority groups, and even more to staff who were LGBT. A small core was still peddling misogynistic so-called 'jokes,' some of them obscene. It was hard to pin down because the few individuals involved made their feelings known in crude banter, facial expressions and whispered comments, all difficult to log with any degree of accuracy. Plans were made to address the problem with Rae, as the group's chair, accepting responsibility for taking the complaint forward. By the time she arrived home, she was exhausted. She ate the take-away burger she'd collected from a café a few blocks away from her flat, gulped down a mug of tea, had a quick shower and fell into bed. She was asleep within seconds.

Barry was left alone in the office, thinking about the possible links between the two bodies they'd pulled from the pool. What could possibly connect a middle-aged detective sergeant and a small woman, possibly of Asian origin, even if Blackman had been working 'off-piste'? He thought of Kevin and Lydia's comments about Blackman's behaviour in the days before he vanished, and Ameera's preliminary findings about his network and database activity. Something had been going on. Blackman had somehow become embroiled with people who didn't play light-hearted games, and most certainly didn't play any games by the rules. Barry took his thoughts home with him. Somehow, somewhere, the puzzle would start to fit together.

* * *

Sophie was walking slowly back to the hospital car park in Gloucester at the end of visiting time, her arm through that of her grandfather, James Howard. He wasn't unwell, but it was clear that his mobility had deteriorated during the past couple of years.

'So, what you're saying, Granddad, is that you didn't realise how ill she was.'

'No, I didn't,' he said. 'I think it's taken everyone by surprise, even the doctors. We weren't trying to hide anything from you, Sophie, really. It's true that we wouldn't want to overburden you needlessly with the aches and pains of old age, but cancer is a lot more serious, and we'd have told you if we'd known. She's been in remission for some years now. I suppose we thought it might be permanent. The wishful thinking of old people.' He stopped and looked up at the night sky. 'Drizzle. Rain on its way.'

'Well, let's get you home. I'll come in for a coffee, but I need to get back home after that. I'm so glad we could see you for so long at Christmas because, for the time being, it'll be back to flying visits.'

They got in the car, a new Lexus that she hadn't had for long.

'A new case, I take it. I saw on the news that a policeman's body has been found. Not anyone from your unit?'

She started the engine. 'No, thank God, but I knew him, of course. Strange character.'

'But you'll be in charge?'

'Afraid so. Although Barry's taking more and more off my shoulders. I've got this expansion to plan for. It's got to work, you see, Granddad. We're ruffling a lot of feathers by pushing ahead with it and we'll be making enemies, though they haven't stuck their heads above the parapet yet. Don't worry. I'm tougher than I look.'

CHAPTER 11: FIRST DAY

Friday morning

At first glance the office looked totally chaotic, but Mia was sure there had to be some system at work. Yes. All of the stacked boxes bore a code in different colours. If she could just find the person who'd organised the system, she'd be able to get started. She went in search of Jane.

'Ah, well, there's a problem there,' the office manager said. 'It was Rosie who did it early last week. But you know where she is, in hospital recovering from her injuries. I've just got to remember what she told me. If I remember right, you should find a box marked "Important Documents." The colour code plan is near the top, I think. Let me know how you get on. By the way, there's another document for you to sign. It's an NDA — a non-disclosure agreement. You can't inform anyone of anything you might come across while working for us.' She handed Mia a document and a pen.

Mia left Jane and returned to her task of sorting and emptying the boxes. Having to sign that agreement was a real nuisance. So much for stumbling across some juicy case and using it to kick-start her planned career in journalism. Still, it was early days yet.

She found the master plan and by lunchtime had made good progress in reducing the size of the piles. Some of the files remained in the office she was in, others had to be delivered to various departments. This gave Mia a chance to introduce herself to her new colleagues. Having to explain that she was Rosie's temporary replacement initiated short conversations about her role and even her interests, giving rise to several social invitations for the weekend. Life was definitely looking up.

Jane, her boss, paid another visit late in the afternoon. She looked around at the neat stacks of boxes. 'My goodness, you've done well. I thought it would be a two-day job, but you've completed most of it already. How would you feel about doing some overtime tomorrow morning and getting it finished? That would mean I could use you on something else on Monday, and we'll gain a day.'

Mia smiled at her. 'It's okay by me. The money would come in handy.'

'Just take that set of files in the corner up to Commercial Contracts, then you can stop for the day. And well done. I'm not often impressed by temps' work.'

Mia watched Jane leave. Maybe she'd misjudged her boss when she'd likened her to a dragon, although it was early days yet. She turned to the set of folders she had to move. It really needed two trips upstairs to the Contracts office, but that might mean she missed her bus, and then she'd be late for that evening's outing with a fun-looking pair of young women from the accounts department. She picked up the folders, held them in place with her chin and made her way out of the office. She almost made it up the stairs but caught her heel on the last step, stumbled slightly and the top folder fell off, spilling most of its contents across the floor. She placed the rest of the pile on the carpet and gathered the loose papers together.

Hang on. What was this? One of the clipped sets of papers had the name Suleiman Hamdi written across the front. Bateson's must be the law firm that looked after Suleiman's affairs in the UK. She took a peek inside.

* * *

It was late afternoon when Mickie Rollins saw the intimidating figure of Vinny Foster swagger onto the forecourt of his garage. Mickie was making a mug of coffee when Vinny came in.

'I think the Jeep's ready,' Mickie said. 'Crustie's been working on it for most of the day. We had to rejig a few other jobs, so I hope you appreciate it.'

Vinny grinned. 'Course, Mickie. You're a great team, you and Crustie, that's what I always says.' He took the proffered steaming mug. 'Listen, that cop's body's been found over at Norden. Summat's gone wrong.'

Mickie looked at him warily.

'We gotta be careful about it, Mickie. I know that guy was doing stuff for you and Crustie, but he also did stuff for Suleiman that you didn't know about. He was getting greedy and sloppy and he had to go.'

'We was using him to spot worthwhile cars for us. Course we knew he was involved with Suleiman too, but not what he was doing. So?'

'You know the rule, Mickie. The fewer that know, the better. So what could've gone wrong?'

'You saw. You was there. We dumped the body in the pool, but it must have got snagged or something. Maybe someone spotted it. Don't worry, it'll be fine.'

'Yeah, but that's the pool we dumped that crazy woman from Suleiman's in. What if she's found? We'll be in deep shit then. And I didn't see you tip him in. I was back keeping watch. Remember?'

Mickie held his hands up. 'Calm down. It's fine. Crustie went back a couple of nights ago to have a quick look-see. It was all quiet. No sign of it being drained. Trust me, they're still in the dark.'

Vinny frowned. 'Okay, Mickie, if you say so. But Suleiman's not a happy bunny, and it'll just get worse if any word of that other business gets out. And I, for one, don't wanna get on the wrong side of him. You know what he can be like. He holds monster-sized grudges.'

* * *

The problem with agreeing to do overtime the next morning was that Mia couldn't afford to be quite so freewheeling as she usually was when out pubbing and clubbing with her friends. Maybe that would be a good thing. She didn't really know Nikki and Abi from the accounts department, nor did she know the other people they met up with, apparently all from Bateson's.

'Sorry. I was a bit late leaving work, and I missed my bus. But thanks for waiting.'

Mia soon realised that one of the young men had his eye on her. He didn't wait long before he squeezed in next to her at the bar and offered to buy her a drink. He was tall, fair and handsome enough and Mia was tempted to respond to his overtures. She was warned off by Nikki during their first visit to the toilet.

'He's a right wanker,' she said in no uncertain terms. 'Far too full of himself and probably only interested in getting you into bed. He's tried it on with all of us. Steer clear, that's my advice. Now Jacob, he's a different matter. None of us has ever got very far with him. He's really shy, and at work he's always helpful in a quiet way. Mind you, if you get off with him, we'll all be really jealous.'

Mia was only drinking at half the rate of the others, who grew more raucous as the evening wore on. By eleven thirty she decided she'd had enough and started making her excuses. As she made her way to the door, she realised that the dark-eyed Jacob was following her.

'Do you mind if I come part of the way with you?' he asked. 'I think I've had enough too.'

Mia smiled. 'Of course not. I'm at work tomorrow morning and I don't want to be hung-over, not on my second day, not while I'm working for Mrs Trilsbech, and not while I'm on a temporary contract that could be ended at any time.'

'Very wise,' he said. 'Actually, she's my aunt. I haven't told any of the others, so please keep it to yourself. Where do you live?'

'I'm renting a tiny flat near Parkstone station. I was lucky to find somewhere so quick. I walked out of my last job — it was a live-in arrangement.'

She told Jacob of her reasons for quitting her post with the Hamdi family.

'We do quite a lot of business with the Arab set,' he said. 'Most of them are absolutely fine, but a couple are anything but. I suppose it's like people everywhere. But Hamdi's the worst. It's best not to cross him.'

She wondered whether there'd been some kind of friction between him and the man but decided not to ask about it just then. She was beginning to feel tired. They parted ways near the Parkstone area.

'Are you free tomorrow night?' he asked. 'How about some food? I like Italian. What do you think?'

'That would be great,' she said. 'And there'll be no work the next day, so I should be able to relax a bit more.'

'Okay, it's a date. I'll message you.'

Mia turned into her road and he waved goodbye. Things were just getting better and better.

CHAPTER 12: LUXURY

It was Friday morning and PC George Warrander and his boss, Sergeant Rose Simons, were in the small staff canteen at Blandford police station before the start of the morning shift.

'You mean we get to be in plain clothes while we're assigned to them?'

Rose frowned melodramatically. 'You can be as plain as you like, Georgie boy. Me, being able to trace my descent from the court of Louis the Umpteenth at Versailles, I'll be wearing clothes of style and grace. Stella McCartney, maybe. Versace, possibly. You know the sort, that upmarket stuff at the cutting edge of fashion that suits me so well.'

'Boss, we're likely to be tramping across muddy fields. Does Stella McCartney design wellie boots?'

'This is exactly the kind of problem we fashionistas always face. Here we are, trying to brighten up everyone's dull lives, and we get pulled back to earth with a clunk.' She looked at her watch. 'Better get moving. We're meant to be at some kind of morning briefing with the great goddess and her motley crew. Are you still on good terms with her? You know why I'm asking, don't you?'

George nodded. 'Yes, Jade and I are still together. Everything's fine, boss. It's just a bit awkward with work, that's all.'

'Awkward? Sorry, I've never experienced that particular feeling. Now, do I have time for another bacon buttie before we head off?'

When they finally arrived at the incident room in Wareham, George was dressed to blend with the crowd, in chinos and a winter jacket. Rose was wearing a cherry-red leather jacket and black jeggings.

'Don't you look the part, Rose,' Rae said. 'Great colour combination.' She was wearing her usual dark blue trousers and pale blue top.

'I do have a life outside the job, you know.' Rose sounded offended. 'I'm not always the scruffy sod people seem to think.'

'No, I mean it. That look suits you.'

'Yeah, well, Tony likes it.'

Rae raised her eyebrows. 'It's a year now, isn't it? It sounds as if you two are quite serious.'

'I take life as it comes. Have we arrived in time?' Rose said.

'Yes. We've got a few minutes to spare, so I'll bring you both up to date. Barry's in with the super. Did he explain that you're here to replace Tommy while he's off sick?'

Rae gave them the details of the case they were investigating, and of the road accident that had nearly killed the unit's junior member.

They were soon joined by Sophie and Barry. Rose asked a few shrewd questions and noted that it was always Barry who replied. *She's grooming him to take over. It's obvious. Is there another change in the pipeline?*

Finally, Sophie spoke up. 'I have a feeling there's more to this than meets the eye. It seems sensible to assume that the same people were involved in the deaths of Stu Blackman and the Filipino woman we found.'

'So, we've narrowed down her origins?' Rae asked.

'DNA,' Sophie said. 'We pushed it through as a priority. The results came in early this morning.'

'We need to think about where she might have lived,' Barry said. 'A large number of people from the Philippines work in the health service. Others are in domestic service or the hotel industry. Things like cleaning, cooking, housekeeping and so on. Which is where you two come in. We need to find out if anyone went missing back in the summer.'

'Hospitals, clinics and the like?' Rose said.

'Exactly. Then we'll move onto hotels and employment agencies, those who keep private houses staffed.' He looked around. 'Who does what?'

'George and I know a lot of the local hotels,' Rose said. 'We can start there if you like.'

'Leave the hospitals to me, then,' Rae said. 'I'll be happy with that. Then we can all move onto the employment agencies if we haven't got anywhere.'

'Sounds good,' Barry said. 'I might get started on the agencies once I've cleared my backlog. But first I want to probe Stu Blackman's background a bit more. Let's see where we've got to by late afternoon.'

* * *

It was proving difficult to find out anything about Blackman's life in or out of the force. He had kept a low profile at work and seemed not to have any close friends. His closest buddy in bygone years had always been the late Phil McCluskie, but Barry doubted whether even that friendship had stretched to their off-duty hours. Since McCluskie's death, Stu had become a loner at work, almost a recluse. He had always taken his full complement of holidays but seemed not to have talked about them very much, apart from an occasional brief mention to one or two colleagues on his return. Spain, the Balearics, the Canaries. These seemed to have been his favourite destinations. Maybe they needed checking out.

Barry paid another visit to Blackman's small house. It was neat and functional inside. A fairly new and expensive car stood in the driveway, the only item of value other than the house itself. It all gave the appearance of a man living within his means, just as his bank account had suggested. There were no signs here of a corrupt cop on the make.

Through the lounge window, Barry saw a neighbour working in his garden, so he made his way out. Ryan Stirling, a fit-looking man in his seventies with wispy fading hair, said he was a retired civil servant. He told Barry that he'd rarely seen Blackman.

'Just occasionally, if I happened to be out in the front garden when he came home of an evening,' Ryan said. 'We just said hello and not much more.'

Barry's interest was pricked. 'Not even at weekends?'

Ryan shook his head. 'No. Not more than a handful of times in the three years I've been here. I assumed he was always working.'

Barry was puzzled. Blackman had become notorious in the police for avoiding weekend work whenever he could. So if he hadn't been here, where had he been?

Ryan went on. 'Mind you, he liked his holidays. That's the one thing he did open up about once or twice. The hotels and villas he stayed in sounded fabulous. He never showed me any photos though.'

'Any visitors? Did he have people coming to see him?'

Ryan shook his head. 'I can't recall any, ever. He was a bit of a recluse, to be honest.'

Barry thanked him and went back inside. This was a puzzle. What on earth did Blackman do on his days off? He went back into the kitchen and poked around. One small bowl held sets of keys, so Barry emptied them onto the table. A set of house keys, car keys, a key to the garage and another to the shed. That left a key ring spare with two keys on it. He picked them up for a closer look. They looked to be door keys but didn't match any of the others. He pocketed them and drove back to the station in time to join the others for a hurried lunch.

In the afternoon, Barry decided to phone around some of the local travel agents and had soon assembled a picture of the holidays Blackman had enjoyed in recent years. It seemed a promising line of enquiry, so he started to compile a list of exactly where he had been and the types of accommodation he had used. Now he was making progress. All the hotels were luxury, high-end places whose prices made Barry's eyes water. It was the same for the villas. Even though Stu was single, with no family to support, those kinds of costs would have only just been manageable on his sergeant's salary. Was there more?

Barry took the keys out of his pocket and turned them over in his hand. He made more calls, this time to estate agents and letting agencies. During the seventh of these calls he suddenly hunched forward, pen in hand. Blackman apparently had weekend access to an apartment in an exclusive block in Poole that had previously been on the agency's books. No other details were available, but it was still on the company's reserve list. Barry noted the address, called to Rae, and as the two detectives set off for the car park, he told her what he had discovered.

'But his bank account didn't show anything like a regular rent payment, did it?' Rae said.

'Maybe he has another,' Barry suggested. 'One that he kept hidden. Once we've had a look at this place, I'll follow up with the letting agent. We might find out more that way.'

The address Barry had been given was for a small apartment block situated in a quiet residential area just off the approach road to Sandbanks. The building appeared to house about six flats and was surrounded by well-maintained lawns dotted with flower beds and shrubberies. A car park was situated to one side, divided into marked bays. Rae drew to a halt in a slot for visitors.

'I can't believe this,' she said. 'How could he afford the rent on this place as well as his other home?'

Barry merely frowned. The larger of the two keys slid smoothly into the front door lock and they stepped into a clean and airy hallway. They climbed the stairs to the second floor and found the door to flat five. Again, the key slid in smoothly and the door opened silently. The interior of this flat was very different to Blackman's house. It was decorated and furnished in contemporary style, the predominant colours grey, blue and silver.

Rae shook her head, looking almost bewildered. 'This is so unlike Blackman,' she said. 'It's actually elegant, for God's sake. He couldn't have done this. Either it was like this when he took it, or he paid a fortune for an upmarket interior designer.'

'Or it isn't actually his,' Barry said. 'Once we've finished here, we need to visit that estate agents and get the rental details.'

The main bedroom was furnished in deep burgundy. A large TV was positioned opposite the bed. Barry flipped through the DVDs lining the shelf below.

'Porn,' he said.

Rae examined the back of the TV.

'It's got an internet connection,' she said. 'He could watch stuff online as well. I'd guess these DVDs are a bit old hat nowadays. This place is weird, boss. I just don't get it. What was Stu doing with a place like this? It's so unlikely that it actually jars. I can't equate it with the Stu Blackman I knew. He always had some greasy food stain somewhere on his clothes. That, or dried ketchup on his tie.'

Barry had switched his attention to the wardrobes and drawers.

'Not much in these,' he said. 'Which makes sense if he was only here at weekends.'

They returned to the hall in time to hear a key turning in the entry door. A short, thin woman in a cleaner's uniform appeared. When she saw them, she gasped and put her hand to her mouth.

'Police,' Barry said, sliding his warrant card out of his jacket. 'No need to panic.'

The woman was dark haired and olive skinned.

'Are you from the Philippines?' Barry asked.

She nodded, her eyes wide with fear. 'Yes. I no have good English. But I legal. I clean flats.'

'All of them or just this one?'

'All. I come every day. I clean flats and stairs and corridors. I no trouble. Please.'

What's your name?'

'Tala Buena. I no trouble.'

'Don't worry, Tala. We're interested in the person who lived here. Did you ever meet him?'

'No. He only here weekends. I always clean daytime in week. I never see him. Other people here sometimes during week.'

'Who employs you, Tala?'

She suddenly looked fearful, glancing around nervously. 'I no trouble,' she said again. 'I in Britain legal.'

'I'm not concerned about that, Tala. Can you just tell me who you work for?'

Tala was now trembling, her eyes filled with tears. She suddenly turned on her heels and fled through the open door.

Rae was about to follow, but Barry put a hand on her arm.

'Leave it, Rae. She's terrified, but I don't think it's just about her legal status here. She's scared of whoever she works for, and we can probably find out who that is at the estate agent's office.' He looked around. 'There's nothing here. No letters, bank statements or forms of any kind. You're right. It is kind of weird, but I guess we've finished here for now. Let's be on our way.'

CHAPTER 13: INTIMACY

George could sense that his boss was becoming increasingly impatient as the morning wore on. Rose Simons just wasn't cut out for office work. The sighs became louder as the minutes ticked by, the phone slammed down more forcefully. She fidgeted in her seat, scratched her head and clicked the button on her retractable pen as if she were in an amusement arcade. Much more of this and she'd explode. Maybe it was time he suggested a change of tack.

'Boss, we ought to pay a visit to this hotel up near Bere Regis. The manager said she could give us the lowdown on the agency staff situation in the area. What do you think?'

'What do I think? I think, yes. Absolutely, yes. I'm just about tearing my hair out sitting here at this desk.'

'Really? I hadn't noticed.' He kept his eyes on his screen, somehow managing to keep a straight face. 'I'll just finish this report.'

A few minutes later, they grabbed their coats and made for the exit. Outside the front entrance, Rose stood on the steps taking in deep breaths of cold January air.

'Thanks, George,' she said. 'You're a real diplomat. Now, let's hit the road and target some low-life.'

He frowned. 'Um, boss, I don't think this hotel manager is low-life. She's offered to help us, remember.'

'Ah, but you never know where intel can lead, Georgie boy. What we find out from her could crack the case wide open.'

Shaking his head, George followed his boss to the car. There were times when he still didn't know if she was joking or not. What was she like with her boyfriend, Tony? The mind boggled.

'Hurry up, George. We haven't got all day. Mindless thugs don't wait for you to zip your jacket up, you know.'

It only took them fifteen minutes to drive to the Firs Country House Hotel, a converted manor house set in several acres of grounds just outside the small market town of Bere Regis. George stood for a moment and admired the ornate facade, then he followed his boss up the steps to the entrance. At a reception desk cleverly designed to look antique, Sharma Franklin, the manager, was waiting for them. She took them into her office, which, in contrast to the reception area, was completely modern. She sat them down at a low table.

'It's hard to keep housekeeping staff once the universities start back,' she said, pouring three coffees from a cafetière. 'So we have to use every means at our disposal to ensure we have enough people. Most of them come from agencies abroad, in places like Romania. When you phoned, you were asking about staff from the Philippines, which is why I suggested you come and visit. It's a bit delicate, you see.'

Rose said, 'You can tell us. We're both experienced detectives who know to treat information with caution.'

Once again George was struggling to keep a straight face.

'Well, there are a lot of Filipino staff in the UK. In this area a lot of them go to work in private houses in the wealthier parts of Poole. Most of the rest work for the NHS, which doesn't leave many for hotel work.'

'What's special about Poole?' George asked.

'A lot of the big properties down at Sandbanks are owned by oil-rich people from the Arab countries. They use a lot of live-in workers and they seem to like Filipinos. We can't compete in terms of wages.'

'That's very useful to know, Mrs Franklin,' Rose said. 'Have you got all that noted, George?'

He nodded.

'By the way, I'm not a Mrs, Sergeant. I'm a Ms and proud of it,' the manager said. 'The thing is, Sergeant, we occasionally hear rumours that some of the staff aren't treated very well. They stick it out because of the money they can earn.'

'Oh, sorry. Do you have contact details for these agencies? If so, George here can make a note of them.'

George duly wrote them down. 'Well, thank you again,' Rose said.

'When you say the staff aren't treated well,' George said, 'what do you mean exactly? Can you give us any examples?'

Sharma frowned. 'The trouble is, it's mostly hearsay, and it isn't all employers. But a few of them treat their staff the way they did back in their home countries. They're not used to having people they see as servants answering them back or standing up for their employment rights. It makes them angry, and they can react by punishing their staff. So there have been stories of slaps and suchlike, even of people being locked in their rooms for speaking out of turn. And that means Europeans are cautious about taking roles as domestics in these households. Filipinos are a bit more compliant. In the end, even they don't always stay long. There's a big turnover.'

They stood up and made for the door.

'Well, that went well, don't you think?' Rose said as they left. 'It's a lovely place, isn't it? You'd think she could offer us a discount or something.'

'Not allowed, boss.'

Rose scowled. 'Of course not. Just testing you.'

* * *

Sophie came into the incident room for the 4 p.m. meeting with her reading glasses perched on the end of her nose. She held a printout that she was studying intently. The others watched her frown.

'It's a summary from the vehicle forensics unit. The tyre tracks near the pool were from Firestone tyres and they say the weight distribution tends to support Dave's initial suggestion that it was a four-by-four and probably a Land Rover Discovery. Can you start checking that out on the database, George, once we've finished the meeting? Maybe the local dealers as well?'

'Of course, ma'am,' he said.

Rose looked aggrieved. 'Isn't that a bit sexist? Just because he's a bloke you think he's better suited to a vehicle enquiry. Ma'am.'

Sophie frowned, clearly discomfited. 'Not at all, Rose. He's the junior officer here and it's a pretty low-level task. But if you really want it, you can take it. It's no skin off my nose. We can put George onto a different task.'

'I know my SUVs,' Rose said. 'Tony's got one and he's always droning on about them. I even listen some of the time.'

Rae looked at Barry and raised her eyebrows a fraction. His mouth twitched at the corner. George kept looking at the desktop.

Sophie cleared her throat. 'Well, that means you can take on the follow-up from what you found out at the hotel, George. We want to know about the agencies that supply house staff to these people across in Sandbanks, and in particular if they know of anyone who's gone missing. Okay?'

George looked pleased. 'Sure.'

Rose looked less happy but said nothing. She was one of Sophie's favourite people in the county police force, but that didn't win her any privileges. Sometimes her take-no-prisoners approach to life, usually such a bonus, could count against her, and this was one such occasion. *She brings it on herself*, Sophie thought, somewhat sadly.

'How did you get on with checking for missing hospital staff?' Sophie asked Rae.

'Well, firstly, there is a big ethnic contingent in the local NHS, we all know that. But there didn't seem to be any record of a worker vanishing. The bigger hospitals are still doing checks for me, but they don't expect to find anyone who fits the description of our body. They all say they'd expect it to be flagged up quickly, so they'd be on an emergency contact list. But there's no one on that list currently, leastways not anyone that matches our person in any important way. I've still got a few local clinics to check, but that's less likely. They'd have already informed us if the employee went unaccountably missing. The ones I've spoken to have all said the same thing. They wouldn't just shrug their shoulders and not report it, not if a member of staff failed to turn up for more than a few days.'

'Okay. Let me know when you've finished. What do you think, Barry?' Sophie said.

The DI chewed his lip for a few seconds. 'There is something niggling away at me. It's the Stu Blackman thing. We've kind of assumed that the only connection between him and the other body was that they both ended up being dumped in the same pool. We think it was probably the same people responsible. We're assuming from what that young girl overheard that he was bent in some way. Maybe he was feeding them information about cars for a backhander but got greedy or careless and they decided to dispense with him. But would a disagreement over some cars end up with him being killed? Most car thieves aren't murderers. What if it was something different entirely? What if he stumbled on some other aspect of what they were up to? What if he found out that they'd already murdered someone, then let slip what he suspected? You know how he had a habit of blabbing.'

'You're absolutely right, Barry. It makes total sense. We need to shift focus.' Sophie looked attentively at her second in command. 'You know, Barry, you're the right person in the right job at the right time. We both should think this through and see if we need to open up some other avenue.'

The others sat looking at the two senior officers, their glances flickering between Sophie and Barry. It was as if they were eavesdropping on an intimate exchange. Rae was the first to move away, and the others followed her. Rae realised that she was missing Tommy Carter's presence in the unit. He might only have been with them for a few months, but his gently engaging personality was endearing. With the chief, Sophie Allen, being out of the office so much recently, the remaining three had formed a close link. But now, with Sophie back and Tommy in hospital, that relationship had been disrupted. And George and Rose had their own close-knit working connection. For the first time, Rae felt herself to be an outsider. She would get on with the task in hand, but maybe another visit to Tommy in hospital this weekend wouldn't go amiss.

* * *

It was Saturday morning, just after breakfast, and Tommy was still propped up against the stacked pillows. As Rae approached, he gave his usual uncertain grin.

'Morning, boss,' he said.

She placed a large paper bag on his bedside table and hauled a chair closer. 'Hi, Tommy. I knew Olivia was coming in to see you last night, so I thought I'd wait until this morning, though it's a bit early for visiting. I spun a yarn at the nurse's desk so they'd let me in. How are you feeling this morning?'

'Not too bad. They seem to think I'm on the mend. How are things going at work? Any more news on what happened to Stu?'

Rae glanced around and saw there was no one within earshot. 'We think he was caught up in something dodgy, and it might be murkier than we first thought. I'm only telling you this because you were working with him recently. I want you to think back over any conversations you had. Think whether he might have dropped any clues. You know how he liked to blab about things . . . I don't mean right now. Take your time over it and let me know if anything occurs to you.' She reached for the paper bag and took another surreptitious look around. 'I've brought you some of my neighbour's flapjack. It's just the best stuff you'll ever taste. You deserve something nice, stuck in hospital like this.'

'It's not that bad, boss. Olivia comes to see me whenever she can, and the staff here know she's a nurse, so I think they take extra care.'

'Quite right too. Only the best for Dorset's finest. The nurse said some other officers came in to see you yesterday. Road traffic accident team?'

He took a bite of the flapjack Rae had offered him and nodded. 'They confirmed what the chief told me when you were here on Thursday. The vehicle hit me front on, so the driver must have known what they'd done. Someone's taken a good look at my bike. They think it was quite a big vehicle, something like a van or an SUV. Dunno how they can tell that.'

'They put everything together, Tommy — the skid tracks, the damage to the bike and where you ended up. There were also a few bits of debris left beside the road.'

'Well, anyway, they also found some paint marks from the car on the bike. That helps, I suppose.' He took a sip of water from a tumbler on the bedside table. 'Are you all coping okay?'

'We've got Rose and George with us. They're both enjoying the experience of being in plain clothes. Well, at least George is.'

Tommy didn't react. Rae realised that his short time with the VCU hadn't given him much exposure to Rose Simons, though he must have come across her when he was at Weymouth CID. Rae recalled that Tommy wasn't very perceptive when it came to analysing people's personalities.

He frowned. 'There was something. Stu Blackman. He made a few comments about rich Arabs and he sounded kind of narked, as if it was personal — you know, as if one of them had upset him. I'll keep thinking about it, okay?'

'That's good, but don't worry too much. We just want you well again and back with us. Have they given you any clue as to when you might be out?'

'It might be sometime next week if things go well. But I won't be able to drive or even walk very much. I feel useless.'

Rae patted his arm. 'It's all right, Tommy. We're pretty adaptable. We can always find you things to work on at home using a laptop once you're well enough. Leave it with me.'

CHAPTER 14: MISTER SNAKE

Saturday morning

Crustie watched the police squad car drive away, then returned to the workshop. Mickie had come through from the office and was waiting for him with a mug of coffee.

'What do you think?' Mickie asked.

Crustie took a large mouthful and shook his head. 'I don't like it,' he said. 'There's somethin' goin' on.'

'They're visiting everyone, Crustie, that's what they said. But it's a lot of time and effort for a hit and run where no one ended up dead. What's it all about?'

Crustie shook his head and grimaced. 'I reckon it was an off-duty cop. They didn't say so, but they was talking to each other just as they left. I followed them out on the sly. Summat about someone being laid up in hospital and the unit being understaffed. Has to be, innit? They were laughing about it.'

'Christ,' Mickie said. 'It just gets worse, don't it? Vinny didn't tell us who or what he'd hit. I thought he was being a bit cagey when he brought the Jeep in. Good job you got it fixed quick. If it had still been here, we'd have been right up shit creek.'

'They looked at all the other four-by-fours out on the forecourt,' Crustie said. 'Why'd they do that? It's a good job ours are parked out back. They didn't check there. They were looking at the tyres.'

'What? And we're in the dark now, what with Blackman gone. Do you think it might be something to do with finding him?'

Crustie shrugged. 'I still don't see 'ow they found him so quick, Mickie. I've been turning it over in me 'ead. How'd they do that? He could have been in 'undreds of places. How come they went straight there?'

'Either someone's talking or we were spotted. It can't be anything else, can it? I been thinking about it, same as you. I dunno which one's worse. It's only Vinny who was there and knew where we put him. Either he's blabbed or he's double-crossing us. Or someone else saw us.'

Crustie finished his coffee and blew his nose on a grubby handkerchief. 'Vinny wouldn't double-cross us, Mickie. We've been together too long. And if he's blabbed, who to? Suleiman? Why would Suleiman grass us up to the cops? He fucking hates cops. He's mental about it. Come to that, so's Vinny.'

'Which means someone saw something last Sunday night, even watched what we were up to. I dunno who, or how, but it happened. I'm gonna have a look at some maps. Maybe it was someone local, out poaching or something. I'll do a bit of digging around. I know someone in Stoborough who's always grateful for a bit of cash.'

'Mickie, if they decide to drain that pool, we're done for. I still say we should of dumped them at sea.'

'Oh, yeah? So they wash up somewhere — some beach, most likely? It's what I said at the time, Crustie. At least in a pool you know they'll stay put.'

'Well, they 'aven't, 'ave they? Not Blackman, anyway.' He paused. 'What if they're stringin' us along?'

'What do you mean?'

'What if they found 'er body and kept quiet about it? What kind of shit would we be in then?'

'But you said the place was just like normal when you went for a look-see.' Mickie was looking uneasy now.

'Yeah, it was. The thing is, Mickie, if I can have these thoughts, so can Vinny and Suleiman. And if they've got any doubts about us, you know what they'll do, don't you?'

Mickie said nothing for a while. 'I'll sound Vinny out. We all go back too far for him to drop us in it now. I still think he's on our side.'

'Okay, but be careful. He's getting deeper and deeper into Suleiman's pocket, if you ask me.'

* * *

At about the same time, in nearby Sandbanks, Vinny Foster was just leaving the luxury waterside home of Suleiman Hamdi. He climbed into his Jeep and breathed a sigh of relief. He always felt the same when he left a meeting with the wealthy Arab — relief that he was still breathing and in possession of all his limbs and digits. It wasn't as though Suleiman had ever threatened him, not directly. And he'd never witnessed the man doing anything sadistic or punitive. He just exuded an aura of cruelty, power and menace. His eyes roved all over you when you were talking. He gave the impression that he could see into your thoughts. Suleiman never said very much, but what he did say was to the point. No one ever argued with him or suggested an alternative course of action. Vinny had noticed that those who did weren't around for very long. He never asked where they'd gone. Probably better not to know.

He was about to start the engine when he saw a small, dark car pull into Suleiman's driveway. Obviously, someone in favour. He'd always been told to leave his car out on the road when calling at the hallowed portals. Vinny watched carefully. A tall, thin man dressed in dark clothes got out of the car and looked around, as if checking for possible onlookers. He walked to the side door, the staff entrance that gave quick access to Suleiman's office. Vinny recognised 'Mr Snake,' Abdal Shariq.

Vinny pulled out into the road and drove to his office above a small grocery shop in Poole town centre. The last time he'd seen Shariq was after Suleiman's New Year's Day drinks reception for his employees and occasional helpers, an affair that only lasted an hour or two but couldn't be missed for fear of insulting the great man. It was at the reception that he'd first learned of the friction between Suleiman's elder daughter, Shazia, and that uppity local trollop, Mia Lockhart. The girl had been there, along with the other household staff, displaying a black eye and bruises to her face. Christ. Her appearance had provoked a few minutes of tension, until Suleiman offered to pay the girl off. For a few brief moments, Vinny thought he'd seen a different, less confrontational side to the hard Suleiman. Then the very same thin, snakelike man had appeared from out of the shadows and conducted a whispered conversation with Suleiman. It had been obvious to Vinny who the conversation had been about — Mia. He saw the two men stare in her direction. He'd wondered for a few days if Mia might come to harm, but she'd worked her week's notice without any further problems. Or had something else happened that he hadn't been told about? If the angry Shazia had hit her a second time, she might be looking for revenge but not telling anyone. Should he warn someone of the danger?

Maybe the guy really was just Suleiman's security adviser as he claimed and was keeping his eye on all the day-to-day affairs of the staff, but Vinny had taken note of his sinister, malevolent air. It was probably safer to leave things well alone. Much safer. Anyway, another visit to Mickie and Crustie was called for. Vinny felt as if he was being pressured from all sides. He seemed to be trying, like a juggler, to keep several sharp knives in the air at once. Any one of them could drop, slicing a blood vessel, maybe even killing him. How had things got this tense?

He ate his lunch — a sandwich — and climbed back into his Jeep. It was gloomy and overcast by the time he arrived at Mickie's premises. God, how he hated January. Short daylight hours and cold, wet weather. He hurried into the showroom through a heavy shower.

'You've only just made it, Vinny. I was just gonna lock up and go home. The weather's kept buyers away,' Mickie said.

Vinny looked around. 'Where's Crustie?'

'Already gone. It's Saturday. The workshop's only open in the morning. Even so, he was here until an hour ago. He's a good bloke is Crustie. Goes above and beyond. What can I do for you? Not another crunch in the Jeep, I hope?'

'That cop, Mickie. Blackman. Suleiman wants to know why he was found so quick. You know what that might mean.'

Mickie didn't say what was really on his mind, that Suleiman should have thought of that before he had the guy killed. That was the problem with psychos like him, they had a habit of acting first and thinking later.

'Yeah, well, that's been bothering me and Crustie as well. Either someone's grassed or we were spotted at some point. It can't be anything else, can it? What do you think? You were there, keeping watch.'

'No one grassed, Mickie. We're sure of that. So we were spotted. The question is, who by?'

'Leave it with us. We'll do a bit of quiet checking. But there's something else you need to know. You see that damage to your Jeep? You said you hit a hedge. Well, we had cops round this morning, looking at every job in the workshop. They said there was a hit and run with a cyclist and they were looking for four-by-fours with front damage. You gonna tell me about it, Vinny?'

Vinny shook his head. 'Nope. You don't need to know.'

'Yeah, I appreciate that. If we don't know, then we can't get in trouble, can we? Sensible. That's the way I normally like it. No questions. Then I can deny stuff. But this is different, Vinny. That cyclist you hit was an off-duty cop. So they're pulling out all the stops. They'll be nosing around for weeks.'

Vinny shrugged. 'Just keep 'em away from me, Mickie. I know how smooth you can be. I can't do that. I get too angry too quick. I hate cops. They always seem to needle me, and I can't help reacting. Even fucking Stu Blackman, and he was on our side. Supposedly.'

'What did go wrong with him? Suleiman never told me the whole story.'

'You don't need to know the full ins and outs of it. Take it from me that he rubbed Suleiman up the wrong way. Stupid prick. Just think of all he gained by staying sweet. All the benefits he had. That flat he used. The women. What was going on inside his thick skull?' Vinny shook his head and ran his fingers through his grizzled hair. 'Anyway, you need to find out why the cops were onto it so quick. Suleiman wants an answer soon.'

'Leave it with me. I'll do a bit of digging around,' Mickie said.

'By the way, that slimy looking guy is back. You know, Suleiman's helper? I dunno his real name. Do you?'

'Mr Snake, you mean? Don't know much about him. Don't want to, either. He gives me the creeps.' He gazed at Vinny for a few moments. 'It figures, don't it? He appeared again just around Christmas. A couple of weeks later Blackman gets done in. But why's he around now? Is someone else being fingered? Listen, Vinny. Me and Crustie are safe, aren't we? You'll warn us if Suleiman starts rumbling about us, won't you?'

'Yeah, of course. Don't worry. Whoever's in the firing line, it ain't you two.'

CHAPTER 15: LA SCALA

Mia pushed open the door of the La Scala Italian restaurant and stepped inside. She hadn't been in this one before — the prices had always scared her away. A staff member hurried across to her, a questioning smile on his face.

'You have a booking, madam?' he asked.

Mia looked around and spotted Jacob waving from a corner table.

'I'm meeting someone here. I've just seen him, over there.' She waved back to Jacob.

Her coat was taken, and she was escorted across the room. Jacob rose to greet her.

'You look stunning,' he said.

Mia glowed with pleasure at the compliment. So all the time she'd spent getting ready had been worth it. She'd tried on three outfits before settling on the deep-red dress and black boots.

'Thanks,' she said, slightly breathlessly. 'You look pretty good yourself.'

It was true. He too looked as if he'd taken some time over his appearance, unlike some of the other young men Mia had dated recently, who seemed to think it was appropriate to turn up for an evening out in an old T-shirt and grubby, ill-fitting jeans. She sat down and ordered a white wine, then gave Jacob another smile. 'It looks lovely in here.'

'I like it,' he said. 'This evening's on me, by the way.'

Mia frowned slightly. 'I'd prefer to pay my own way,' she said. 'I don't want to feel under any obligation to you.'

Jacob's smile faded. 'I hope you don't think I'd ever consider it like that.'

'No, of course not. But if we share, it puts us on an even footing.'

'Do you always insist on sharing?' he asked.

'I didn't used to, but then I found myself in a couple of awkward situations. It was obvious what they thought. Then, in my recent jobs, I listened in on a few conversations and saw the way that some men were thinking. I don't want to put myself in that kind of position again.'

There was a short silence. Clearly Jacob was thinking things through. 'I meant the compliment about your looks, by the way. It wasn't rehearsed or anything.'

She smiled at him. 'Neither was mine. You do look good.' She took a sip of wine. This was proving to be a bit awkward, but she didn't want to surrender her principles, not this early in a possible relationship.

He sat silently for a few moments and took a sip of his lager. 'I suppose I can see what you're getting at. I hadn't thought of it like that, that if the man pays for the date, he expects something in return.'

'I had a proudly feminist teacher in the sixth form,' Mia said. 'She took us through all the tricky man–woman social interactions and how they might pan out. I've never forgotten what she said. And temping in hotels when I was a student taught me a lot. Some of the behaviour — on the part of men and women — had to be seen to be believed. Domineering men and manipulative women. It isn't healthy.'

'You sound as if you've got a lot of life experience.'

She laughed. 'I've managed to avoid most of the worst types of incidents.' She picked up her menu. 'So, what do you recommend?'

He seemed to relax. He was back on familiar masculine territory, being asked for advice and guidance by a woman.

'All the pasta dishes are great. So are the pizzas. I don't know about anything else.'

Mia scanned the rest of the menu. There were some fish and chicken dishes. The bream in Mediterranean sauce looked a good choice, along with a side salad. Maybe potatoes? She looked up and caught the eye of a waiter, who was quickly alongside the table. They placed their order.

'You mentioned the Hamdi family last night and that you thought it best not to cross them,' Mia said. 'Any particular reason? Does he have a reputation?'

Jacob took another sip of beer. 'It's just the rumour mill. He tried to get one of our staff sacked when some property transaction didn't run as smoothly as he wanted. It was a bit vindictive since it wasn't our guy's fault. It was the vendor's solicitor. Hamdi tried to throw his weight around. He even threatened to cut his contract with us and find a different law firm. Apparently, one of the partners told him to go ahead if he felt that strongly. It was all rather nasty.'

'So, did he go?'

Jacob shook his head. 'Not yet anyway. I don't think the partners would fight too hard to keep him. Someone overheard a couple of the bosses talking in the lift. It was beginning to dawn on them that he might be a crook. We're a legitimate legal practice and want to stay that way.'

'What kind of crook?' Mia tried not to sound too keen.

Jacob shrugged. 'You might know more about that than me. You worked in their house, didn't you?'

'Well, I didn't see much of him. It was his spoiled brat of an older daughter who bugged me. She really threw her weight around. His wife is a bit of a mouse, but she's got royal connections, apparently. Some sheikh back in the Gulf.

My guess is Hamdi uses that to gain influence. The younger daughter, Gamila, is nice. She was quite friendly, we even went shopping together.'

Mia didn't want to arouse Jacob's suspicions, particularly in light of the documents she'd seen on Friday, so she changed the subject.

'Nikki and Abi think you're the cutest guy in the office,' she said. 'They say that you steer clear of all the girls though. Is that true?'

He laughed. 'Not deliberately. When I first started at Bateman's I already had a girlfriend, so I wasn't really interested. Then, when that went tits up, I couldn't be bothered, partly because I guessed they'd been gossiping about me. Then you appeared. It's as simple as that.' He finished his beer. 'Shall we get a bottle of wine? What do you think?'

'Why not? I think that's our food coming.' Mia gave him a happy smile.

They chatted amicably while they ate. Mia told him something of her background in Bristol. Her mother had died when Mia was in her early teens and she loved her father. She disliked his new partner, a brassy blonde who clearly saw sex as a tool, a legitimate carrot to dangle in front of a man in order to get her way.

'I can't stand more than a couple of days at a time at my dad's house now, not with her there,' she said. 'It's as if she's bewitched him. It breaks my heart.'

Jacob had a less dramatic childhood, but he'd always had the feeling that he was somehow a disappointment to his parents because of his perceived academic failings. He'd moved out of the family home in Bridport a year earlier after landing the job with Bateman's, an apprenticeship as a legal clerk.

'So, you're local to Dorset?' Mia asked.

'I've always lived here,' he said. 'I've only ever been away for holidays and family events. I guess that makes me boring.'

She shook her head. 'Not really. It's a lovely county. And if you're happy in a place, why move? I'd like to look for a job in London. I want to be a journalist, so I can't see myself staying here.'

Jacob looked surprised. 'I thought you were just an ordinary office worker.'

Mia finished a mouthful of food. 'I've got a degree in journalism, but there's not many openings these days. I'm sure they operate a kind of old boys' network, which counts against me, 'cause I don't have any contacts. What I need is a killer story to write freelance and get me noticed. And how likely is that?'

Jacob laughed. 'Not likely round here. It's a bit of a dead zone for things that the papers might be interested in. What about TV journalism?'

'It's worth thinking about. But I like writing. And TV can be a bit shallow unless you're careful. We were told on the course that news only makes the TV screens if there's a bit of visual drama in it. Something can be really important, but if there isn't any good video, it gets downgraded.'

Jacob looked surprised. 'Is that really true?'

'Absolutely. That's why they interview so many onlookers or neighbours when something happens. They've usually got nothing important to add to an event, but it creates a bit of emotional drama. It's what viewers seem to like.'

They finished eating at about the same time and laid down their forks. A waiter was with them almost instantly, removing their plates and asking if they'd like dessert. Mia glanced at the menu again.

'Oh, panna cotta. I just love it, even though it's bad for my figure.'

'I think your figure's lovely,' Jacob said.

Mia laughed. 'Okay, I'll go for it.'

* * *

Mia leaned back against her doorway, her arms around Jacob's neck, pulling him in hard. Their tongues were intertwined, sliding around, probing. A sudden flurry of chilly rain fell, blowing into the side of their faces. She pulled away.

'Eugh. I hate cold rain, especially when it comes on suddenly like that. Um, do you want to come up?'

He didn't hesitate. 'Yeah, of course.'

She pulled her keys from her pocket and unlocked the door. They went in, closing the door firmly behind them.

Across the road a black-clad figure slid out from behind a clump of bushes, made its way to a nearby car and started the engine. Within seconds the vehicle, a small dark saloon, had driven off, vanishing into the damp night.

CHAPTER 16: MARRY YOU

Sunday morning

Mia was sitting with Jacob at the small table in her kitchen, gazing at him while he crunched on a slice of toast, liberally coated with marmalade. A small dollop was left below his bottom lip after he finished eating. She reached across and delicately transferred the sticky lump to her finger, then poked it forward, offering it to his mouth. He closed his lips around it, sucking noisily.

'Tasty,' he said. 'Just like you.'

'Cheeky. I'll have you know that I don't make a habit of this. I'm known for my discerning nature.'

'So, I'm highly favoured?'

Mia laughed. 'Oh yeah, you certainly are. Particularly in the light of some of the things we did last night.'

'What are your plans for today?'

She shrugged. 'I don't have any. Having free time is new to me. I've been cooped up in someone else's home for the past six months. I always worked on Sundays. I feel kind of liberated.'

Jacob was facing the small window in the kitchen. 'The sun's shining. How about a walk? Tell you what, let's take the

Sandbanks ferry across to Studland and walk along the beach. I like a bit of fresh air.'

'Done!' she replied. 'Isn't there meant to be a great pub in the village? We could have lunch there. We could get the bus. It stops just along the road here and goes across the ferry to Studland and Swanage.'

'Even better. I like the way you think. I'll need to go back to my place for a change of clothes, though.'

An hour later the couple met at the bus stop and were soon on the upper deck, travelling west towards the chain ferry that ploughed back and forth across the narrow mouth of Poole Harbour. The bus route took them through the so-called Millionaires' Row on the Poole side and a huge National Trust nature reserve on the Studland side. They got off the bus immediately after the ferry crossing and headed away from the road, along the three-mile beach.

'It's so different in winter,' Jacob said. 'It's almost empty, and whoever's here is in thick jackets, gloves and hats. There are a lot more people around in summer.'

'I'm not surprised,' Mia said, her cheeks already pink from the chilly air. 'It's beautiful. I can just imagine how fun it must be for kids with all those dunes to play in. How far is it to the pub?'

'About two miles, I guess. There's also a really good café on the beach at the busy part.'

They trudged on, facing into the wind. Mia couldn't believe how much her life had changed for the better in the few days since she'd left her job at the Hamdi's house. She'd spotted it from the bus as they'd approached the ferry, its cream-coloured walls just visible through the trees. It had been hard not to shudder. Best forgotten. Now she'd found a great man, had enjoyed a lovely evening with him and, to cap it all, experienced a night of passionate sex. It just went to show how life could be a series of ups and downs. She'd been lucky to find that small flat as well, even though it was a share with two other girls. They'd both been away for the weekend, which had meant that she and Jacob had the place to themselves the previous night. If things went well with her job, maybe she could start looking for a place of her own in a couple of months.

Jacob broke into her thoughts. 'See that sign? There's a section of the beach beyond it that's open to nudists. There can be quite a few in summer.'

'I guess we won't see any at this time of year.'

He shivered. 'I don't think so, but you never know.'

'Have you ever tried it?' Mia asked.

'Well, yeah, of course,' Jacob said. 'It's only a bus ride away. I came with a previous girlfriend last year.'

'I'd love to try sunbathing in the nude. Even better, swimming. I bet it's liberating.'

'I didn't go in the water. I'm a bit of a coward. Might be fun, though.'

Mia laughed. 'As long as there aren't any jellyfish or other snippy-snappy things in the water. Could be a bit dangerous that.'

As expected, everyone on the beach had their jackets buttoned up, their hats and gloves firmly in place. Mia and Jacob kept moving. As they approached the busier section of the beach, they spotted a group of windsurfers out at sea, scudding across the grey waves.

'I tried that once too,' Jacob said, 'but I kept falling off. I guess it's not for me.'

Mia squeezed his arm and poked him in the ribs. 'Maybe you need to show a bit more staying power.'

In another half hour they were inside the old village pub. A log fire roared in the grate and a small table beside it was free.

'That's lucky,' Jacob said. 'We're early for the crowds. It'll be heaving in another half hour.'

They ordered their food, collected their drinks, and returned to their table.

'What are you thinking?' Jacob asked.

'That I want to marry you,' Mia said, and clapped a hand to her mouth. Her cheeks turned bright red. 'God, did I really say that?'

* * *

Mia and Jacob separated at the end of the afternoon, just as darkness began to fall. Mia's flatmates were home, and after a brief chat with them, she retired to her room with a mug of tea. She extracted her old and rather battered laptop and switched it on. She created a new folder, *Journalism Work*, then opened a new file, *SH*. She started to write:

BACKGROUND

Middle-aged. Probably early or mid-forties. Medium build and keeps himself very fit. Dark hair and neatly trimmed beard. Very wealthy.

Always wears smart clothes. Usually grey suits and polished shoes. Probably expensive.

Has a very intimidating manner. Minimal conversation. Guttural accent. Always looks watchful, alert. Eyes always on the move but not in a nervous way. Controlling?

Family home in Sandbanks. But also has property back in his home country. Does he have influential links there?

Wife, Nadira, is very silent. Intimidated? Two daughters. Younger, Gamila, is nice but a bit spoiled, quite generous. Older, Shazia, is a cow of the first order. Short temper, violent. Like her father, maybe? Though he keeps it under control.

WORK

Not rich from oil, apparently. Trading stuff. What? Might be arms, from an overheard conversation back in the autumn. But still very wealthy. Other Arab people nervous around him — noticed while serving at receptions and parties at the house.

PROPERTY
Main house is luxurious. Employed an upmarket interior designer to fit it out. Just discovered from a document at the office he owns a small block of luxury flats on the edge of Sandbanks. Not sure the family knows about them.

CARS
Owns several expensive cars. Daughters have a sports car each. Wife always driven by chauffeur when she goes out.

OTHER
SH is up to something. Don't know exactly what. Maybe he's not playing straight with his own government. There's something secret going on.

Mia yawned. Maybe she'd watch television for a while with her flatmates, then have an early night. She saved the file with password protection then switched off the laptop and put it away. She needed to find out in more detail what Hamdi was involved with. Maybe there were more records at the office that might prove useful. It might also be worthwhile paying a quick visit to the block of flats. No one had ever mentioned them when she was working at the house. The reason for that might be obvious — the other family members didn't know of their existence. Now, why would that be?

CHAPTER 17: EXPERIENCED INVESTIGATORS

Monday morning

George breathed a sigh of relief. Rose Simons was back to her usual bubbly self. He'd felt uncomfortable ever since the meeting on Friday, when Rose had shot herself in the foot with her outburst about men and cars. Both of them had subsequently got stuck into their allocated tasks and had made good progress in narrowing down their search. Now, they were out, working their way through a list of vehicle dealers in Poole, with this one, Sunnyside Cars, in the middle. Apparently, it dealt in high-end SUVs, both supplying second-hand luxury models and servicing them. As they strolled across the forecourt, Rose pointed out various models to George. They were approached by a man who'd come out of the showroom, a salesman's breezy smile on his face.

'Good morning,' he said cheerily. 'Michael Rollins. I'm the owner and manager. Are you looking for a particular model?'

'Might be,' Rose replied. 'I'm just pointing out some to my young assistant here, George. He's a beginner when it comes to cars. That's a nice Merc across there. Pricey, I bet.'

'Well, yes, if you look at it like that. But you get what you pay for, that's what I always say.'

'I'm a Land Rover sort of person, myself,' she said, smiling in a sickly way that George thought made her look both sinister and slightly ill at the same time. He looked away quickly to prevent himself from laughing.

'Really? What model is your favourite?' the dealer said.

Rose gestured airily. 'Well, you know, pretty well all of them. I'm not picky.'

'Is that what you're looking for this morning? A Land Rover?'

A mechanic in grubby overalls came out of the workshop and walked towards them, wiping his hands on an oily rag. He stopped a few yards away and looked suspiciously at Rose.

'Well well, Sergeant Simons,' he said. 'Dorset police's finest. And in plain clothes. Or 'ave they sacked you at last?'

'Oh, Crustie, how could you think such a thing? There are times, you know, when the most experienced investigators in CID need to call on my in-depth knowledge and experience of local crooks. And this is one of those times. I didn't know you were back in Poole. You must've been keeping quiet. You've always liked Land Rovers, haven't you?'

Crustie turned to his employer. 'She's not interested in buyin' a Land Rover, Mickie. She's up to somethin'.'

'Just having a look around. I'm allowed to do that, aren't I?'

'Well, you would be if it weren't for the fact that we was visited by some other cops a couple of days ago. They were just "havin' a look around" too. What's going on?'

'Traffic division, I'd guess. Yeah? Nothing to do with me, Crustie, not in my new hush-hush, top-secret role. I get my orders direct from Number Ten now. Sorry, but can't breathe a word of it. National security and all that. You still got a Land Rover, Crustie? It's that one parked out the back, I'd guess, in the staff bay. We've already had a snoop around.'

The two Sunnyside Cars men stood and glowered. George saw just how much his boss had managed to discomfit them, totally and utterly. He'd have to give her an easy ten out of ten for this performance.

'Bye, then,' she said. 'Might see you around.'

George followed her back to their car.

'Well, would you believe it,' she said. 'Crustie Valentine's back in the area. He was the best vehicle man in the business years ago. Totally bent. Serviced the cars for most of the crooks in the county. Disappeared after her imperial ladyship took down the Duff and Frimwell gang. That says a lot, doesn't it? You know something? I don't think we need to look much further. There's something going on here that could be very murky indeed. Let's go back and share the info. It'll be glory days for us, Georgie boy. Probably champagne all round.'

* * *

'The treads don't match.' Dave Nash was using a magnifying glass to inspect the high-resolution print of the photos from George's phone. 'Sorry to disappoint you, but they don't match the tyre prints from beside that pool.'

'You can be that sure?' Barry asked.

Dave looked up and frowned. 'Of course. But it's not all bad news. These tyres are new, recently fitted. You can see the chalk marks still on the sidewalls. Within the last week, I reckon.'

Rose and George, both of whose faces had dropped on hearing Dave's first pronouncement, brightened up.

'All the tyres? How likely is it that someone needs to change all their tyres at the same time?' Rose said.

Dave smiled. 'Yes, all of them. And you're right. It's not common, but it does happen. Wear is usually uneven between front and back, so tyres tend to get changed in pairs. But they can overlap. And remember this is a four-wheel drive. That might alter wear and tear on the treads when the second set of wheels are engaged.'

'It's still suspicious though,' Rose insisted. 'Surely?'

'That's for you lot to decide,' Dave said.

'What do you think, Barry?' Rose asked.

'Two things, I suppose. First, Dave's right, this isn't direct evidence. But you're right too. The timing is very suspicious. It fits in so well with what we'd expect from someone as canny as Valentine. No one but him would have thought of changing all their tyres immediately after something like that. He was always a slippery character. In all these years we've never been able to pin anything on him. I have to be honest, I hadn't connected his absence with us breaking up the Duff gang. When was it? Four years ago? Though maybe he never really left, he just moved to this new place and kept his head down.' There was a lengthy silence before he continued. 'It makes sense. They would have had to get their cars supplied, checked over and serviced by someone they trusted. Could you two look into the background of this Sunnyside Cars business? We need to know more about them. But don't visit again, not without my say so. We don't want to spook them.'

'In that case,' George said, 'you need to know that a couple of cops from the Stolen Vehicle Unit visited them a few days ago. Valentine mentioned it. He was obviously annoyed when we turned up.'

Barry grunted. 'Unfortunate. They'd be looking into the hit and run that nearly killed Tommy. But interesting at the same time. All roads seem to lead to Crustie Valentine. I'll need to bring the super up to speed on this. Good work, you two.'

'Any chance of champagne?' Rose asked.

'No,' he said shortly. 'Bacon sandwiches, perhaps.'

'Done,' she said. 'Good enough for me.'

* * *

The website of Sunnyside Cars stated that it had been at its current location for more than a decade. It was owned and managed by the man they'd first spoken to, Mickie Rollins. Publicity material for the business emphasised the company's experience in and knowledge of the luxury end of the SUV market, as well as the skill of their mechanics in servicing this type of vehicle.

'It figures,' Rose said peering over George's shoulder. 'Every crook in the area wants a big, black machine that intimidates people. Stick a big gun on the top and you'd have a tank. They'd probably get one fitted if they could get away with it. How many employees?'

'Five, as far as I can tell,' George said. 'The owner, Mickie, has an assistant in the sales office, and there's a second mechanic helping your old pal Valentine. Then there's the book-keeper and office clerk.'

'Does it all look legit? Any signs of naughtiness going on?'

'I can't tell that, boss. I don't know what to look for. We need one of the proper 'tecs for that.'

'Point taken, George. You're a wonderkid some of the time, but you have your limits.' She looked at her watch. 'I'm getting peckish. Let's see if that ridiculously small canteen here does bacon butties. You never know, we might be able to put it on Barry Marsh's tab. He did promise.'

* * *

Unfortunately for Rose, she was forced to pay up front, which made her glower. They were just starting to eat when Barry and Rae came in, closely followed by Sophie, just arrived from county headquarters. The three collected their snacks and drinks and joined Rose and George.

'What do you think of detective work, George?' Sophie asked.

'I'm really enjoying it, ma'am,' he said. 'Thanks for giving me the chance.'

Sophie took a sip of tea. 'Have you spoken to Jade recently? Is she all right?'

George gulped. 'Yes, last night. She phoned me. She's fine but a bit tired. It's that cold she went down with last week.'

'So, you didn't visit at the weekend?'

'No. She sounded a bit poorly, to be honest. I'll go this weekend. Well, if that's alright with you,' he said, looking awkward.

Sophie looked at Rose. 'I think we can spare him, don't you?'

Rose shrugged. 'I dunno. I'd keep his nose to the wheel and his shoulder to the grindstone if it was me, but I'm a slave-driver.'

'And a mixer of metaphors, Rose. From a personal point of view, George ought to go. I can guarantee that my daughter will blame me if she can't get to see him. Isn't that right, George?'

George looked embarrassed. 'No. That's a bit unfair, ma'am. I've always found Jade to be very understanding.'

'Well, get you!' Rose said. 'Living dangerously, eh?'

Sophie decided they needed to change the subject. 'It's time we reviewed progress. Let's consider all the odd snippets we've gathered and make plans accordingly. Incident room in fifteen minutes. Okay with you, Barry?'

'Of course.'

Sophie finished her cup of tea and left. Barry extracted a ten-pound note from his wallet and slid it across the table to Rose.

'For the bacon sandwiches,' he said.

'Is there something going on?' she asked as she pocketed the money. 'You know, something from on high, a big change in the pipeline?'

'What on earth gives you that idea?' Barry replied. He took a big bite from his cheese and pickle sandwich, deliberately filling his mouth so he couldn't speak.

He and Rae got up to leave. Rose looked at George.

'There's something going on, isn't there, George?'

He shrugged. 'Don't ask me. If there is, I'll be the last to know.' He dropped his eyes.

* * *

Sophie looked around at the assembled crime team. 'Can you start, Barry?'

'I've got the report Ameera sent in about Stu Blackman's network activity, and it has a few interesting bits in it. The most suspicious is the fact that he was accessing information about newly bought high-end cars across the county, including the owners' addresses. As far as I can tell, the dates he accessed the database don't match up with any thefts, but several of them were stolen later. It looks very suspicious.'

'So, he might have been feeding the details to a gang of car thieves?' she said.

'I don't see any other explanation, ma'am.'

Sophie frowned. 'What kind of cars were these?'

'Mainly BMWs, Mercs and Land Rovers. And that fits in with other comments we've picked up. Lydia told us he acted suspiciously a couple of times when he was at Bournemouth, all linked to the same kind of activity — expensive cars.'

'Who could he have been working for?' Sophie asked.

Rose snorted. 'That's an easy one. The dealer at that place in Poole, Sunnyside Cars. Crustie Valentine's place.'

'Any evidence, Rose?' Sophie said.

She shook her head. 'The car crime unit don't know of anything. It was all news to them.'

'There is another possibility, ma'am,' said Rae. 'It was something Tommy mentioned to me a couple of days ago when I went in to visit. Apparently, Stu made some comment to him about greedy Arabs but didn't explain what he meant. Tommy said it sounded personal. What if there's some kind of system involved — you know, like stealing cars to order? Maybe they're stolen and then driven out of the country to the Middle East. I bet there's a ready market for high-end cars out there.'

'So we've got two possible avenues to explore,' Sophie began.

George raised a hand. 'Sorry, ma'am. I just thought you ought to know that one of the cars in Crustie's workshop had a sticker on it in Arabic. On the back window.'

'Ah. There might only be one avenue, is that what you're saying, George?'

He looked flustered. 'I don't know. Maybe.'

'Okay, so we look for any links between Crustie's place and some of those rich Arabs across in Sandbanks. Good. Who's next? Rae?'

'When Barry and I were at this flat that Stu used at weekends we were disturbed by a cleaner coming in. She was from the Philippines. Tala Buena, that was her name. I can't find her on any agency list I've checked so far. Either she's illegal or she's someone's permanent employee. She looked very scared, kept saying she was legal. If that's true, she was scared of her employer rather than deportation. I'm still trying to trace her details.'

Sophie looked thoughtful. 'And the second body in that pool was someone from the Philippines, according to the DNA profile. It's all a bit of a coincidence. The thing that disturbed me about her was the crushed toes. Has anyone found any more incidents of that kind?'

She looked around at her team members, who all shook their heads.

'Anything else, Rae?'

'Not really. I was hoping that the night-vision photos we took of the prowler near the pool would show us something, but they're disappointing. Whoever it was kept his hood up the whole time, and there isn't a clear shot of his face.'

Sophie cleared her throat. 'Okay, thanks everyone. It's me last, then. The report's come back on that suitcase that we pulled out of the mud when the pool was drained. It was full of clothes. It looked as though they'd been carefully packed. We'll get more details as the forensic team get to work on them.'

CHAPTER 18: WATCHFUL EYES

Rae was perturbed. How come she couldn't find anything about Tala Buena, the frightened cleaner? Of course, there was always the possibility that she wasn't actually legal. More than a possibility, really. Wealthy families from the Middle East were known to try all kinds of ruses to sneak their favourite domestic workers into the country. Was this such an example? The benefits of having illegal immigrants as house staff were huge. They couldn't leave. They could be paid minimal wages, were expected to work long hours and treated in whatever way their employers liked. In short, they were modern-day slaves. Of course, there was always the possibility that the woman had given them a false name. But Rae didn't think this was the case. She'd just been too frightened. The name had come out too automatically. And she'd sounded almost indignant when she'd said she was in the country legally.

Maybe she just needed to be patient and wait for the Home Office to get back to her. It always took a while for them to respond to an official immigration records check. The other option was to return to the flats and wait to speak to the woman again.

Rae slipped her jacket around her shoulders and set off for the car park. It was late afternoon by the time she reached the flats. She let herself into the block and had a quiet look at the three floors. There were three apartments on each floor, with a lift and a flight of stairs connecting them. There was no one about, although she could hear a television inside a few of them. There was a service cupboard on each floor, complete with vacuum cleaner, brushes and other cleaning products, but no sign of a cleaner. Maybe she needed to return in the morning, when Tala was most likely to be on duty.

She returned to the ground floor, passing a tall, very thin man on his way in. He had a prominent nose, olive skin, dark hair and a growth of stubble on his chin. He gave her a piercing stare and no answering smile. She walked on, trying to look nonchalant, but he had thrown her. There was something extremely intimidating about him.

Rae glanced around quickly as she reached her car. He was at the first floor landing window, looking out at her. That look, so full of menace, was almost upsetting. Something wasn't right. She slid into her car and started the engine, looking around her. A shiny black saloon occupied the previously empty parking slot close to the main entrance. She made a mental note of the registration number as she drove out. Suddenly, she noticed a figure lurking in the shadows beneath some shrubs. It was a young woman. Rae drove out onto the road and found a place to park nearby. She made her way back to the flats.

The young woman was still there. Rae had been half expecting to see Tala Buena, but this woman was smartly dressed in a grey coat, dark trousers and shiny, medium-heeled shoes. Rae watched her for a few minutes until she turned and went back to the road, making for a nearby bus stop. Rae joined the queue behind her.

'Sorry, but can you tell me where this bus goes?' Rae asked.

The young woman turned. She was a little shorter than average with dark hair and a smooth, pale-olive complexion. 'Up through Parkstone and on to the town centre.'

'Oh, that's fine. Thanks. You live close to the town centre, do you?'

The woman smiled back. 'Parkstone. I could walk, but it would take me almost an hour and that's a bit much after a day's work.'

'I know what you mean. That's where I'm going, Parkstone, though I don't really know the area. It's nice, is it?'

'Yeah, though it's new to me too. The trouble is, I'm in a pokey little room in a shared flat. Once I get settled into my new job, I may look for somewhere a bit bigger. What about you?'

'Well, actually, I live in Wool but I'm here visiting someone. That's why I wasn't sure if this was the right bus. I think it's near the station, but I could be wrong. I have been known to end up in totally the wrong place before now.' Rae laughed. 'Do you work around here?'

'No. I'm at a solicitors' in the town centre. I was just looking for a client.'

Just then a bus appeared, and the conversation stopped while the small queue of people climbed on board. Rae was pleased to see that several double seats were free. She sat beside the young woman.

'I'm Rae Gregson, by the way.'

'Mia.' The young woman smiled. 'Mia Lockhart. What do you do?'

'I'm in the police,' Rae said.

'Oh.' Mia seemed nonplussed. 'You're not in uniform.'

'No. I'm a detective.'

'Are you on duty?' Mia asked.

'Yes, sort of.'

Mia said nothing for a while, then, 'What are you investigating?'

'The murder of a police officer near Wareham. I'm following up one of the leads.'

'Oh, yes, it's been in the papers. Was it someone you knew? That must be awful.' Mia's eyes were wide.

'Yes, I did know him. He'd worked with me on several cases.'

Mia frowned. 'Oh, this is my stop.' She pressed the bell.

Rae slid out of her seat as the bus pulled in. She moved to the front and checked that Mia was following, then stepped down to the pavement. She turned to the young woman as the bus drove off.

'I'm telling you because I spotted you watching that block of flats. You must have seen me come out.'

Mia nodded. 'Yes. Look, I can't tell you why because I don't really know, myself. It's probably just something silly. But I'm not up to anything illegal, honestly. Working at a solicitor's, I'd lose my job if I got involved in anything shady. That was the only time I've ever been there.' She stopped. 'This is where I live.'

Rae stood in front of her. 'Look, Mia, it might be better if you stayed away from those flats for the time being. Be cautious if you don't know what you're dealing with. Here's my contact details. Phone me if you think I can help. Promise?'

Mia nodded her head solemnly.

'The thing is, if I spotted you watching the place, someone else might have. A man arrived just as I left. Did you recognise him?'

Mia shook her head. 'I don't think so. It's hard to be sure. I did meet quite a few Arabs in my last job. He might have been one of them. I'd better go. I'm meant to be going out with friends tonight, and I've a lot to do.'

'So why *were* you there?' Rae asked.

Mia took the proffered card, turned and unlocked the door. 'I don't really know. It was just something curious that I spotted at work. It was probably just me being nosey. Look, I've really got to go.' She gave Rae a brief wave and went inside.

* * *

Mia looked out of her bedroom window. The detective had gone. What had she been doing at the very apartment block that she herself had been watching? Why were the police interested in the place? And ought she take the warning seriously? She didn't quite know what to think about that detective. She reminded Mia of some of the sportier teenage girls of her schooldays — tall, big-boned and always keen to strong-arm others into taking up hockey, cross-country running or even, latterly, rugby. Mia had always hated sports. She glanced at the card the detective had given her. Detective Sergeant Rae Gregson. So, not just a mere junior detective. And she hadn't actually come across as being in any way bullying. In fact, she'd seemed genuinely concerned for her.

Mia wondered about telling Jacob about her suspicions to see what he advised, but she quickly rejected the notion. She didn't want to put the relationship at risk this early. And there wasn't an obvious way of seeking his view on the detective's advice without telling him why she'd been watching the apartment block. Maybe better to keep things quiet and think it through herself. After all, there was no reason to rush.

She changed into jeans and a sweatshirt and returned to the kitchen. It was her turn to prepare the evening meal. One of her flatmates was a vegetarian who ate fish, and she'd be in tonight. Was there a more correct name for people like that? Pescatarians? Mia looked in the fridge and the cupboard. Pasta with some peppers, mushrooms and that unopened packet of salmon fillets. A jar of tomato sauce and *hey presto* — dinner.

She heard the front door slam and Jodie, the flatmate in question, came into the kitchen.

'Looks good,' she said. 'It's a bit chilly out there, so it'll be great to have something hot. Have we got any wine left over from the weekend?'

Mia shrugged, concentrating on chopping an onion, so Jodie had a look in the fridge. 'Woo hoo! More than half a bottle of red. Let's have some now.'

Just after they'd finished eating, Mia's phone pinged. She glanced at the display. It was a text message from a number she didn't recognise. *You're at risk from SH. C U at Ashley Green. 9 p.m.* Mia looked at the message in puzzlement. How did whoever sent the message know of Mia's altercations with the Hamdi family? She showed the message to Jodie.

'Well, you told us about your clash with the daughter. Anyone else?'

Mia realised that she'd probably told at least half a dozen people about her reason for walking out on her job at the Hamdi house. Probably more. Sometimes she'd been in pubs and clubs, talking loudly across noisy tables. Lots of people could have overheard. Even so, she was reluctant to venture out on the basis of a strange message like this. That detective had told her to be cautious.

'I'll come with you if you like,' Jodie suggested.

'Would you? That would be so great.' Mia was relieved.

The two young women left just before nine to walk the short distance to Ashley Cross Green, the local play park and green space. A light drizzle was just beginning to fall, so visibility was poor. Mia pulled her hood up and put her gloves on.

CHAPTER 19: OUTMANOEUVRED

Tuesday morning

'Maybe another visit tomorrow morning is called for. Cleaners tend to start work early and finish by mid-afternoon.' While he talked, Barry scrolled through something on his computer. He leaned back. 'But you're right. It's important that we speak to her again. She was definitely frightened of something, wasn't she? What was her name again?'

'Tala Buena,' Rae said. 'I'm having trouble finding out who exactly owns the flats, boss. I thought they'd all be owner-occupied. A couple are, but most are rented, owned by a company called Sandline Developments.'

Barry looked up. 'That name rings a bell. It's cropped up recently, but I can't remember where.'

'Okay, I'll check. Another strange thing. When I called there late yesterday afternoon, there was a young woman watching the place.' Rae told him about Mia.

'Well, you gave her the right advice, Rae. She said she worked at a local solicitor's office?'

Rae nodded. 'I don't know which one. Something was bothering her, but she wouldn't tell me what. It was all a bit odd really, though maybe it was just her overactive imagination.'

'Well, we meet enough of that in our line of work, don't we?' Barry said.

Rae changed the subject. 'I did what the super asked. There are no other records of victims with crushed toes on the central database. It looks like a one-off.'

'It was always going to be a thin lead,' he said. 'But who might do such a thing, and why?'

'A punishment of some kind,' Rae said. 'It's kind of medieval, though, isn't it? Sounds sadistic.'

Barry walked to the window and looked out, where rain was just beginning to fall. 'There are enough sadists about. Even if there's just one person in a million with a sadistic personality disorder, that means there are likely to be sixty-five in Britain. Five in the South West, which means one in our area. But the proportions will be a bit higher than that. Maybe a lot higher. The chief will know. She's full of those kinds of statistics.'

'What a horrible thought.' Rae looked dismayed.

Barry shrugged. 'Look at some of the living conditions we've found people in here, particularly children. We've both been into homes where it must be hell for the kids. They're breeding grounds for the cruel tyrants of the future. Casual violence is the norm in some places.'

'Well, from what Rose told us from interviewing that hotel manager, some of the big houses across in Sandbanks have a preference for Filipino house staff. Most will be perfectly normal employers, but there could be a nasty one there somewhere. Is it worth following up?'

Barry grimaced. 'I'll have to check with the super. We need to know what we'd be getting into.'

'Any news about the clothes that turned up in that suitcase? What about them?'

'Yes, as it happens. An email came in this morning. Here. I've printed the report off.'

The two detectives read it closely. The case had probably been in the water for about six to eight months, maybe the same length of time as the body. There was some deterioration of the clothes because of being under water for so long, but some of the labels were still legible.

'Does that match our thoughts about the length of time the body was there?' Rae asked.

'Yes, so it's very likely they went in at the same time as the body. I was wondering if I might pop across to see Tommy a bit later. I could kill two birds and visit forensics as well, get a closer look.'

He took a sip of coffee and ran his fingers through his hair, leaving a few ginger tufts sticking up.

* * *

Sophie was back in the incident room by late morning, having attended a reorganisation meeting at headquarters. Plans for the inter-county serious crime team had moved to the practical planning stage, so developments were gathering pace. She made herself a coffee and went to find Barry.

'Anything new?' she asked.

'It's the usual slow grind,' Barry said. 'Discovering bits and pieces of information that might or might not be relevant. Looking for connections.' He pulled a face.

Sophie laughed. 'The bread and butter of detective work. How we all love it.' She took another sip of coffee.

'The thing is, ma'am, there might be a thread, but it's potentially a bit tricky. Rae found out that the block of luxury flats in Poole is owned by a company called Sandline Developments. I thought I'd come across the name before, so I did a bit of checking. It was in one of the emails that Ameera found in Stu Blackman's account. It came from someone at Sandline, but it wasn't about the flat. It was a one-line message about a Mercedes sports car that needed to be red rather than black. It was from someone called Shazia Hamdi.'

'The implication being that Stu was to search for one,' she said.

'Well, that's the most likely interpretation, don't you think?' Barry said. 'The thing is, we need some advice on how to handle it from this point. Some of Sandbanks set are high-ranking diplomats and the like. To get to the bottom of it all we may need to start asking questions, and that could ruffle some feathers.'

'You're right. I may have brushed aside the difficulties when we talked about it yesterday. I'll need to make a sensitive phone call, but I've got to think it through first. Can you both concentrate on this for the time being? Do some more digging but keep it to yourselves. I don't want Rose or George involved. And no person-to-person interviews without checking with me first.'

Sophie made a call to her boss at headquarters to keep him in the picture. She then sat drumming her fingers on the table for a few moments before putting her coat on and going outside. She looked around. Too many opportunities for prying eyes, the same as inside the building. Fortunately, she had another option. It was only a ten-minute walk to her own house close to Wareham quayside, and a stroll in the chilly January air would help get her thoughts in order.

She went into her empty house, poured herself a glass of cold water and took out her mobile phone. She stood holding it for a few moments, then made the call.

The response was almost immediate. 'Hello, Sophie. Good to hear from you. You're lucky. I have ten minutes to spare while I munch my way through a tasteless Whitehall sandwich. Such is life. Is there a problem?'

'No. Well, not in the reorganisation. This is to do with our current case.'

'Ah. That'll be your dead colleague, I expect. My commiserations. I don't see how I can help, though.'

'He was on the make, Yauvani. He was supplying information to crooks. But we also found another body, and we haven't released that to the press yet. But that's not why I'm phoning you. We suspect a link to someone from the super-rich Arab set in Sandbanks.'

'Anyone I need to know about in advance? Not a diplomat?'

'I don't think so. The name is Suleiman Hamdi. My understanding is that he's some kind of arms dealer.'

'Ah, I see. Then I'm glad you've told me. Okay, leave it with me. I'll keep the Met out of your hair. Listen, can I make a visit? Would that help? It would have to be official, of course. Maybe I could see your chief constable. As Home Secretary, I think I'm allowed to do that, particularly as I'm new to the job.'

Sophie reflected that she was talking to someone vastly more adept than her at high-speed scheming and manipulating. In fact, Yauvani was in a different league entirely. 'Of course. But we'd need to get the timing right.' She could hear the sound of pages being flipped over. She'd lost control of this conversation.

'I'm free Friday morning thanks to a cancelled meeting. I'll get my staff to set the wheels in motion. It'll be like a breath of fresh air — literally. Let's hope the weather's good. Isn't it always, in Dorset? Look forward to it. Sorry, I've got to fly. Lovely to hear from you.'

Sophie sat open mouthed looking at her phone. Dammit, if she'd realised what the outcome would be, she might not have made the phone call at all.

'Ah well,' she said to herself. 'Just go with the flow.'

She finished her glass of water and set off back to the station. Barry would have a fit when he heard what was about to happen.

* * *

'What? The Home Secretary? How?' He ran a hand through his hair.

Sophie put her hands up in mock surrender. 'I thought I was being clever, Barry. Getting her onside to keep the Met at bay.'

'I didn't know you'd kept in contact,' he said.

'Well, I don't have to tell you everything, do I?' She sounded indignant.

He looked horrified. 'I didn't mean it that way. I don't know what I meant. It came out wrong, sorry.'

'I came into contact with her quite a lot back in the early autumn on that case with the migrants. I liked her. I may not agree with her politics, but we got on well on a personal level and we stayed in touch. She got Ken Burke's job as the Home Office junior minister after he died, made an immediate impression with some new policy decisions and got the top job in the New Year reshuffle. She's very astute, Barry. And she'll be coming to see us at the end of the week. So no *faux pas*, please.'

Barry backed out of her office, his face red with embarrassment. Still trying to work out what had gone wrong with the conversation, he made himself a cup of tea. Out of habit, he got one for Rae as well. She looked at him closely when he placed it on her desk.

'Something wrong, boss?'

'Just put my big feet right in it with the super.'

Rae smiled knowingly. 'I bet you didn't really. I bet it was a half-and-half kind of thing. I saw her when she came in just now and she looked tormented. Has something happened?'

'The Home Secretary's paying us a visit on Friday. The press will be in tow, big time.'

Rae gaped. 'What? What on earth's been going on? Some clever scheme of hers must have backfired. Serves her right. Outmanoeuvred by a politician. Ha!'

CHAPTER 20: IN THE WOODS

Amy Birkbeck was often a little late getting home from school. Most days she took her time tidying her things away in her locker, sorting out what she needed for the night's homework and chatting to her friends. Then there were the after-school clubs she attended twice a week. Cross-country running on Mondays and junior wind band every Thursday. She often took the later bus which meandered in a vaguely south-easterly direction from Wareham. She preferred this one because it was always quieter than the bus that left five minutes after school finished. A bus full of exuberant teenagers tended to create a cacophony of noise, and she was unable to distinguish what her friends were saying. Today, however, she hurried to catch the earlier bus. She'd spotted the way the weather was set to change overnight and wanted to check the bat boxes, which she had left alone since the dreadful events of the previous weekend. She was home within ten minutes.

She ran into the house, startling her mother.

'Goodness, Amy. You look in a bit of a rush. Do you want a bun?'

'In a bit. I'll get changed first. Gotta check the nests and boxes before it gets too dark.'

Her mother frowned, but Amy was already gone, thundering up the stairs to find her jeans and warm sweater. She ran back down, grabbed a fruit bun from the kitchen table, swallowed most of a glass of water, slipped into her olive-green anorak and made for the door.

'Bye!' she called to her mother.

She cannoned into her father as she hurtled down the steps.

'Bat box check,' she yelled. Her father watched her run past, his mouth open.

The woods were silent. The recent windy conditions had stripped the final few dead leaves from the bushes and trees, but today the air was still. A few birds could be heard in the distant trees. There was no other sound. It was important to check the boxes after a spell of windy weather. During the previous winter, Amy had lost a nest when a falling branch had crashed into a bat box on its way down, dislodging it from its mounting. She'd never found the hibernating bats. She hoped some of them had been lucky and had found somewhere else to snuggle down, but some might have fallen prey to the hungry predators that tended to prowl the woods in the cold winter months. She headed for the pool and rounded a corner, to find herself face to face with a tall thin man coming from the opposite direction. After a moment's hesitation, she kept going, trying to look nonchalant and pretending she hadn't spotted him. Which was stupid, really. How can you not spot someone so close to you? She passed him and kept going until she reached the next bend in the path, then turned slightly to glance behind her. He had stopped and was looking back, following her with his eyes and frowning.

Amy kept going and rounded the bend. She was now hidden from view. She turned off the main path and sprinted through the thickets as fast as she could, dodging between the tall beech trees in the direction of home. She ran as if she was on the home straight of a competitive race, with the winning tape ahead of her. She steered clear of the spots where leaf litter had accumulated, trying to keep the sound of her footfall to a minimum. She reached the boundary fence and vaulted across it, then, crouching low beside a tall hedge, she ran towards the farm. The twilight would help keep her hidden. She hurtled into the farmyard and again cannoned into her father, who was coming from the milking shed.

'A man,' she gasped. 'In the woods. Near the pool. He stared at me.'

She started to cry.

* * *

Theresa Jackson, who'd acted as the family liaison officer a week earlier, soon arrived at the farmhouse, closely followed by Rae Gregson. Rae listened while Theresa used her skills to calm Amy down and get a coherent description of what had occurred.

'Do you think this was one of the men from a week ago?' Rae finally asked.

'No, not the ones at the pool,' Amy muttered. 'Oh, I don't know.'

'You said last time that both men wore hoodies, and you couldn't make out their faces,' Theresa said.

Amy nodded, still tearful.

'You said one man was tall and thin, the other shorter. Is that right?'

'Yes,' Amy whispered, 'I know. This man was tall but different. I could see his face. He had a dark beard. He stared at me. He had black hair as well.'

'So, are you saying he was someone else?' Theresa went on. 'Not one of those two men at the pool?'

Amy nodded again, looking miserable.

Rae looked at Theresa. 'I still don't like the sound of it. Barry's heading up there now with Rose Simons and George Warrander in tow. Let's hope it was all a misunderstanding.'

'No,' Amy insisted. 'It wasn't. Honest. The way he looked at me. It was like he *knew*.'

'You don't think he followed you?' Rae asked.

'I don't know. I'm deaf!' She burst into tears.

'I'm sorry, Amy, I didn't mean it like that.' Amy was clearly frustrated with her deafness.

Was the man she'd just encountered connected to the bodies found in the pool? Was he the taller of the two men she'd seen last weekend, the one who'd tipped Stu Blackman's body into the pool? Or was he someone different, but still involved in this strange, interlinked set of mysteries? Or was he just some poor innocent, out for a quiet late-afternoon stroll in the woods? Rae told herself to give the young girl the benefit of the doubt. She was genuinely scared by the man's hostile demeanour. So not the last option. Amy obviously thought he wasn't one of the two who'd dumped Blackman's body, which left the middle option. In which case, why had he been there?

'Anything else you can remember about his face, Amy? Did he look really tanned?' Rae had surprised herself by asking this last question. It had seemed to just pop out of her mouth before she'd thought about it.

Amy's brow furrowed in concentration. 'Not really.' She suddenly sat bolt upright. 'That night. There might have been another one. They were moving away, and a sort of shadowy figure came up to them. He hadn't been there at the pool. He'd stayed back.'

'Like someone keeping watch?' Rae asked.

'Yeah. Just like that.'

'You're very observant, Amy. You're one of the best witnesses I've ever talked to,' Rae said.

'Well, I'm bound to be, aren't I? I can't hear stuff very much, so I see things instead.'

* * *

Barry had arrived at the pool within ten minutes of receiving the message, with Rose and George following behind. There were no vehicles parked in the approach lane, and no sign of anyone in the vicinity of the dank pond. The trio checked the surrounding footpaths but, again, drew a blank.

'He's gone,' he said to the other two after a hasty scout around the area. 'But there's a fresh set of tyre tracks and some footprints. He most likely left in a hurry.'

'Or he was just some guy out for a stroll,' Rose suggested.

'Rae's just been in contact,' he said. 'She thinks it was probably genuine. But she also wonders if he was someone new. She didn't say why she should think that, but she'll explain soon enough. I'll need to get forensics here to record those traces.'

'Why would someone be here in the first place, sir?' George asked.

'We need to discuss that back at the incident room once we've got all the details. Right now, I've no idea. I can't see it. If it was one of the guys from that Sunday night, he's being a bit reckless coming back during daylight. If it was someone else, as you say, why were they here? It's a puzzle.'

'There's something else, sir,' George said. 'It's only just occurred to me. The two men who run that car place in Poole—'

'You mean Crustie Valentine and Mickie Rollins?' Rose said.

'Yeah, them. Well, I don't know why I didn't think of it at the time, but their heights match the description that young girl gave you.'

There was a short silence. 'Ooh, George,' Rose said. 'You are a clever one. Even I hadn't thought of that.'

Barry was annoyed. Why hadn't this been spotted earlier? Full marks to George for thinking of it now, but a whole day had passed since Rose and her sidekick had visited the car dealership. This was the problem with using untrained officers as stand-in detectives. George had potential, but Rose was a uniformed cop through and through. She didn't view things through a detective's eyes.

'Right,' he said. 'This is important. We need to bring it to the super's attention, and fast.'

CHAPTER 21: MISSING

Jacob Foster was becoming increasingly agitated. He'd heard through the grapevine that Mia had failed to appear for work that morning. Had she fallen ill? Was it a family emergency of some kind? He tried calling her mobile but there was no answer. He decided to take the bull by the horns and ask his aunt Jane, Mia's boss.

'I'm a rather annoyed, to be honest. I thought she had good potential, but to just not turn up without sending a message is a bit much. I'll have to have some straight words with her when she does appear.'

'I'm sure there'll be a good reason,' he said.

'How would you know, Jacob? Ah, I see. You've become friends, have you?'

'Well, yes. And she's not the sort to let anyone down unless it's an emergency.'

'I don't see how you can have that much confidence in her, Jacob. You hardly know her.'

'Aunt Jane, if you do find out why she's not in, please let me know. I'm worried about her.'

She scowled and walked away, muttering.

No news came. That evening, Jacob called at Mia's house on his way home. A young woman came to the door who introduced herself as Jodie. Jacob explained why he was calling.

'It is a bit weird,' she said. 'She's not here, and I'm not sure where she is. We went out last night after she got a strange message on her phone. But we got separated. I thought she'd come home by herself. I was in really late and went straight to bed. But she's not around and her coat's missing, the one she wore last night.'

'Do you think we should tell the police?'

Jodie looked surprised. 'Isn't it a bit soon for that? Maybe she had to go and visit her family in a hurry. I don't know much about them though. I don't even know where they live.'

'Her dad's in Bristol, but I don't know where. What was the strange text you mentioned?' Jacob asked.

'She said it was from an unknown number, but it was something about someone she knew called Hamdi. Mia was to meet the person at Ashley Green at nine. The thing is, she seemed pretty unsure about it. She wasn't going to go, and then I said I'd go with her, so she changed her mind. When we got there, I saw some of my friends at the bar opposite and they called me over. I was going to wait but Mia spotted someone she recognised. She said something like, "It's alright. I know her. You go in. I'll be with you in a couple of minutes."'

Jodie clapped her hand to her mouth. 'I've only just remembered that last bit. She never joined us in the bar.'

'Did you see who it was? Who she spotted?'

Jodie shook her head. 'Not really. I think it might have been a woman, but that could be because Mia said "her." It was drizzly and misty, so you couldn't see very far.'

Jacob stood thinking. 'It might be better if we tell the police, don't you reckon?'

'Yeah. God, I feel really guilty now.'

* * *

DC Jimmy Melsom was annoyed. Yet again, he'd been asked to shelve his plans for the evening and put in a few extra hours to cover for a colleague off sick with flu. It was getting ridiculous, and all because of the cuts. This was what happened when you reduced staffing levels to the bone — overworked and overstressed cops who felt undervalued. And he was one of the lucky ones, with an understanding boss who tried her best to stay one step ahead of looming disaster. Like him, DS Lydia Pillay had been about to set off for home when the call came in. He knew that she would normally have taken it herself, but it was close to his route home, so she'd reluctantly asked him to volunteer to check it out. What about the so-called Missing Persons Unit? Wasn't it their job? Why weren't any of them available? They seemed to have a cushy life. Come to think of it, did that unit still exist now that Stu Blackman was dead?

He drew up outside the address he'd been given. The door opened before he'd even rung the doorbell, and Jimmy found himself face to face with an anxious-looking young man.

'Are you the police?' he asked. A young woman hovered behind him, peering apprehensively over his shoulder.

'Detective Constable Jimmy Melsom. I've come in response to the call you lodged earlier. Someone's gone missing, you said. Can I come in so you can tell me what's happened? It's a bit cold out here.'

He followed them into what looked to be a shared kitchen and dining area. Another young woman was already there. 'Tea or coffee?' she asked.

He shook his head. Any more coffee and his stomach would burst. 'Just tell me who you are and what's happened.'

Jacob and Jodie told him of the previous evening's events. Jimmy's ears pricked up when he heard the name Hamdi. Someone else had mentioned that name in the last couple of days. Who was it and what was it to do with? He couldn't remember. He realised that the young woman was still talking.

'Say that again,' he said.

'I said I feel so guilty. Mia wasn't going to go because she felt uneasy about it. She only changed her mind because I said I'd go with her.' Jodie repeated what she'd just told Jacob.

Jimmy noted it down. 'Did you get a good look at this person by the park entrance?'

Jodie shook her head. 'No. It was kind of misty and drizzly, and I wasn't really paying much attention. I feel terrible about it.'

'It's not your fault,' Jimmy said. 'Could you take me to this park?'

'Yeah, it's only a couple of minutes' walk away.'

'We'll take my car,' Jimmy said.

Jodie and Jacob collected their coats and followed Jimmy to the car.

As Jodie had said, the park was just a couple of blocks away. Jimmy pulled into a free parking spot and they all climbed out. Jimmy looked around, noting the proximity of the bar to the park entrance. It looked as though the bar had CCTV, maybe some of the other premises did too.

'So where was this person standing — the young woman Mia recognised?' Jimmy asked.

Jodie pointed directly across the road to the park entrance. 'Just there.'

'On the pavement or on the path just inside the park entrance?' This might seem a minor point, but it was an important one.

Jodie thought for a few seconds. 'I'm pretty sure she was standing back, just inside the park.'

Jimmy nodded. In that case, they might have walked further into the park after they met.

'I'm going for a quick look across there. You're welcome to come,' Jimmy said.

'Of course,' Jacob said. 'I know it fairly well, so I might be able to help.'

Ashley Green was small, less than a hundred and fifty metres across at its widest point, so the walk to the far entrance only took a couple of minutes. The path led them past the central pool and fountain, then beside the wooded area, although the trees were bare at this time of year. As he went, Jimmy took note of the layout. None of the five entrances were gated, although the Church Road entrance at the far side was in a much quieter location. There were also parking bays tucked up close to the entrance. He nodded to himself.

'Okay, let's go back,' he said.

He called at the bar and spoke to the duty manager, had a closer look at the neighbouring premises and then drove them back to the house.

'I'd like to have a quick look at her room before I leave. Would that be okay? Has anything been touched?'

Jodie, climbing the stairs behind Jimmy, said that Mia always kept her room tidy. 'Much neater than me,' she added in a stage whisper. 'And no, I haven't touched anything. I just took a quick peek inside.'

Jimmy asked her and Jacob to remain outside on the landing, slipped on a pair of latex gloves and entered the room. He had a quick look around and opened all the drawers and cupboards. After five minutes, he came back out.

'I don't want anyone going in,' he said. 'Just in case forensics are needed. Did she have a tablet or laptop?'

Jodie nodded. 'Yeah, a silver laptop. It's always on the side of the desk —' She clapped her hand to her mouth. 'It isn't there, is it? She didn't have it with her last night, so where has it gone?'

* * *

Back in his car, Jimmy phoned Lydia. 'It's a strange one. I wouldn't normally be bothering you this late, boss, but something definitely isn't right. It didn't look as though the place had been searched before I got there, everything was fairly neat, the clothes all hung up in the wardrobe or put away in drawers, but her laptop is missing. Boss, she mentioned the name Hamdi, which got my attention. Where have I heard it recently?'

'Barry Marsh was here a few days ago asking about Stu Blackman. There was some vague connection to Hamdi, but

I can't remember the details. I'll call him. Have you secured the room?'

'Yes, and the bar opposite the park entrance has a CCTV camera that faces out, it's for keeping a check on the outdoor tables at the front. I've asked the manager to keep the recording for that night. We might be lucky, boss.'

'Well, let's hope. Go home now, Jimmy, and get some sleep. We'll meet up first thing in the morning. If it's something that touches on VCU work, we need to be on the ball.'

'Aren't we always?'

'Ha ha.'

CHAPTER 22: TALA

Wednesday

Lydia and Jimmy arrived at the incident room in the middle of the morning, having spent the previous two hours at the home of the missing woman, carrying out a closer search alongside a forensic officer from the county team. The two senior VCU detectives were waiting and listened carefully to Jimmy's account.

'We mustn't assume that the cases are linked, not without any clear evidence,' Sophie said. 'But it's an awfully big coincidence. We'll know when we find out more about this Mia person. What have you found so far?'

'It was her boyfriend who reported her missing,' Jimmy said. 'He says she told him at the weekend that she'd worked as a domestic for the Hamdi family. She and Jacob only got together at the weekend, but it sounds like they got serious pretty quick. He seemed a decent enough bloke to me. We've got a statement from him and he knows he'll be a suspect, but I don't think he's the type. What do you think, boss?'

Lydia pursed her lips. 'I agree. He didn't set off any warning bells with me. He seemed a nice guy, and genuinely upset by what had happened. Though I only had a few minutes with him before he had to set off for work. Nothing suspicious about the other flatmates either. Two young women who were just as puzzled as him.'

Sophie had worked with both Lydia and Jimmy in the past, and trusted their judgement, particularly Lydia's. She'd once been Sophie's protégée in the VCU, a spot now occupied by Rae. 'What do we know about this Hamdi family?' she asked.

Barry shrugged. 'Not much. The name cropped up when we were looking into what Stu Blackman might have been up to. Ameera found an email from a Shazia Hamdi when she was tracking through his network activity log. Something about a red Mercedes. I don't think there's anything else.'

'Well, this guy Jacob Foster, the missing woman's boyfriend, knows a bit about the family,' Jimmy said. 'He's an office worker at a local solicitor's and met Mia there. She started with them last week. They deal with some of the family's legal work. He said that Suleiman Hamdi's a nasty piece of work and very wealthy. Shazia's his daughter. One interesting thing he told us is that Mia, the missing girl, had a run-in with one of the daughters while she was working at the house. According to Mia, the daughter assaulted her, so she walked out. She got a pay-off. It could be this Shazia.'

Sophie was fingering her lips. 'Rae met this Mia woman very briefly, late on Monday afternoon. Apparently, she was watching a small apartment block that Hamdi owns. She thought she was being unobtrusive, but to Rae she stuck out a mile, so she tried to warn her off. She told Rae that she'd spotted something odd at work involving Hamdi but didn't elaborate. Any ideas?'

Lydia shook her head. 'Not really. This is news to us.'

'Did this Jacob say whether Mia had ever mentioned any Filipino people on the staff at the Hamdi house?' Sophie asked.

'No. Not that he told us. Why?'

Sophie stayed silent for a few moments. 'Because we found another body in the same pool as Stu Blackman, but it had been there a lot longer. It's still undergoing forensic tests, but it looks like it's a female from the Philippines. We're waiting for forensic confirmation before we release the news to the press.'

A long silence followed, broken eventually by Lydia. 'You know that Filipinos are a favourite choice for domestic staff in Sandbanks, especially among the Arab community?'

Sophie nodded slowly. 'Yes.'

'We've been finding out more on the quiet,' Barry added. 'It's ongoing.'

'Well, we'll let you know anything we find out, of course,' Lydia added. She frowned. 'Some of these people will have diplomatic immunity, won't they?'

Everyone looked at Sophie. 'Possibly. Probably. Anyway, if we're cautious, there shouldn't be a problem. We've got the Home Secretary on board.'

Everyone looked surprised, but no one said anything. What could they say? This was deep water into which they most certainly didn't want to plunge.

* * *

Jimmy paid another visit to the bar at Ashley Green, interviewed the staff and took away a copy of all the CCTV footage from Monday evening. Lydia walked through the small park with a forensics officer, looking for residual signs of a struggle. Rose and George carried out a house-to-house enquiry of the residential properties on the opposite, quieter side of the green, where a vehicle could have waited for a few minutes if Mia had been abducted.

'We seem to be taking this disappearance a bit seriously, boss,' George said to Rose as they left the fifth house. 'Fine if it's a kiddie that's gone missing, but not someone in their twenties and there's no evidence of violence.'

Rose shrugged. 'Maybe we're not getting the whole picture, Georgie boy. To be honest, my head's reeling a bit. Maybe this detective lark isn't for us after all. I'm starting to miss roaring around the streets in the squad car looking for common thieves, thugs and hooligans. They're usually more brainless than me, so we have a good chance of catching them. This stuff is all too clever for a thicko like me, George, but you should be able to keep up — unless you've been contaminated by my radiant stupidity.'

They stopped chatting while they waited for a response at the next house. The door was opened by an alert-looking elderly woman. Rose introduced herself and repeated the question she'd asked at the previous houses.

'Yes, there was one of those big black-type cars waiting across the road for a few minutes in the evening.' The woman stepped out a few feet and pointed to the bay window on the left. 'I sometimes sit there to take my late evening cup of tea at this time of year. It's nice when the Christmas lights in the park are still up. I couldn't see them because the car was blocking my view. It was really big, with blacked out windows. It was only there for a few minutes and was gone by the time I finished my drink, so I could see the coloured lights again. They're taking them down at the end of the week, you know. Shame. They're so pretty.'

'Can we come in and have a look?' George said.

She led them into the room in question and showed them the winged armchair and small table in the bay. The homeowner, Pauline Smith, was right. There was a good view across the park from there.

'Did you see anything else unusual, Mrs Smith? Either about the car or anyone round about?'

She shook her head. 'Not really. It did have its engine running, I remember that. It always annoys me when I'm out walking along a pavement and a car's belching out exhaust fumes. It makes me cough, so I hold my breath when I walk past them.'

'How come you saw that on Monday night?' Rose asked. 'It was dark.'

The lady pointed across the road. 'Streetlight.'

'Okay. I think we'll need a short, written statement from you, but we'll be back for that,' Rose said. 'It'll give you a bit of time to think of anything you might have forgotten.'

No other residents had noticed anything amiss on the evening in question. Rose and George returned to the cars where the other detectives were waiting. Lydia asked everybody to tell her what, if anything, they'd found, so Rose told her about the car Pauline had seen. Jimmy had obtained copies of the bar's CCTV recording.

Lydia had found no obvious signs of a struggle. 'No bloodstains and no new scuff marks on the grass. Nothing out of the ordinary. It's all a bit mystifying.'

* * *

Rae Gregson was sitting in her car in a corner of the car park by the block of flats, pretending to read through some documents. She'd been watching the entrance for more than an hour, but Tala Buena, the frightened cleaner, hadn't shown up. What would they do if she didn't appear? There seemed to be no trace of her in any official records. Had she given a false name after all?

Rae glanced up as a small car drove in and stopped in a bay close to the entrance. A small woman clambered out and glanced around. It was Tala. Rae watched Tala make her way to the front porch and let herself into the building. Rae waited ten minutes, then followed Tala inside, letting herself in with the keys found at Stu Blackman's house. Would the cleaner make a start on the ground floor first and work upwards, or start at the top and work down? None of the doors on the ground floor were open and there was no sound of a cleaner at work, so Rae went up the stairs to the first floor. There, she found the service cupboard open and heard the tinny sound of a radio. A trolley was standing outside the flat next to Blackman's, which had its door open. The music was coming from an old, battered transistor radio sitting on the trolley alongside a collection of cleaning materials and tools. Rae had seen similar trolleys in hotels. She stepped inside the open door just as Tala was coming out. Just as she had done before, Tala gasped and put a hand to her mouth.

'Hello, Tala. No need to panic. I'm not here to arrest you or anything. I just want to ask you a few questions. Can we go back inside, please?'

Rae made sure she was standing between Tala and the door in case the cleaner made a dash for it. Tala nodded, so Rae pushed the door shut with her hip. The lock engaged with a satisfying click. She looked around her. The furnishings and fittings in the flat looked almost identical to those in Stu Blackman's apartment. Maybe it had been a contract job. She followed Tala through to the kitchen and they sat down, Rae positioning herself closer to the door. Clearly Tala thought it inappropriate for the cleaner to use the lounge.

'I want to know about this apartment block, Tala. Who owns it? Do the occupants own their flats or do they all rent them?'

Tala, still nervous, looked at her. She was sitting on the edge of her stool, taut as a bowstring. Rae wondered if she was considering making another attempt to flee. 'They rented. All them, 'cept penthouse.'

'And who has that?'

'Him. Mr Hamdi. He keep that one himself.' Her eyes dropped to her lap. Clearly there was something troubling her.

Rae nodded. 'Does he own the building?'

'Yes. He boss. The others, they rent from him. He important man. He own lots of places. He rich.'

'He owns other properties in Poole? Do you clean them too?'

'That my job. I clean all his places 'cept his main house. Pay is good.'

'Do you see very much of Mr Hamdi?'

Tala shook her head. 'No, not since I leave working in his house. I see his manager, Mr Shariq. He pay me.'

'Is he tall and thin? Does he drive a black car?' Rae was wondering if he was the man she'd seen there on Monday.

'Yes.' Tala had become even more nervous, her eyes were darting about the room.

'Do you get paid in cash or do you have a bank account?'

Tala sat up straight, which brought the top of her head level with Rae's shoulder. She sounded affronted. 'I here working legal. I have all documents. Me, I not benefit cheat.'

Rae decided to change the subject. 'Did you ever meet Mr Blackman, the man who rented the flat we saw you in the other day?'

'Mr Blackman, he nice man. He tip me and give me present at Christmas. He only there at weekends.'

Rae was surprised. Stu wasn't known for his generosity. 'Really?' she said.

'When he have girlfriends to visit, he tip me to stay away. They dress nice.' Tala smiled. 'He have party with them. Sometimes extra cleaning next day but I not mind.'

Time to attack from another angle. 'So, how long have you worked here, Tala? As the cleaner?'

'Since summer. I work in Mr Hamdi's house before that. I take Janella place here.'

'Did she leave?'

'She went back. Mr Shariq told me.' Again the evasive look.

'She went back where?' Rae asked.

'Home. To Pilipinas. She come from Mindanao, not like me. I from Manila.'

Rae was silent for a few moments as she thought through the implications of this. 'Why did she go home?'

Tala shrugged. 'She lazy. Not do her job properly. That's what Mr Shariq say.'

'Did you think that?'

Tala shrugged again. 'No. She always work okay. But she was nosey. She try to find out about people. She laugh about them to me, about their secrets. I not like that. I keep away from trouble.'

'Do you think Janella got herself into trouble somehow?' Rae asked.

'I don't know. But she got sacked and went back.' By now, Tala was looking utterly miserable.

'Did you see her before she went?'

Tala shook her head. 'I too busy. I working in big house and have lots to do.'

'Have you kept in touch with her?'

'She not answer my messages. Don't know why.' Tala shrugged.

Rae could see that Tala was getting increasingly edgy. 'What was Janella's last name, Tala?'

'Ramos.' Tala looked at her watch. 'I got to work. I be late. I get into trouble.'

'Okay. Where do you live?'

Rae noted the address, thanked Tala and left. Was it too much to hope for that the mystery of the woman in the pool had just been solved? And what was to be made of the fact that yet another mystery seemed to be linked, somehow, to the mysterious Mr Hamdi? She phoned her boss, climbed into her car and drove away.

* * *

In a silent corridor in Whitehall, a hushed conversation was taking place.

'Home Secretary, we must send in officers from the Met, surely? Some of these people are very influential with their governments. We can't have county plods stomping all over the place with their big feet and putting our international relations at risk. It's unthinkable.'

'No. We'll leave it to them for the time being. Sometimes we have to trust our local police forces. This is one of those times.'

'But, Home Secretary, it could go horribly wrong. The consequences might be serious. Is there something you're not sharing with us?'

'Yes. I know the officer in charge. Do you think I'm a fool?'

'I'm so sorry, Home Secretary. I didn't mean to imply . . .' A pause. 'Of course. That would explain your, er, somewhat hastily arranged visit on Friday.'

'You're reading too much into it, David,' she snapped. 'And don't assume I'm incapable of organising something without you and the other aides. I make my own mind up about things. I always have done. I'm not sure I like having my motives questioned by advisors, however well-meaning, so it might be better if you backed off a bit. Otherwise, there might have to be a parting of the ways.'

Yauvani Anand smiled to herself as the bumptious, and now red-faced, staff member hurried away along the corridor. These people needed to learn that she was her own person and expected things to be done her way. And that she didn't always play by the rules. Well, they would have to either learn or find themselves new jobs, because she wasn't about to change.

CHAPTER 23: AT HAMDI'S HOUSE

'Okay.' Barry slid his phone back into his pocket and turned to Sophie. 'That was Rae. She's in place. She's also confirmed that Janella Ramos had an account at one of the local banks. It hasn't been touched since July. We have enough to go ahead. And something else as well. Shariq drives a black Mercedes saloon, one of the smaller models.'

They climbed out of the car and made their way up the driveway towards the gleaming white house. The air was heavy with the scent of pine trees and the sea. They could hear the crash of the waves, although the house and shrubbery hid the view of the beach. A gardener was sweeping leaves and pine needles from the path ahead of them. He looked up at their approach and eyed them suspiciously.

They mounted the steps to the capacious porch. Barry rang the bell and looked around curiously. So this was what one of those ultimate luxury homes on 'Millionaires' Row,' as Sandbanks was called, looked like from up close. The term was rather outdated now. You'd need a lot more than a million to buy one of these properties at current prices. He realised that Sophie was watching him, a slight smile on her lips. She gave him a wink, something she hadn't done for a long time. It brought back memories of their early days with the VCU when he was still a detective sergeant. How things had changed. Here he was, a DI, wearing a new suit and new shoes, having just climbed out of a new car.

He looked back at Sophie and returned the smile. She still scrubbed up well. Not that he would ever dare use a phrase like that to her face. But she'd always been a bit of a looker with an eye for nice clothes. Really not bad for someone approaching fifty.

He cleared his throat. 'How are we going to take this, ma'am?'

'Oh, you lead. I'll sit and smile. I might throw in a couple of red herrings to see how he reacts. That's assuming he's in, of course.' So she still had that mischievous streak too.

The door opened to reveal a middle-aged housekeeper in a black uniform and a haughty manner. 'Yes?'

'Detective Inspector Barry Marsh. This is Detective Superintendent Sophie Allen. We're from Dorset police and we'd like to see Mr Hamdi, please. May we come in?'

She stood back, ushered them into a large hallway, showed them to a cushioned bench seat and asked them to wait. Barry looked around. He was far from being an expert in interior décor and furnishings, but even he could identify the Middle Eastern feel. And the probable expense.

'Lovely, isn't it?' Sophie said.

Barry shrugged, and she laughed. 'I can guess what you're thinking, Barry, and I agree. But it doesn't stop me from admiring it.'

The housekeeper returned with a tall, bearded man in a beautifully cut blue suit, white shirt and red tie. He was pulling at his cuffs. Barry noticed the cold, wary eyes and the scar on the right side of his forehead which stretched from his hairline almost to the outer corner of his eye.

'Who are you and what's this about?' Hamdi said. He waved the housekeeper away. 'My housekeeper wasn't clear.' He spoke precise, well-enunciated English with a Middle Eastern accent.

Barry repeated his previous introduction. 'We didn't give the reason for our visit, maybe that's why she was uncertain.'

They shook hands. Barry noted the man's hesitancy as he went to briefly shake hands with Sophie. Was he unused to dealing with women in senior roles?

'Well, I'm a busy man and you've interrupted a meeting with a client. We'll talk in the drawing room.'

He led them to a spacious, high-ceilinged room decorated in deep-red velvet and gold and gestured for them to sit down at a low table.

'We're investigating the murder of one of our colleagues, Mr Hamdi. You may have seen on the news that Sergeant Stuart Blackman's body was found last week. We'd like to know if you had any dealings with him, for whatever reason.'

A few moments of silence ensued. Barry could sense some rapid thinking going on in Hamdi's head.

'I wonder if I need my lawyer present.'

Barry shot a glance at Sophie. Things had already accelerated to a point beyond what he'd expected. She cleared her throat. 'Of course, you have that right, Mr Hamdi. If that is your wish, then we'll book a time for a formal interview at the police station. But it is our intention to keep this low-key at present. As I say, the choice is yours.'

There was another silence as Hamdi's gaze flickered from one to the other, finally settling on Sophie. 'I have contacts in the Home Office. And the Foreign Office.'

'You and me both.' Sophie looked at him levelly. 'And mine will be more senior than yours, Mr Hamdi. You can be sure of that.'

He continued his bleak stare for a few seconds longer. 'I'm willing to continue for now, but I only have a few minutes.'

'Thank you. It's not our wish to cause any unnecessary upset. Please answer DI Marsh's question.'

'I may have met your officer on one or two occasions. He sometimes rented a property owned by a company I have links with.'

'Where was this, may I ask?' Barry asked.

'The company owns a small apartment block a mile or so away in Parkstone. As I said, he had occasional use of one of the apartments.'

Barry opened his document case and extracted a single sheet of paper. 'Can you explain this, Mr Hamdi?'

Hamdi studied the page. It was the email sent from Hamdi's daughter to Stu, about a red Mercedes sports car.

'Yes, well, that's one of my daughters. Clearly she wanted advice.'

'Is that the company you referred to? Sandline?'

Hamdi nodded, almost imperceptibly. 'Sandline Developments.'

'Do you have a preferred dealer for your cars, Mr Hamdi?' Barry asked. 'We noticed that there are about ten vehicles registered to the various family members in this household.'

'Not exclusively.'

'But have a number of them come from Sunnyside Cars, down near the harbourside?' Barry asked.

'It's possible. Is there a problem?'

'Not necessarily. Was this car for your daughter?'

'It was a birthday present for my younger daughter, Gamila. Shazia was arranging it,' Hamdi said.

'What about hiring household staff and filling vacancies? Do you have a preferred agency for hiring personnel?'

'I think we mainly use the VF agency. But this is not something I get involved with. I leave it to my household manager.'

'Oh, I see. Who is that?' Barry asked.

'I don't see the point of this.'

'Did your company, Sandline, employ a cleaner, Mr Hamdi?' Sophie said. 'One by the name of Janella Ramos? She was from the Philippines.'

Hamdi looked puzzled. 'Why are you asking me this?'

'We found her body too. In the same flooded pit as DS Blackman. So we have a double murder on our hands. Didn't she work in this house at one time? Her bank details suggest she was employed and paid by Sandline. The regular monthly deposits suggest they were wages. Or have I misinterpreted something?'

'I can't recall all the details of everyone who's ever been employed in my properties. I have staff to deal with that kind of thing.'

'Would that be Mr Shariq?' she said.

Hamdi seemed nonplussed for a moment, then rose to his feet. 'Yes. Now I need to get back to my meeting. And I want my lawyer present when we talk again.'

The two detectives took their leave. Barry handed Hamdi his card. 'As soon as possible, Mr Hamdi. Before the end of Friday.'

Sophie turned to go but then spun back.

'Oh, I nearly forgot. You had a young woman by the name of Mia Lockhart working as a member of your household staff until very recently. She lived in, we believe. She seems to have disappeared and we're concerned for her safety. Better make that arranged meeting this afternoon because we need to interview everyone who knew her. Meanwhile, DI Marsh and I want to speak to your household manager and look at the staff records. Now, please.'

He almost trembled, barely able to suppress his anger. 'Do you have a warrant?'

'Why? Do you have something to hide?' Sophie retorted.

'Of course not,' he spat out. 'But I have the right to insist.'

'Yes, you do. I'm a superintendent, Mr Hamdi. If you force me to get a warrant, be assured that I will do so without the slightest difficulty and be back within the hour with a full squad of search officers. That warrant will be for the whole house and every room in it. I'm happy to take that line if you force me to. I thought you'd prefer to keep it low-key, but the choice is yours.'

Hamdi glowered at her. He rose from his chair and pressed a small button on the wall by the door. 'I'll leave you with Mrs Sayegh, the housekeeper. She manages all the staff. Please wait here.'

'Where were you on Monday evening, Mr Hamdi?' Sophie said.

He frowned. 'I was here, at home. I had a meeting with my lawyer about a property deal we have planned.'

'What time did the meeting finish?'

'About ten, I think. Why?'

'Isn't that obvious? We're trying to establish the whereabouts of everyone of interest at the time Mia Lockhart disappeared.'

He stared at her angrily for a few moments then left the room, closing the door behind him.

Sophie took the opportunity to make a brief phone call to Rae, while Barry had a quick look around the room. He could hear quiet voices outside the door but couldn't make out what was being said. The door was opened by the housekeeper who'd welcomed them to the house — although 'welcome' wasn't the right word for their frosty reception. Her attitude had, if anything, become more hostile.

'We'll use my office,' she said curtly, turning on her heels and stalking away towards a door at the far end of the hallway. Sophie and Barry followed her to a small room with racks of storage boxes lining one wall, a desk and filing cabinet set against the opposite one, and a low cupboard placed under a small window in the short fourth wall, facing them as they entered. The room obviously doubled as both a storage facility for cleaning equipment and the housekeeper's office. A laptop sat open on the desk.

'What do you want?' the housekeeper demanded.

'Mrs Sayegh, isn't it?' Sophie said smoothly. 'Ideally, we'd like your co-operation, but your hostile attitude seems rather to preclude that. We don't intend to be unpleasant, so please relax. We're here in an attempt to find out what happened to Janella Ramos, who may have worked here until last summer, and also Mia Lockhart, who definitely did work here until a couple of weeks ago. Both have disappeared. We're very concerned for Mia's safety. Your staff files would be a good starting point, but first we want to ask you a few questions.'

Barry had endured some awkward interviews in his time, but few had been as monosyllabic as this one. The housekeeper was frosty in the extreme, treating each question as if it were a trap set to test her loyalty to the Hamdi family. In one respect, he couldn't help but admire her attitude. But it made trying to gain information hard going. The woman maintained her disdainful look throughout the session. Finally, Sophie decided to draw an end to it.

'Let's talk to the gardener instead,' she whispered to Barry. 'He might be more helpful.'

He wasn't. The middle-aged man, Nasir Dawoud, was cautious in the extreme. It transpired that he wasn't just a gardener, he was a general handyman who held similar roles with three other households in the same street. Much of his time was spent outside in the gardens of the four properties, but he also did painting, general repairs and even some low-level electrical work.

'Is your time split evenly between the houses?' Barry asked him.

'No. I am here for three days each week. The other places, maybe half a day.' He spoke slowly. Was he being cautious?

'How long have you been working here, Mr Dawoud?' Barry asked.

The man pursed his lips. 'A year. I was lucky to get the job, I think. I lived in London before that.'

'Doing the same kind of work?'

'No. I worked in a café. But I prefer to be outside in the open air. It suits me better. I am from a farming family.'

'Why did you come to Britain, if that's the case?' Barry asked.

'My family were all killed in the civil war. There was nothing for me there, just more death and destruction. I am saving to study for an agriculture degree. I may go back if the war ends.'

'Do you know the members of the family here, Mr Dawoud?'

He shrugged. 'Some of them. But not close. Mrs Hamdi, she is very nice. The others don't bother me.'

'Do you remember Mia Lockhart? She worked here as household staff until two weeks ago,' Barry said.

'I saw her sometimes. She caused trouble.'

Sophie watched him closely. 'What do you mean?' she said.

He shrugged. 'She didn't know her place. She argued. That is not the way.'

'Did you know she is missing? That no one knows where she is?' Sophie asked.

Another shrug. 'It is no surprise. But I cannot comment. It is not my place.'

Barry took out a photo of Stu Blackman. 'Did you ever see this man here?'

Dawoud shook his head. 'No. I don't remember him.'

'What about a cleaner, Janella Ramos? Is that name familiar?'

He looked down at his feet. 'She worked here then moved somewhere else.'

'What was she like, Mr Dawoud?'

'I stay away from her. She was trouble. She was always laughing with men. All men. She tried to find out things and make money.'

'Was she trying to blackmail someone? Is that what you're saying?'

'I don't know. I stay away from it all. I just get on with my work.'

'Do you know Mr Shariq?' Barry asked. 'He works for Mr Hamdi, doesn't he?'

Silence. Dawoud was clearly flustered. His eyes flickered from Barry to Sophie and back. He shook his head. 'No.'

He picked up a rake and moved away to a heap of dead leaves on the lawn.

The detectives returned to the house to interview Mrs Hamdi, who was waiting to meet them in the hallway. She was a soft-featured woman, immaculately dressed in pastel-coloured clothes and a cream headscarf. She was much less hostile than her husband and housekeeper, but despite her apparent openness they learned little from her. She denied all knowledge of anything relating to the investigation and claimed she'd been at home with Gamila, the younger daughter, on the evening of Mia's disappearance.

* * *

Jane Trilsbech, Mia's boss at Bateson's Solicitors, looked troubled. Lydia thought she understood why. The office manager had freely admitted that her first instinct upon learning of Mia's non-appearance at work had been cynical, dismissive. She'd immediately assumed that Mia was just another unreliable young temp, unable to commit to solid, hard work.

'I admit I was wrong to make that assumption,' Jane said. 'But it happens so often, temps letting us down. If I had a pound for every time someone didn't turned up, I'd be a rich woman.'

Lydia suspected that this was a gross exaggeration, but she smiled anyway. There was no point in upsetting the woman.

'So, in fact, you found her a hard worker in the few days she was here?'

'That's right. She only needed a day and a half to complete a job that should have taken two. And she did it better than I'd anticipated. Moving premises meant that a lot of stuff was boxed up, and her job was to get it back to its rightful owners. It could have resulted in chaos, but she somehow got everything to its rightful home.'

'So you might have kept her on if she'd wanted a permanent job?'

'Yes, provided things continued the same way. She was on a three-month trial. I've racked my brains, but I can't remember her giving any clue as to where she might be. She never mentioned any family, other than to Jacob. He's my nephew, by the way.'

Lydia raised her eyebrows. 'He seems a nice young man.'

'He is. Reliable and trustworthy. He won't be involved in Mia's disappearance, Detective Sergeant, not in any way.'

'Suleiman Hamdi is one of your clients. Is that right?'

'Yes. I can't tell you what work we do on his behalf though. I think you'd need to see one of the senior partners about that.'

'Yes. Maybe you could clear the way for me. Right now, if possible.'

'Do you suspect foul play of some kind? Jacob said Mia had told him of a run-in with someone in the Hamdi family.'

Lydia shook her head slowly. 'Let's hope it hasn't come to that.'

Lydia's visit went downhill from that point on. The one senior partner who had a few minutes to spare was decidedly unenthusiastic about revealing anything that might be interpreted as dishing the dirt on one of their clients.

'Mia couldn't have seen anything about the Hamdis in the course of her work here?' Lydia asked him.

The man harrumphed. 'No. Of course not. Everything is securely stored under lock and key. She was only a lowly temp worker.'

'You're saying that all the documents relating to the Hamdis were secure? That Mia couldn't have seen anything, despite the fact that her job was moving files to their new homes?' Lydia said.

He hesitated. Clearly it had only now dawned on him that Mia had been transferring all kinds of documents between offices.

'Well, I assume not.'

'What's the nature of your work for Mr Hamdi?' Lydia asked.

'I can't disclose that.'

'Let's consider a possible scenario. Somehow, while moving folders, Mia caught sight of something relating to the Hamdi family. Could it have been something that put her in danger? Mr Halliwell, something isn't right here. I'd like you to do a very thorough check and contact me if you find anything.' She handed him her card.

Halliwell frowned. He looked troubled.

'Please do it as quickly as possible,' Lydia said. 'Otherwise, I shall be back with a warrant.'

* * *

Shazia, the elder of the two Hamdi daughters, came across as very self-confident. What was she, twenty? Twenty-one? She gave a strong impression of being self-controlled and sophisticated, although Sophie wondered if she'd led a comparatively sheltered life because of the wealth of her family. She was tall and slim and wore a brightly coloured shirt with a complementary headscarf. The outfit went well with the tight jeans she wore.

'I don't see why you need to talk to me,' she said as she sat down. She sounded hostile. 'Surely other people can tell you what you need to know?'

'That's not how it works, Shazia,' Sophie said. 'If a serious crime's been committed, we need to speak to everyone directly.'

'So, what's the problem?' Shazia snapped.

'Mia Lockhart hasn't been seen since Monday. It's possible she's been abducted, so we need to speak to everyone who's had anything to do with her recently. You had an argument with her that led to her leaving her job here. That was just over two weeks ago. Is our information correct?'

'Yes, but if you think I had anything to do with her vanishing, you're mad. Why would I bother to get involved with a servant? One goes, we just get another. I wouldn't demean myself.'

'You aren't concerned about her safety, then?' Sophie asked.

Shazia shrugged. 'I don't feel responsible one way or the other.'

'What if she's come to harm?'

'Well, I hope she hasn't, but it's got nothing to do with me. Why would it?'

'Because my understanding is that you hit her around the head with a table lamp, causing fairly severe cuts and bruises to her face. You were lucky she didn't press charges,' Sophie said.

'She hit me back, so she couldn't have been too badly hurt. And she got a pay-off from my dad. She's got no complaints.'

'Do you live here all the time, Shazia?' Barry asked.

'No,' she replied somewhat haughtily. 'I'll be back at uni next week.'

'Where's that?'

'Bath. I'm studying geography and politics.'

'So, it's really only in the past few weeks, over the Christmas break, that you came into contact with Mia?'

'Suppose so. But I was home a couple of weekends and she was around then. She started in late summer, a few weeks before I left for uni.'

'Was there friction between you before this latest flare-up?' Barry asked.

Shazia glared at him. 'What do you mean by friction? All I expected is that she'd do her job properly. If she didn't, she deserved a reprimand. That's not friction.'

'But by all accounts, Mia was conscientious and worked hard. Are you saying different?' Barry said.

Shazia shrugged. 'I only came into contact with her a few times.'

Barry was beginning to shift around in his seat, obviously frustrated. 'Was there any other time that a disagreement with her became violent? Did you hit her more than once?'

Shazia looked angry. 'I don't know. Anyway, she played on that image, of the reliable and conscientious worker. It was all a show for my parents and Mrs Sayegh. When they weren't around, she could be a real problem. She goaded us.'

'Us?'

'Me and Gamila. Gamila can be a bit slow, a bit too trusting, and Mia ran rings around her. When I was home, I tried to even things up a bit, stop her from exploiting my sister. Look, I haven't done anything to her. If she's gone missing, it's got nothing to do with me. I wouldn't lower myself.'

'Where did you go to school, Shazia?' Sophie asked suddenly.

The young woman turned to face her. 'Why? What's that got to do with anything?'

'Just answer the question, please.' Sophie too was becoming exasperated by Shazia's continued animosity.

'Trilton Grange, in Hampshire. We were both there. Gamila was a couple of years below me.'

Sophie knew of the school, an expensive and exclusive boarding establishment for the daughters of the rich.

'What did you mean by saying that Mia exploited your sister?' she asked.

Shazia shrugged wearily. 'They went shopping together a few times. I think Gamila was buying Mia expensive clothes from some of the boutiques, and that's not right. She was only a servant.'

'Is that what the friction was really about?' Sophie asked.

'Well, it didn't help. She was obviously abusing my sister's trust. Look, I've got to go. I'm meeting a friend for lunch and I don't want to be late.'

'When do you return to university?' Sophie said.

'Next week.' Shazia rose and walked out.

* * *

Jimmy Melsom yawned, scratched his chin and ran the CCTV footage again. The problem was the drizzly, misty rain that had been falling on the night Mia disappeared. It blurred the image and made it difficult to make out any detail. True, there was a figure standing on the opposite pavement, just inside the entrance to the small park. Was it a young woman? It was hard to be sure, yet Jodie had been certain that Mia had recognised them. Hooded and well wrapped against the chill of the January night air. And beyond? In the indistinct shadows beneath the clump of trees? Was that dark blur another person sliding deeper into the gloom?

CHAPTER 24: HAWK

Rae was sitting in her car, parked in a side street that gave a good view of the entrance to the Hamdi house. She'd arrived at the same time as her two senior colleagues and had been waiting patiently, watching the broad sweep of the tree-lined driveway. It wasn't a long wait. Only ten minutes after Sophie and Barry entered the house, a car appeared around the side of the building. It was the same black Mercedes saloon that she'd seen at the apartment block on Monday.

She started up, radioed in with her position and pulled out into the road behind her quarry. Where would he be going? The flats? Or maybe Sunnyside Cars? It was neither. The luxury car moved smoothly along the harbourside road heading for the town centre, where it came to a halt in a small car park on the edge of the commercial district. Rae followed it in and parked in the last free bay, several rows beyond the plush Mercedes. Rae ran out to purchase her ticket and slapped it on her windscreen. Where was he? She caught sight of his tall form just rounding a corner near the shopping area and hurried to catch up. There he was, entering the side door of a large clothing store. She followed but lost him among the aisles of clothes. The shop had three different ground-floor entrances, and all were busy.

Muttering a curse, Rae went back to the car park. How had he managed to get away from the car park so quickly? She glanced at the Mercedes. No wonder. It was displaying a season ticket. Rae returned to her own car, got in and waited. She gave up after an hour. Maybe he lived locally and was staying put for the day. She drove away, frustrated. She called Barry, then drove west from Poole to Purbeck, intending to catch Amy Birkbeck when school finished. She needed more information about the man she'd seen in the woods. There was a chance it was the same person.

* * *

By late afternoon, Rae was in the Birkbeck's farmhouse kitchen, warming herself by an old-fashioned range and sipping tea from a mug with a bright-yellow duck design on it. Amy was tucking in to a second fruit bun selected from a freshly baked batch.

'I'd like to take Amy back to the pool if she'll agree and if you give permission,' Rae said to the Birkbecks. 'Sometimes going to the actual location jogs your memory. We often use this method when we're trying to get a clearer description of someone or something that happened. One of you can come too, if you like. I can drive us up, so it'll only take fifteen minutes or so.'

'Oh, can't we walk up the track?' Amy said. 'I can show you my bat boxes and some of the bird nesting sites on the way. It'll be really cool.'

Rae gave her a tired smile. 'Okay. But as long as we get there before dark.'

She swallowed the rest of her tea, and Amy went to collect her coat. Her parents decided to remain in the warmth of the farmhouse. Rae wondered if they'd not been sleeping well since the bodies were discovered. Both looked tired and worn.

'Would you like to stay for dinner? I've got a casserole in the oven,' Geraldine asked.

'I'd love to, but I can't, I'm afraid,' Rae said. 'It's pretty relentless at the moment. We've got an end-of-day briefing in Wareham in an hour or so and I've got to prepare my report. Then we'll be assigned work for the evening.'

'Tell you what, you can take your portion with you, then you won't have to cook anything when you get home.'

Rae was almost overcome with gratitude at Geraldine's kind thought. 'That'd be lovely. Thank you. When an investigation like this is on, we don't get much chance for proper meals, it's all sandwiches and takeaways. The boss usually makes up for it with a slap-up meal when it's all over — or a wild party.'

'I bet you have to watch how much you drink, if it's your boss in charge. It can't be too wild, surely?'

Rae laughed. 'You don't know my boss. She knocks back more beer than any of us. She even tried the yard of ale once at a charity do. It wasn't a pretty sight.'

'Is this the one you call the super? The blonde woman?' Geraldine asked.

'Yes. Er, you won't repeat what I just said, will you? I only got my promotion to sergeant a couple of months ago. I don't want to lose it already.'

Amy reappeared and the two of them set off. They plodded up the track, Amy pointing out various features, mainly nesting sites, some of them summer visitors — swallows in an old barn — or permanent residents such as fieldfares in the woods. They slowed as they reached the network of paths near the pool.

'It was here,' Amy said. 'I was going this way, like we are now, round that corner, and he was just coming the other way.' She pointed.

'Well, let's stop here for a few minutes. I want you to think about what you remember, okay?'

Amy screwed up her face in concentration. 'It's like I said — he was tall and thin. He had a bit of a fierce look, like a hawk.'

'You didn't mention that before, Amy.'

'No. It just came to me. I think because we were talking about birds. His nose was a bit like a hawk's beak. I don't think he was one of the men I saw before.'

'What about his height? Was he about the same height as that clump of bushes over there? They must have been behind him.'

Amy pondered this for a short while then went over to them. 'This is where he was when I saw him first. You stand here.'

They swapped places. 'He was taller than you. His head blocked out those holly berries behind you.'

Rae joined her and turned to observe the view. 'That would make him about six foot two. Okay. Anything else?'

'Not really. Oh, except he had scary eyes.'

'Well, that's all really useful. Shall we get back?'

'Why are you so interested in him? Just now, I mean?' Amy asked.

'I think I may have seen the same man this morning in Poole,' Rae said. 'Your description matches him.' She didn't elaborate.

They returned to the farmhouse. Rae told Amy's parents that she was concerned for the girl's safety.

'I don't mean to alarm you, and please don't get paranoid, but I'd recommend that you be extra cautious for a while,' she said. 'Amy, from now on you're not to go out into the woods alone. In fact, you shouldn't be anywhere alone, even going to and from school. Geraldine, keep your doors locked at all times. Get security chains fitted to both doors and engage them before opening the door to anyone who rings or knocks. Do that right now if you can. The hardware store will still be open in Wareham. Amy, you must promise me that you'll always be with someone when you're out. Keep your mobile phone with you. Here's my number. Call me any time, day or night, if you need to. And I won't mind if it's a false alarm. I'll make sure a squad car passes by regularly and that we keep an eye on the area, but we can't be here twenty-four hours a day. Do you all understand? Amy, do you promise?'

They nodded.

Rae continued. 'It won't be for long. But there've been some pretty awful goings-on in those woods, and Amy's been spotted there. We can't take any chances.'

* * *

'It's been two days now, and still no sign of Mia, despite the efforts of our search teams. It looks like our worst fears have been realised, doesn't it? She's been abducted.'

Sophie was chairing the early-evening briefing. Her team all looked tired and somewhat dispirited. They had been working around the clock for more than a week and the strain was beginning to show.

Barry reported on the events so far. 'Mia was employed as the assistant housekeeper at the Hamdi house and had been there for almost six months when she left abruptly, early last week. Apparently, there'd been tension between her and Hamdi's elder daughter, Shazia, for some time. There was another dispute between them during her final weekend in which the daughter struck Mia on the head with a small table lamp. Mia tried to turn away, so it caught her in the face, bruising her temple. Apparently, there had been a couple of prior assaults on Mia, but this time she reacted and slapped Shazia back. That, of course, was a step too far, so she was dismissed. We suspect that by then, she had already decided to walk out.'

'What Barry isn't telling you,' Sophie added, 'is the difficulties we had in extracting any of this information from the staff. They all seem to be terrified for some reason, but we don't know who they're frightened of. It could be Hamdi himself — he's a deliberately intimidating figure. But there's some other shadowy man around. This man does not appear in the household's staff records.'

'That'll probably be the man I tried to follow,' Rae said. 'He's the same one who was at the flats a couple of days ago. He might well have seen Mia lurking near the entrance. What if he's some kind of hitman? I reckon he might also have been the man young Amy Birkbeck spotted at the pool.'

'That reminds me,' Sophie said. 'The DNA profile has come back for the second body and it confirms what we thought. Significant links to the Philippines. Rose, I want you to trace those clothes in the suitcase. Most were cheap, but a couple of items looked pricier. Someone in a local shop might remember selling them.'

'Okay.' Rose didn't look very happy.

'Sorry, Rose, but someone's got to do it. I want George out with Rae, trying to identify this man she and Amy Birkbeck spotted. Lydia and Jimmy will be co-ordinating the search for Mia. We'll ramp it up a gear first thing tomorrow morning when Greg Buller's squad can be fully deployed. Barry and I will be back at the Hamdis' continuing our interviews with the staff. There's something not right in that household, but it's hard to pin down. All the staff are so bloody wary, as if they're scared stiff of letting something slip. But before we all head home for a few hours' sleep, we've got one last task tonight. We're going to conduct a search of all those flats that Hamdi owns. Get your coats, everyone.'

* * *

The search of the apartment block took the team less than an hour. Rose and George examined the gardens, the shrubbery and the small outhouses that lay to the side of the block and found nothing suspicious. Lydia and Jimmy visited all the ground-floor apartments, while Sophie and Barry went through the three on the upper floor. This was a search, not just a visit, and so they had to explain to the occupants as gently as possible that every room and cupboard was to be inspected. Sophie held a master key that opened every apartment in the block. It had come to light during the interview with Mrs Sayegh, the Hamdi family housekeeper. Barry had spotted it hanging on a solitary hook in her office and had asked about it. They'd been surprised that the key was kept where anyone could have access to it. And was it common for such a key to even exist? Landlords had the right to keep a key for each rental property they owned, but a master key?

There was no sign of the missing woman, nor any indication of anyone having been held against their will.

CHAPTER 25: GAMILA

Thursday morning

Sophie and Barry were back at the Hamdi house, continuing their enquiries into Mia's disappearance. They only had one family member left to interview — the younger daughter, Gamila, who hadn't been at home the previous day. They'd also spoken to all the household staff but hadn't yet managed to find the elusive tall, thin man, although they had finally discovered what his name was — Abdal Shariq. His role in the ménage was still unclear.

'No one's helping us, Barry. Everyone in the family and on the staff seems to be holding back. What are they hiding, and why?'

Her second in command had already noticed this reticence. 'They're all scared, ma'am. Even Hamdi himself. The thing is, they might be scared for different reasons. Some of them are scared of Hamdi himself — his wife, for example, and most of the house staff. But there's always a slight wince when we ask about this tall man, Shariq. You know, a sort of involuntary gasp.'

'I'm glad you noticed it too. I thought it was just my imagination.' There was a knock at the partly open door and a nervous face peered through the gap.

'Are you ready for me?' the younger Hamdi daughter asked, sounding almost timid.

'Yes, come in and sit down,' Barry said. He stood up and indicated a chair. From the way she dressed it was immediately obvious that Gamila was nothing like her older sister. Her face was round, accentuated by the dark blue headscarf she wore, with flat sandals the same cream colour as her loose-fitting top and trousers. It was totally unlike Shazia's skinny jeans and high heels.

She settled herself into a chair and gave them a wary look.

'No need to be anxious, Gamila,' Sophie said in an attempt to put the girl at her ease. 'We just want to clear up one or two points about your relationship with Mia Lockhart. I expect you're aware that she's missing.'

'Yes. I hope she's alright. I probably knew Mia better than anyone else in the family.' She spoke with a slight accent, similar to that of her parents and unlike Shazia, who had shown no trace of one. In terms of self-confidence, it was immediately clear which daughter took after the shy mother and which the domineering father.

'When did you last see her?' Sophie asked.

'The weekend after your New Year.'

'Our new year?' Sophie asked.

'Yes. Our Islamic New Year is in your summer. But my father likes to have a reception here in early January for his English friends, and the family are expected to attend. It suits us because it means that Shazia can be there. Father likes that. She's very confident and she chats to everyone.'

'Was this the occasion when there was trouble between Mia and Shazia?'

Gamila paused. 'Yes,' she said in a low voice. 'Mia was serving the drinks. Somehow, she spilled some over Shazia's dress. Shazia was upset. It was new and she thought Mia had done it on purpose.'

'Why would she have thought that?' Sophie asked.

'They'd argued earlier in the day. Shazia said she hadn't cleaned the rooms properly, there was still dust around. We had someone off work sick, and I think Mia had been given extra work to do. She wasn't very happy.' Gamila sounded reluctant, as if she didn't want to speak about it. Sophie wondered if she'd been primed to say as little as possible.

'Do *you* think she spilled the drink over Shazia on purpose?' Sophie asked.

'No,' Gamila said emphatically. 'Mia wouldn't do that. It was busy and she was carrying a tray. Someone backed into her. That's what she said, and I believed her. But Shazia wouldn't have gone after Mia after she stopped working here. She's my sister. I know her. She might have a temper, but she wouldn't really harm anyone.'

Gamila looked uneasy, even frightened when she said this, and Sophie wondered how true it was, considering how confrontational Shazia been on the previous day.

'Shazia said you sometimes went shopping with Mia. Is that true?' Sophie asked.

'Yes.'

'So you got on well with her?'

'Yes. She was nice. And she showed me the best shops for clothes and presents.'

'And you sometimes bought her clothes as gifts?'

'Yes, because she was helpful.'

Sophie decided to change tack. 'Do you know Abdal Shariq?'

Gamila seemed wary. She avoided Sophie's gaze. 'He sometimes does work for father.'

'Was he at the party you talked about?'

'I think so.'

'What kind of work does he do?'

'I don't know,' Gamila said quietly. 'Sometimes he's here, then he seems to disappear for a while. I don't really know much about him.'

'Does he make you nervous, Gamila?' Sophie said.

'A little. All men do. Shazia's much more confident than me.'

'Are you close to Shazia?'

'Of course. She's my sister. I love her. She's much cleverer than me and I know she feels protective towards me. I sometimes think I disappoint her.'

Sophie expected Gamila to look up at her then, but she kept her eyes lowered.

'Where were you on Monday evening, Gamila? At about nine o'clock?'

'I was here, with my mother. She's teaching me embroidery.'

'Thank you for your help. We may need to see you again. By the way, do you work or are you at university too?' Sophie asked.

'I work at a local accountant's office. I started there after I left school. I did business studies as one of my A levels.'

'Was that where you were yesterday?'

Gamila murmured something and got up. She made her way out, her eyes still on the floor.

'She's uneasy about something,' Sophie said. 'But what? That's the key question.'

'They all are,' Barry said. 'Well, that only leaves this Shariq man to talk to. What do we do about him? We still don't know what his role is.'

When they found Suleiman Hamdi to ask about Shariq, he was of little help.

'Abdal isn't really an employee,' he said. 'He's a security consultant and has useful contacts. He finds people for us all. He arranges things for us.'

'Who do you mean by "us?"' Barry asked.

'The Arab community here. But he probably has other clients.'

'What kind of things?'

Hamdi hesitated. 'Things to do with our safety. There are many people who wish us harm.'

'Can you give me his contact information, please?' Barry said.

Hamdi said nothing.

Sophie was exasperated. 'Do I have to threaten you again? We will take you to the station if you refuse to answer our questions. Just give us his number. And no tricks, or we'll be back.'

Scowling, Hamdi dictated a telephone number. 'I have no address for him,' he said.

* * *

Gamila stood with her eyes shut, leaning against her firmly closed bedroom door. She felt sick. It wasn't anything new. She'd felt nauseous with anxiety for most of the past week. It was like living inside a nightmare. How had things managed to spiral out of control so quickly, despite her best efforts? The worst of it was that she had no one to talk to, no one to confide in. Her mother, the one person she'd always felt close to, had snapped at her at breakfast when she'd tried to initiate a conversation. 'I don't want to know,' she'd hissed. 'Don't tell me of your scheming. I've had enough of it all.'

She heard the front door close, so she walked to the window and looked out. There were the two detectives making their way towards their car. How clever were they really? Would they spot that everyone was telling them lies and half-truths? Would they sense the shimmering threat of intimidation that lay over everyone connected with this household? It was like a suffocating blanket, clogging up relationships that should be open and easy.

Gamila opened a bottle of mineral water and stood sipping it slowly, trying once again to spot a way out of the maze she was trapped in. Once again, she failed. She opened the bottom drawer of her bedside table and moved a layer of socks and pants aside. The small silver-coloured laptop was still there. She covered it up again and closed the drawer. How much longer would she have to keep it hidden?

* * *

They waited until they were back in the incident room before Barry tried the number.

'Well, there's good news and bad news,' he said to Sophie. 'The bad news is that he claims to be in London at the moment, so it's not possible for him to see us right now. The good news is that he's returning tomorrow morning. He's agreed to come here tomorrow afternoon. He sounded very co-operative — strange, considering the job we've had getting information out of the others.'

'There's plenty of time between now and tomorrow for that attitude to change,' Sophie said. 'Let's wait and see.'

'Time's ticking by, ma'am,' Barry said, 'and we don't have much of it left if we're to find Mia.'

Sophie looked him in the eye. 'What are the chances, Barry? What have they ever been? She might well have been dead since Monday night. You and I both know it, even if the others don't. These are people who feel justified in killing a cheerful, hard-working cleaner because she got too nosey, and then dumping her body in a foul, muddy pool. People who can kill a cop because they probably got tired of his whining and his habit of trying to dig up dirt on anyone he came into contact with. And then, along comes Mia — young, innocent and a bit too interested in whatever secrets they have. No, the more I think about it, the more likely it is that we're looking for a body, not a living, breathing kidnap victim. Not that it changes anything, of course. We keep looking anyway.'

CHAPTER 26: BLUE VINNY

Vinny Foster sat in his first-floor office, gazing out of the window at the near-empty street below. He was feeling ostracised. Why was no one talking to him? On an average day in normal times, he'd often find himself at the centre of a whirlpool of activity. His phone would be ringing, people would be calling in, his inbox would be full. Not today. During the past week, he'd had just one visitor, the gaunt and intimidating Mr Snake. Not that he called him that to his face, of course. It had been 'Mr Shariq'. He'd tried 'Abdal' once, and Shariq's expression had been cold enough to freeze the tea in their cups. Only one other person had a look like that — the boss, Hamdi himself.

Why was he being left out in the cold like this? It was as if he'd become tainted somehow. Even contacts from some of his more orthodox, long-term clients had been thin on the ground of late. Though that could be his own fault. He could make more money, and faster, by concentrating on his new venture with Hamdi. He'd been neglecting his other activities recently, so was it any wonder that many of his older clients were looking elsewhere? He couldn't really blame them.

He sighed. Maybe he needed to knuckle down and rebuild those old networks. The trouble was, he'd have to do it without Stu Blackman's secret contact list. Maybe he and Hamdi had been too quick to react to the perceived threat that Blackman had posed. Well, it was too late to do anything about that. Then there was the other problem, the fact that the cops were probably out looking for him because of that altercation with the crazy cyclist. How was he to know the fucker was a cop? And to cap it all, that bloody pain in the neck Mia had vanished. Christ. It wouldn't be long before the cops started hounding him about that too. What a life. Maybe it was time he went to see Mickie and Crustie again. At least they might tell him if they'd found anyone to replace Blackman as an information source. Though realistically, how likely was that?

He stood up, collected his coat and made for the door. He opened it and found himself face to face with a tall, dark-haired woman. She smiled thinly at him.

'Mr Foster? I'm Detective Sergeant Rae Gregson. Do you have a couple of minutes free for a chat?'

Shit. Should he just push her down the stairs and do a runner?

* * *

Rae looked around at the blue painted walls, the blue furniture and the blue curtains. Even the chairs they were sitting on were blue, although they could do with a good clean.

'Nice colour, Mr Foster. Like blue, then, do you?'

He scowled. 'Not especially. I rent this place. It was like this when I moved in.'

'When was that?'

He shrugged. 'Five years ago, maybe? Look, I was just about to go out. I can only give you a couple of minutes.'

'Well, I'm sure that will be long enough. I've only got two or three questions for you. You know Mia Lockhart?'

He nodded slowly. 'Yes.'

'Are you aware that she's disappeared?'

'I think I caught something on the local news,' he said.

'Tell me how you know her, please.'

Rae noticed how slow he was to respond to her questions. He obviously needed a few moments to formulate an answer.

'I run a personnel agency. Mia is on my books.'

'When was the last time you saw her?' Rae asked.

His gaze wandered around the room then returned to Rae's face. 'Wednesday last week.'

'What was the nature of that meeting?'

He curled his lip. 'She'd just walked out on a job and wanted me to find her another one.'

Rae watched him carefully. 'And?'

He shrugged. 'That's not the way it works, and I told her so. If someone gets fired, I do my best for them, but if you walk out, that's your decision. You've got to take the consequences.'

'Anything else? Did you follow it up?' she asked.

'Yeah, sort of. I'm not a complete bastard. I gave her some cash to tide her over and told her I'd see what I could do for her.'

'Did you arrange her latest position, the one she started last week?'

'Where was that?'

'I'll take that as a no. So you are aware that she was looking for another job in a hurry?'

Again, the pause. Rae could almost see the wheels whirring in his head. This was the beauty of turning up to speak to someone when they weren't expecting you. He could, of course, refuse to answer or insist on having a lawyer present, but doing so would indicate that he had something to hide.

'Well, she did say she was looking for something else, but she isn't really on my books, not as a general job-seeker. Potential employers use me to find suitable staff, not the other way round.'

Rae frowned. That was as clear as mud. 'Isn't that what all employment agencies do?'

'What I mean is, it's a fairly specific area I deal with.'

'Geographical or job type?' Rae asked.

'Both. Mainly domestic staff, and just Poole.'

'Not Bere Regis?' Where had that flash of inspiration come from? Rae was puzzled by her own suggestion. It had seemed to come out of nowhere.

The effect on Foster was startling. It was if an electric shock had been applied to his spine. His eyes widened momentarily, and he jerked forward in his chair. 'What?'

'Bere Regis. Do you have clients in that area?'

'There might be one or two. Why?'

Rae realised why the name of that particular village had popped into her head. There was an old, sepia-tinted photo of Bere village centre hanging on the wall directly opposite her, clearly labelled with its name. Why had the man reacted so strongly? Curious.

'How far north does your client base stretch, out of interest?' she asked.

'I have a couple in the Blandford area. Look, I specialise in finding domestic staff. I don't see why that's of interest to the police.'

'Mia was employed as an assistant housekeeper at the Hamdi house in Sandbanks. You found her the job there, so I assume Suleiman Hamdi is one of your clients.'

He reverted to his previous wariness. 'Yes.'

'And Mia must also be on one of your lists. She must have registered with you at some point?'

'Yes.'

'When was that, Mr Foster?'

'More than six months ago, back in the summer.'

'Do you have a record of her on your system?'

'I expect so.'

'Well, can I have a look, please?'

Rae could sense his hesitation. Was he about to refuse?

'I insist, Mr Foster. If you don't show me what information you have on her, I'll apply for a warrant. That might not be in your best interest.'

He held his hands up. 'Okay. Point taken.'

He stood up and crossed the room to a desktop PC, so old that it took several minutes to boot up. Rae watched as the operating system loaded.

'You do realise that this system is no longer supported by the software company? That means there are all kinds of security loopholes,' she said.

'So? It does me okay.' He looked at her challengingly.

'You hold personal information on your clients. You are required by law to keep it secure and do what you can to prevent data theft. That means using up-to-date software. You'll need to upgrade in order to comply, Mr Foster.'

'Christ. This bloody country,' he said. 'Why can't we just be left alone to get on with our jobs and our lives?'

Rae frowned at him. 'I don't agree with you there, Mr Foster. I think people have a right to insist that their personal information is kept secure, which is what the law does. Haven't you heard of identity theft? Anyway, let me have a look at Mia's record.'

She walked across and peered at the dusty screen. Much of the information confirmed what the police knew already. Mia was twenty-two, had graduated from Bournemouth University with a degree in journalism, and had worked for the Hamdi family until two weeks earlier. Rae turned back to Vinny.

'Who's your contact at the Hamdis', Mr Foster?'

'The housekeeper, Mrs Sayegh. She phones me when she needs staff.'

'So, have you supplied a replacement for Mia?'

'Yes, though it's only a temp. I ain't managed to find anyone permanent for them yet. It's tricky with the new term about to start at the university. I'm still looking.'

'Do you know Abdal Shariq?'

He looked down at the desktop. Once again, she had shaken him. At times like this, Rae loved her job. A simple question could have the effect of a verbal hand grenade exploding. It was fascinating.

'Well?'

'I came into contact with him a couple of times.'

'When was the last time?'

'At Mr Hamdi's New Year reception.'

'You haven't seen him more recently than that?'

'No.'

He was lying. His office was just around the corner from the department store where Shariq had done his vanishing act the previous day. He'd probably been here when she was scanning the street outside for him. And Foster had that shifty look in his eyes again.

'So, he didn't visit you here in this office yesterday afternoon?'

'If he did, I was out.'

'Did you speak to him at that New Year reception?' she asked.

'Only in passing.'

'Did you witness the altercation between Mia and the older Hamdi daughter?'

'Not really. I was aware of some incident. It was dealt with pretty quick.'

'But Mia lost her job because of it,' she said.

'That's what she told me.'

'Did she give you any details?' Rae asked. 'Any long-running friction between the two of them?'

'No.'

He was lying again, of course. Mia was certain to have let her feelings about her employers known to the agency that had found her the job. So, she could only conclude that Foster knew when it was best to keep his mouth shut. His loyalty wasn't to the workers on his list but to his clients, the wealthy families and firms looking to employ staff. Particularly to the Hamdi family and Shariq, Amy's Mr Hawk. Rae knew it. And from his reaction, Foster could see that she knew.

CHAPTER 27: LUMINESCENT CONDOM

Friday morning

Yauvani Anand, the new Home Secretary, arrived at police headquarters just after nine thirty and spent the first half hour in a meeting with the chief constable and her top aides. She was delivered to the VCU office just in time to have coffee with the three core members. Barry was quiet and Rae even quieter. They left the office as soon as it was polite to do so.

'They're a great team,' Sophie said, noticing Yauvani's raised eyebrows. 'They're just keen to get back to work.'

'Which is how it should be,' Yauvani said. 'That's what policing is all about, surely?'

Sophie poured them both another coffee. 'What's it like being in the top job?'

'Well, you know the general rule. The higher you climb, the further you have to fall. There are two ways you can deal with it. You either develop the hide of a rhino or find coping mechanisms. Sadly, I don't have the hide of a rhino, despite what people think. I'm a self-made woman, Sophie, like you. I've got all these insecurities that white, upper-class males who've been to Eton or Harrow or wherever don't have. So, they keep their knives polished and ready for when it's time to stick them in my back. I have no illusions about it. Sooner or later, it's bound to happen. This is the thing men don't understand. They say we have equality, but they don't have an inkling of what we have to go through to get to positions they take for granted. I'm a woman. I'm from an ethnic minority. I know they're watching me in a way they wouldn't watch a white bloke, just waiting for me to make a mistake. Then they'll pounce. I'm skating on the thin stuff every day, where a man in my position would just plod along on solid ground with few worries. But that's the way of the world as it's currently constituted.'

'Do you want a gin and tonic?' Sophie asked suddenly. 'I keep a secret stash here.'

'Oh, you temptress you,' Yauvani laughed. 'But no. There's a time and a place. Sadly, not here and not now. I have a speech to make, remember.' She glanced around as if to ensure there was no chance of being overheard. 'I wanted to get you on your own because of a snippet I picked up at a reception at their embassy just yesterday. Apparently, they have someone on the inside in the Hamdi place.'

Sophie frowned. 'Really? So things may not be quite what they seem. Interesting. Anything else?'

'I sensed a certain amount of unease about Hamdi. Officially he's here as a key player in their defence procurement team, although he's freelance. I wonder if he's trodden on sensitive toes, so they've planted someone in his entourage.'

'Did you pick up any hints about this insider's identity?'

Yauvani snorted. 'Oh, come on, Sophie. You expect too much. These are Arabs we're talking about. You know what some of them think is the true role for a woman. And I'm from the Indian Hindu community to boot, people who are more often than not only fit to do their laundry. So I was lucky to get even that crumb from the big boys' table.'

Sophie frowned. 'It is good to know though, even though it could complicate things.'

Yauvani smiled. 'Goodness. So I've become a police helper. Do I get a badge?'

Sophie laughed. 'Not another middle-aged woman seeking approval and reassurance. I have some badges left over from a teenage helpers' initiative a couple of years ago. I'm sure I can find one if you insist. I think the colour might even match your outfit.' She pulled one out of her bag. It was bright yellow with dark blue writing that boldly stated, *Dorset Police Young Helper*.

Yauvani Anand, the UK Home Secretary, and probably the most powerful woman in the country, slid her arm through Sophie's. 'Let's do it. Really. I can just imagine the looks on the faces of my senior advisors when they spot it. They'll all be too embarrassed to mention it.'

'It comes with a bright pink balloon,' Sophie said, fishing around in her bag. 'Shall I inflate it? Oh God, it looks a bit like a luminescent condom.'

She blew into the sausage-shaped balloon and managed to get it half inflated before the slightly perished rubber developed a small split. It rapidly shrank, the air escaping with a loud farting sound.

The two women dissolved into fits of giggles as Sophie slid the badge's pin through Yauvani's lapel and handed her the limp balloon.

'I think I'm about to wet myself,' Sophie gasped.

'That makes two of us,' the Home Secretary said. 'Is there a loo close by? Race you.'

* * *

Yauvani looked at the sparse crowd of shivering people in front of her. 'And, finally, I must add the thanks of the government for what these men and women do. Every working day, police officers leave their homes and set off for work not knowing what the day will bring. Not knowing whether they will return safe and sound at the end of it. That's what

Detective Sergeant Stuart Blackman would have felt as he set out for work on that fateful day. I want all the thugs and criminals out there to know that this government will do all it can to support the police in their efforts to find those responsible for violence against its officers and bring them to justice. Good, honest coppers like Stuart Blackman deserve nothing less when they've put their lives on the line for the communities they serve. I have absolute confidence that the local police investigation team will find those responsible. Those killers will have their day in court. Rest assured of that . . .' Yauvani frowned at the notes she was holding in her hand. Good job she'd spotted that final bit of claptrap and refrained from uttering it.

A faint ripple of applause broke out from the scattered onlookers standing in the cold wind outside Wareham police station. News cameras swung away from the Home Secretary and panned across the thin crowd. Most of the people there were local dignitaries, police personnel and reporters, along with half a dozen passers-by who had stopped to see what all the fuss was about. Yauvani stepped aside and waited until the cameras were all turned off before hugging her bright blue coat even tighter.

'It's bloody freezing out here,' she complained to her senior aide as they walked towards the group huddled around the chief constable.

'These things have to be done, Home Secretary,' he said. 'Think what you've done to bolster the local vote.'

'Odd though it may seem to you, David, I do take a genuine interest in what the police do. That was the point of this visit, to listen to their concerns and see how they go about their work.'

'Of course. Inside for a hot coffee?' He glanced at his watch. 'Not much time, though. We have to be back in Whitehall for late afternoon.'

'Who added those extra bits, by the way? If I'm ever given a speech as mixed up as that again, I'll fire whoever wrote it.

I shouldn't have to do as much improvising as that in front of the press.'

'It was a newcomer to the Number Ten team.'

'No surprise there, then. I'd have thought by now they'd have enough faith in me to allow me to write my own speeches in total and not have extra bits inserted. Particularly when the bits they add are as clear as mud. Any half-decent journalist would have had a field day if I'd left it as it was.' Yauvani noticed that his eyes had shifted to her lapel, still displaying the prominent police young helper badge. His lip curled slightly.

'Early days yet, Home Secretary.'

'No, David. That level of interference needs to stop now. I'm fed up with Number Ten advisors trying to dictate what I should and shouldn't say. It wouldn't be so bad if the stuff they added made any sense. Good job I spotted it before I opened my mouth.' She looked across at Sophie Allen and raised her voice. 'Is that offer of a gin and tonic still valid? I need a slug of something to restore my mental equilibrium.'

'We can do better than that. We've got some hot snacks ready.'

'Sounds good. Lead on, MacDuffle Coat. I like it, by the way. It suits you.' She nodded at the deep-red, hooded coat that Sophie was wearing.

* * *

'Well, how do you think the visit went, Sophie?' The chief constable was being her usual probing self. She was leaning against the desk in Sophie's tiny, improvised office in the incident room.

'Good. Fine. She's on our side, ma'am.' This was difficult. Sophie was aware of a tension between them, something she hadn't noticed before when she was talking to the chief. Clearly her friendship with someone who had just been made Home Secretary had consequences. Better to be open about it. 'Look, ma'am, when we became friends, she was just a PPS to a junior minister. There was no way of knowing that her career would take off like this, so quickly. I think even she feels a bit stunned by it.'

The chief frowned. 'I never know what to think about the usefulness of politicians. In the short term, yes, go along with them if it will help the problem in hand. But their career slopes are steeper and more slippery than ours. She's a fast-rising star, but it could all end in tears, and more quickly than she might expect.'

'She knows that, ma'am. I don't think she has any illusions. But with respect, ma'am, she's a friend, politician or not. I'm not using her in any way. I'd be ashamed of myself if that were the case. I'm sorry if it's brought any awkwardness to our situation.'

The chief nodded slowly. 'I wondered if there was something deeper at work because of this extra funding for the reorganisation of your unit. Just keep me posted, will you?'

Sophie smiled cautiously. She knew how perceptive the chief was. 'Of course. There's nothing hidden here, ma'am. I can assure you of that.'

'I spotted the badge on her lapel. Was that one of yours?' The chief seemed more relaxed now.

'It was by way of a joke, ma'am. She gleaned a bit of information from an ambassador in London, realised its value and passed it on to me. I'm still processing it.'

'Well, come on. Do you plan to share it with me?'

'His government have a plant among Hamdi's staff. They obviously don't trust him entirely. It ties in with something we heard. Hamdi works in defence procurement. It's possible he might be double-dealing.'

'What do you mean?'

'He might also have links to the rebels back in Yemen.'

'Did that come from the Home Secretary too?'

Sophie shook her head. 'No. Lydia Pillay finally got some information from the solicitors that employed Mia Lockhart, the missing woman. Mia started there as a temp last week. We think she might have uncovered something about Hamdi's secret dealings. Mia hinted something like that to her boyfriend. Anyway, one of the senior partners told Lydia that they received an unexpected copy of an export license. We're guessing Mia saw the document. It wasn't for a government purchase, it had an address that's in rebel-held territory.'

The chief constable smiled grimly. 'So, what you're saying is that Hamdi is playing arms dealer for both sides? He's able to plan the purchases because he's their government's official procurement person, but some equipment is being diverted?'

'Well, it's only speculation on our part. But Yauvani's snippet about someone on his staff being a government plant now makes sense, doesn't it? Maybe someone at the top got wind of it. The whole thing has become really high stakes, ma'am.'

The chief was silent for a few moments. 'I'm going to have to tell Special Branch. Did you mention your suspicions to the Home Secretary?'

Sophie shook her head. 'Lydia only recently got hold of the information from the solicitor, so I've only just put it all together. What it means is that if Hamdi somehow found out that Mia spotted something incriminating, the outlook for her is bleak. It reduces the chances of us finding her alive, ma'am.'

CHAPTER 28: MESSAGE

Jacob Foster sat morosely at the kitchen table. His two flatmates had given up trying to keep him cheerful, instead resorting to occasionally asking if he was okay. His monosyllabic replies and sullen look precluded conversation, so for the past two days they'd left him alone. Every so often they checked in on him to make sure he was still actually alive and functioning. They'd done so again this morning before they left for work, each poking their heads into his room and then withdrawing.

At least today he'd managed to eat some breakfast — a few cornflakes — even though the food tasted of nothing. Several hours later, he was still there, still looking out of the window at a cold January day. It was late morning by now, but frost still glinted in patches that had seen no sun. He sighed, moved to the toaster and popped in a slice of bread. He took a jar of peanut butter from a shelf in the cupboard. Maybe he was hungry today because he'd managed to sleep for a while last night, the first half-decent night's rest he'd had since Mia went missing. Was he at last starting to accept the harsh reality of her disappearance? Maybe parts of his brain had begun to admit that he might never see her again.

Confused and angry, he felt a burning desire to lash out. Anybody would do — punch, slap and kick, if only to relieve the overwhelming tension that gripped his body. How could this have happened? It was so unfair, to find someone like Mia, fall for her big time and then have her snatched away. He was heartbroken. It was obvious to everyone he came into contact with. Even his boss had noticed the state he was in and told him to take a day off, but what was the point of sitting around here? Though he couldn't keep his mind focussed on anything at work. He felt useless. The police had politely but firmly declined his offers of help. He couldn't even concentrate on his favourite hobby, photography. He'd never felt so low.

The toaster popped up and his mobile phone chirped at the same time. He grabbed the toast, put it on a plate and took it across to the table. He tried to spread peanut butter onto it at the same time as picking up his phone and checking the screen. The message came from a number he didn't recognise. *Don't worry. Mia is safe.* What? Who could have sent that? His hopes soaring like a bird in flight, he called the detective in charge of the case, who said she'd be right over. Oh, God. Was everything going to be all right after all?

* * *

The front door opened almost before Lydia could ring the bell, practically yanked from its hinges by the young man now facing her. He must have been standing behind the door, waiting for her to arrive.

'Hello, Jacob. This is my colleague, Ameera. She's a technical whizz. Can we come in? I want to find out exactly what this message is.'

He almost pushed them into the sitting room. 'It's got to be important, hasn't it?' he said.

'We hope so. I've already been in touch with the SIO to keep her informed. Look, Jacob, it might be what it seems, a message sent to reassure you. But we have to bear in mind that it might be a hoax, sent by someone playing a cruel trick on you.'

Jacob picked up his phone and showed her the message.

'You haven't tried calling that number, have you?' Lydia asked.

He shook his head. 'No. I've done what you said.'

Thank goodness. Lydia had half expected him to have tried, despite her request not to do so. 'That's good. I can guess you were tempted, but we want to do it with some kit running. Then, we might be able to get a rough idea of where it came from. Ameera's got some equipment with her that we want to use. We still want you to be the person to make contact, but only when we're ready.'

Ameera unzipped the bag she was carrying, took out what looked to be a large mobile phone and switched it on. She then took Jacob's phone, had a look at the connection ports, removed a cable from the bag and connected Jacob's phone to the piece of equipment she was holding. Meanwhile, Lydia took Jacob through what she wanted him to say, assuming someone answered. She told him to take it slowly and calmly.

Ameera handed him his phone and he called the unknown number. It rang three times before being picked up, but no one responded.

'Hello?' Jacob said into the silence.

Then, 'You mustn't call. You endanger Mia. Just trust me.'

The call was cut.

Lydia turned to Ameera. 'Was it enough?' she asked.

Ameera was working her way through the specialist software on her unit. Finally, she exhaled noisily. 'Just. It's come from the local mast. They're in Poole.'

'Did you get a recording?' Lydia asked.

'Yes. It's there. What did you make of the voice?'

Lydia gazed at her colleague. 'A strong Middle Eastern accent. At least, that's what I thought.'

Ameera nodded. 'Me too.'

Lydia didn't say anything else, not in Jacob's presence. She was now almost certain that the message wasn't some elaborate prank.

As soon as she was out of the house, Lydia phoned Sophie.

* * *

Something was happening at last. Filled with hope and a sense of purpose, Jacob couldn't bear to sit around any longer. But what to do? He'd been warned in no uncertain terms not to do anything that might derail the police's attempts to find Mia. This was something to go on, though. He had a quick wash, changed out of his sweatshirt and jeans and set off for the office.

It was a Friday afternoon, and like many workplaces, the accounts office at Bateson's was tidying up loose ends in time for the weekend. The unexpected appearance of Jacob caused a stir among his fellow office workers. They saw immediately that this wasn't the lethargic, disconnected Jacob of the days after Mia first went missing.

'Something's happened,' Nikki whispered to Abi. 'Look at him. He's almost back to his normal self.'

He said there was no news and that nothing had changed, but it was glaringly obvious that there was something he wasn't telling them. He got down to work before they had time to ask more, finishing his to-do list well before the end of the day. He spent the rest of the time reading what little he could find about Suleiman Hamdi. All the juicy stuff, of course, would be kept secure, but at least he had two addresses to work with. Would they be worth a look?

After work, he took a bus to Sandbanks and walked the length of the road where the Hamdi residence was located. It ran parallel to the beach, lined with imposing properties that were largely screened from view by walls, shrubs and clusters of pine trees. Hamdi's house was a large, white building set in manicured gardens. Jacob saw several expensive cars parked in the driveway. A smartly dressed young woman with a silk scarf covering her head came out of the front door, made her way to one of the vehicles — a bright-red Mercedes sports car — and drove away. Probably one of the daughters. Jacob waited for a few more minutes, but it was cold and darkness was rapidly setting in. No sense wasting more time here. He retraced his steps to the bus stop and returned to Parkstone, just in time to catch the bus he wanted. He got off a stop before his usual one and soon found the second address he had unearthed back at the office. He entered the gateway to a small block of flats, rounded a corner and stepped back into the shadows. The red sports car that had just left the Hamdi house was sitting at the far end of the small car park, in a slot marked 'visitors.' There seemed to be no one about. Jacob approached the glass doors at the entrance to the building and peered inside. All quiet. He tried the door, but it was locked. He considered various excuses to bluff his way in but decided against them. He needed to think. Did the police know about this place? Maybe he should report it and let them decide what to do. He turned away from the doors and nearly bumped into a tall, gaunt man with an aquiline nose who was just walking in from the street.

'Sorry,' Jacob said.

'Is there something you want?' the man said. He had a strong, almost guttural accent.

'No.' That sounded lame. He needed a reason for being here. 'My cat's gone missing. I'm looking for it.'

The man scowled at him but said nothing. They both turned as the door opened and the young woman with the silk headscarf appeared. Her gaze skated across Jacob and settled on the other man.

'I thought you'd be here already,' she said.

The man frowned and shook his head slightly. 'Delayed. It's okay.'

Jacob sensed tension, possibly caused by his presence.

'I'll be off then,' he said, and hurried away, turning around for a last look when he reached the corner. They were going back into the building. Something wasn't right.

CHAPTER 29: BLOODSTAIN

Rose stared at the report, muttering.

'Some of this stuff is too technical for me,' she said. 'There isn't a summary at the end, so how am I meant to make sense of it?'

George peered over her shoulder. 'It's at the start, just there, on the first page.'

'Why have they done that? That's stupid. Aren't summaries meant to be at the end?'

'I think it's because all anyone wants to see is the summary, so the forensic service decided to move it to the front,' George said. 'I expect people asked for it.'

Rose scanned the bullet list. 'Most of the clothes are fairly cheap, from low-cost shops. There's one expensive dress, though.'

'Is it safe to assume they were all hers?' George asked.

Rose flicked through the report. 'Apparently so. Everything was her size.' She read on. 'And they're all short. Remember, she was less than five foot. Ah, look at this.' She pointed at one short paragraph. 'There was a dry-cleaning label still pinned to the dress. So we can follow up on that at least. We're in business, Georgie boy. Let's get going.'

The dry-cleaning premises was in the Parkstone area of Poole, in the main shopping arcade. They explained what they were looking for to the single assistant in the shop, who turned out to also be the manager. She took the details, turned to the console on the desk and typed in the reference number. She frowned.

'Yes, I can see the details. The lady who brought the dress in was a Janella Ramos.'

'What was the nature of the job? Just a routine cleaning?' George asked.

She examined what was written on the screen, then shook her head. 'No. It was a bloodstain.'

* * *

Barry collected the tall, hawk-nosed man from reception and led him to a small interview room. So this was Abdal Shariq, the intimidating man who seemed to make everyone nervous. Barry could see why. His manner was hard, watchful, distrustful. He looked around him as he entered the room.

'Take a seat, Mr Shariq. I'm Detective Inspector Barry Marsh. The superintendent will be with us shortly. Is there anything I can get you while we wait? Tea or coffee?'

Unsmiling, Shariq shook his head and sat in the chair Barry had indicated. His eyes moved slowly around the room, wary, as if he were a cornered animal.

The door opened and Sophie came in. She held out her hand but Shariq made no motion to shake it. 'Good afternoon, Mr Shariq. Sorry to keep you, but I've had a very busy day. Do you know why we've asked you here? We're investigating the disappearance of Mia Lockhart, who's been missing since Monday. We believe you may be able to help us.'

'Why would I be able to help you?' His voice was harsh. Barry noticed several prominent veins on his forehead. Was it his imagination or did one move, as if he had a slight tic?

'Have you seen her since she left her job with the Hamdi family?' Sophie asked.

He shook his head slightly. 'No.'

'Did you know she'd gone missing?'

He nodded, again almost imperceptibly. 'Yes, I heard.'

Barry wondered if the rest of the interview would proceed like this, in monosyllabic responses to his boss's questions.

'When did you last see her?' Sophie asked.

His expression didn't change. 'At Mr Hamdi's New Year reception.'

'Where there was some friction between her and Shazia Hamdi?'

'So I understand. I didn't see it.'

'What's your role with Mr Hamdi?' she asked.

'I organise security. He is just one of my clients.' He sounded almost challenging.

'Could you explain in more detail, please?' Sophie said.

He shrugged. 'Wealthy people can become targets for thieves and opportunists. I deal with it. I make sure his properties are secure and well looked after. The same with all my clients.'

'Are you involved in vetting staff?'

'If necessary.'

'Did you vet Mia when she started?'

'Yes.'

'Do you vet the cleaning staff?'

He nodded, looking suspicious.

'Did you vet Janella Ramos?'

There was a short, frozen silence. 'Yes.'

That was interesting, Barry thought. He glanced at Sophie and she moved a finger. Time for him to take over. 'Where is Janella Ramos, Mr Shariq?'

'I understand she returned to the Philippines to be with her family.'

'No, she didn't, Mr Shariq. We dragged her body from a muddy pool near Wareham a few days ago. She'd been there since the summer. She was murdered.' Barry kept his eyes on Shariq.

'I know nothing of this.' For an instant, his gaze flickered, he looked troubled. And then it passed.

'We need to make sure the same fate doesn't befall Mia,' Barry said.

'I understand that. I can't help you.'

'Can't or won't?' Barry said.

Shariq didn't answer. Barry was watching him closely. A tension had arisen in the air between them. What was it?

Sophie took over again. 'You'll know that one of our own officers was murdered a few days ago. His body was pulled out of the same pool as Janella's. Both of them seem to be linked to you, Mr Shariq. You and Suleiman Hamdi.'

'What link? How can there be?' His tone was challenging.

'You've been seen regularly at a block of flats in Parkstone, owned by Mr Hamdi. Janella Ramos was the cleaner there until she vanished. Mia Lockhart was at those flats on the afternoon before she vanished. So were you. The pool where Janella Ramos's body was found is near Wareham, and your car has been seen nearby. That's where Sergeant Blackman's body was found. He rented one of those flats for weekend use.'

'*Sudfa*. What do you say in English? Coincidence. I told you, I am Mr Hamdi's security agent. I look after his interests. Visiting his properties is my job. Checking up on staff is my job. These women, they were his staff. That is the only link.'

'Did you ever meet Sergeant Blackman?' she asked.

Shariq's lip curled. 'No.'

'Why were you visiting the woods by Corfe Castle?'

'I wasn't. Who claims to have seen me? Because whoever it was, they've made a mistake. Who was it?'

His attitude was becoming increasingly aggressive. Maybe he already suspected that it had been the young girl, Amy, who'd seen him.

'We've had several teams out watching that road all week. But let me give you a warning, Mr Shariq. We suspect you know more than you're letting on about all this, including Mia's disappearance. If anything happens to that young woman, we'll be back to see you. And if it becomes clear that you are involved, we'll have you. Understand?'

He held her gaze for a while. 'Strange that a police officer feels it so personally. But I hope you find her.'

Barry showed him to reception. When he returned, Sophie was in the incident room, staring out of the window. She was watching Shariq drive away.

'That didn't go the way I wanted,' she said. 'Am I losing my touch, Barry? Did I misread something?'

'Well, if you did, I don't know what it was. I couldn't read him at all, and that's unusual. Nothing seemed to have much of an effect on him. And doesn't that suggest something? If you want to know what I think, he's somehow involved in it all.'

'It was that last comment he made, about me feeling it personally. I wasn't expecting that. I don't think anyone's ever made a comment like that to me before, not a suspect.'

Her phone rang. It was Dave Nash, the county's senior forensic officer.

'That was about the dress found in the suitcase from the pool,' she told Barry. 'Apparently, it might still have traces of blood on it, according to Rose Simons. I've authorised a closer examination and a DNA analysis if any traces of blood survived the cleaning.'

'But haven't we already assumed it was Janella Ramos's dress?'

Sophie smiled. 'Exactly. But what if the blood isn't hers? That might give us a way in as to what's really been going on. Maybe this afternoon hasn't been a total waste after all.'

* * *

Jimmy Melsom rubbed his eyes again. This was the trouble with being the county's acknowledged CCTV analysis expert. You got to spend hours in front of screens trying to match up images. At least most of the film sequences were of a reasonable quality nowadays and could be computer-enhanced, but it still left him wanting to climb the walls sometimes. And this had been one of those times. He went to see Lydia with his findings. She was talking to Barry Marsh. Lydia glanced at the stills he'd extracted.

'Jimmy, this is brilliant. You're a genius,' Lydia said. She turned to Barry. 'These are the final images from Ashley Green for the night we think Mia was abducted.'

Barry was looking intently at the photos. 'That's Gamila Hamdi,' he said. He was examining the image of the young woman in the hooded jacket, standing across the road at the park entrance. He transferred his attention to the other image, the obscure figure in the background, only just visible as a grainy shadow in the original film sequence. Tall, thin, and that shadowy face only just discernible under the deep hood. Barry moved his head slightly, trying to catch the image from the corner of his eye. Was there a hint of a bony nose?

'It could be Shariq,' he said. 'Oh, sod it. We've just had him in for an interview. The boss is going to explode.'

The three of them hurried off to speak to Sophie. She turned visibly pale. 'Get them both in,' she said. 'Right now.'

It was no use. Their phones went unanswered. Sophie and Barry rushed across to Sandbanks but neither Gamila nor Shariq were there. Mrs Hamdi looked genuinely worried when it became clear that Gamila was nowhere to be found. She was clearly apprehensive about Shariq, something she hadn't shown when they'd interviewed her earlier in the week. What did she really suspect about him? She refused to explain.

Sophie and Barry returned to the incident room. Time was fast running out and it felt as if they were getting bogged down in an increasingly glutinous quagmire. Sophie sat with her head in her hands. She heard a cautious knock on her door and looked up. A familiar face peered around it.

'Tommy! What on earth are you doing here?'

'I got discharged early, ma'am. The docs said I'm recovering quicker than they expected. I'm still bandaged up but I'm okay to work as long as it's nothing physical.'

'Did they actually say you were okay to come back to work?' she demanded.

'Um, well, it was all a bit vague. But they didn't forbid me. Is that okay?'

Her mood lightened instantly. 'Of course. And it's the best news I've had this afternoon. You can take over the background work. It'll free up the others to get out more. Tommy, welcome back. You've no idea how much this has cheered me up.'

Once the greetings were over, Rae had a quick word with him. 'Have you been back to the site of the accident, Tommy?'

He shook his head. 'No. I came my usual route, down the main road.'

'Would it be useful to go back for a look? We've got an hour before the late afternoon briefing and we could get there while there's still some daylight left. We can be there and back in half an hour.' She looked across to Sophie.

'Go ahead. Barry and I can reorganise the schedules.'

CHAPTER 30: FURRY DICE

An hour later the unit members clustered around a central table, sipping at mugs of tea or coffee and nibbling biscuits. The mood was still sombre. Tommy tried hard to follow what was being discussed, noting the names of the people involved and jotting down a few points about their profiles. The problem was that he wasn't emotionally involved with the case. Not yet anyway. Tommy was the type of person who needed a real, living face to focus on, something to connect with. And that wasn't happening here. Photos, however good, just weren't a substitute for the genuine thing, a face-to-face encounter and the thoughts and memories that it sparked. He tried his best to focus, but his mind kept drifting away.

The short trip back to the scene of his accident hadn't proved particularly useful, and he had felt unexpectedly tense. It was almost as if his brain was trying to tell him that there were things he should have remembered about the shocking event, even if it had been over in a flash. Maybe his concern about that was preventing him from fully engaging with the discussion. Rose Simons was talking about vehicles — SUVs and four-by-fours — but he was having trouble following what she was saying. Had he come back to work too soon?

His mind drifted back to that steep twist in the narrow lane, the nearby gorse bushes, the overgrown banking.

He suddenly jerked back to full awareness. 'Furry dice,' he said. 'Hanging from the rear-view mirror. Pink ones. I've just remembered.' He looked around and realised that everyone was looking at him. 'Sorry,' he added sheepishly.

'What do you mean, Tommy? What dice and what vehicle?' Sophie asked.

'The one that hit me. I think I've just had a flashback.'

Rae was frowning. 'I've seen a pair of pink furry dice hanging somewhere in the last day or two, just as Tommy described. Oh, where was it?' She massaged her forehead. It didn't help.

The meeting drew to a close and tasks were allocated for the evening and the following morning. Rae drew Tommy aside.

'Are you sure?' she said. 'You don't think you got the image mixed up with something else?'

He shook his head. 'No, I don't think so. It's linked to that downhill twist in the road and those grassy banks. They were there in the flashback.'

Rae went to her desk and sat down to read back through her notebook, examining the entries for the last few days. Where had she been? What visits had she made? One thing was for certain. Those dice hadn't been dangling in any of the upmarket cars owned by members of the Hamdi family. Anyway, aren't such things illegal because of the possible obstruction they'd cause to the driver's field of view? Maybe that depended on the size. She rubbed her eyes again, trying to clear away the seemingly perpetual feeling of tiredness. She hadn't seen it today, with its frantic mix of fact checking, report writing, VIP visit planning, search co-ordination and forensic-log checking, along with ad hoc decision-making. So had it been yesterday, when she'd visited Vinny Foster? *Vinny Foster!* There had been a vehicle sitting in the single parking spot outside his office. A dark-coloured SUV with . . . yes!

Pink furry dice hanging from the mirror. Or was her memory playing tricks on her out of sheer mental exhaustion? No, she was sure she was right. She suddenly sat bolt upright. Of course! It explained the startled look on Foster's face when she'd mentioned Bere Regis to him during their interview. Bere Regis was very close to the scene of Tommy's bike crash. She went to find Barry.

* * *

By the time the two detectives got to Foster's office, the place was empty and locked up, just like most of the other premises along the street. Was it really that late? Rae checked her watch. Seven in the evening! Where had the time gone?

'Do we have a record of his home address?' Barry asked, looking anxious. He was visibly relieved when Rae responded in the affirmative.

'Of course,' she said. 'What do you take me for?'

They drove to the address Rae had noted, a small, semi-detached house in a new development in Upton, on the northern edge of Poole. It was in darkness, with the curtains still open. There was no car in the driveway.

'Let's leave it for now,' Barry said. 'We need to discuss this with the super and think things through. He might be a vital link. Only a few days ago someone said that all roads seem to lead to Vinny Foster, but we had nothing substantial on him.'

'That was you, boss. But it wasn't Vinny Foster, it was Crustie Valentine, the mechanic.'

He laughed grimly. 'Well, whoever it was, we need a good plan of action. You know, Rose told me something interesting. Crustie Valentine is meant to be the best body-repair man in the business. Locally, I mean. Interesting, yes? But we'll deal with Vinny Foster first. Let's get a house search organised.'

CHAPTER 31: SLIMEBALL

Saturday morning

Sophie was addressing her team at the early-morning briefing in the incident room. She was proud of them all. Every single one had arrived for work early and had applied themselves to whatever task they were working on. Their hard work was already bringing results.

'The search of Vinny Foster's home was useful for a number of reasons, even though we didn't find him or anything that would directly link him to Mia's abduction,' she said. 'Not least was that I got to chat to his long-term partner, Maddie Brooks. She's not a happy bunny. She moved in with him just a year ago, but from what she said, I gathered that the relationship has gone downhill since then. It's a common story. While they were living separately, they got on perfectly. Then she moved in and soon found herself doing most of the chores, the shopping, the cooking. She's obviously resentful. He's been secretive with her. Well, that's no surprise to us, is it? He's heavily involved in something devious, apart from knocking Tommy off his bike.'

'Is that definite now?' Barry asked.

'Pretty much so. We found a receipt for bodywork repairs done last week by — guess who — Rose's old friend, Crustie Valentine. Maddie confirmed that he arrived home at about seven thirty that Monday morning in a foul mood. He claimed he'd been out working all night, but she thinks he's got another woman somewhere and he'd spent the night with her. She even suspects who this woman might be, a Bren Docherty who lives in a farm cottage between Bere Regis and Wool.'

'Near that road where Tommy got hit?' Rae asked.

'Exactly. And it explains why he was in such a hurry. Maddie thinks he was racing to get back home before she spotted his absence. Maddie was meant to be on nights that week, but her shifts got changed at the last minute. She's furious, understandably so. She says that she'll probably move out once she's found somewhere to go. As for the rest, we didn't spot anything that directly links him to Mia Lockhart, but a couple of details did come to light. He was clearly in regular contact with Stu Blackman, for one.'

'That message Jacob got yesterday puzzles me,' Lydia said. 'I don't get it. Who could have sent it, and why? Can it be traced?'

'Burner phone,' Barry said. 'No use. And the message came through a wiping service that deleted its route. So no luck there.'

'But the fact that such a clever system was used is a clue in itself, isn't it?' Rae suggested.

'Good point,' Barry said. 'Someone knew what they were doing, so we know we're not dealing with a complete amateur here. But that's all we know. It doesn't help much, does it? Anyway, on to the bloodstain on that dress from the suitcase in the pool, the one we think belonged to Janella Ramos. One of the forensic technicians worked on it through the night and found some useful pointers. The blood is from a woman and the DNA indicates that it's of Middle Eastern origin. So it's not Janella's blood. They'll be running it through the database today to see if it links to anyone already on file.'

'One of the Hamdi women?' Rae suggested.

Barry shrugged. 'Maybe we shouldn't speculate. Anyway, I doubt if their DNA is on file. None of them have criminal records and, as far as I'm aware, they've never been lifted for anything, not even under suspicion. Rose and George spent much of yesterday looking into the background of Janella Ramos and found something. Do you want to explain, Rose?'

Rose took a swig of tea. 'Yeah. She actually lived in one of those flats for a spell, while she was the cleaner. You know, the ones that Hamdi owns. We asked a few of the other residents about her, and some people in the neighbourhood. They all said she was a good worker but a bit nosey. People said she always wanted to know people's business, which sometimes got their backs up. She also had a string of boyfriends — that's if they really were boyfriends. At least one of the residents has an alternative name for them, if you get my drift. The people in one of the local boutiques said that she was never short of a bob or two. You can draw your own conclusions about that. George wondered if she'd snooped a bit too successfully and found out something she wasn't meant to know. Maybe instead of keeping quiet she tried to prise money out of someone, and they weren't best pleased. It makes sense, doesn't it?'

'Good work, you two,' Sophie said. 'That fits in with what Rae discovered from the current cleaner and something the Hamdi gardener said to Barry and me. She might have attempted to blackmail someone and got killed as a result. But who and what did she have on them? It's a puzzle until we can get more details. Maybe we need another look at her bank account, Rae.'

'If the bloodstain was a woman's, that must mean the wife, Nadira, or one of the daughters, Gamila or Shazia,' Rae said. 'Does it mean Janella Ramos was involved in a violent incident some time before she died?'

'It would seem so. But you're forgetting the housekeeper, Mrs Sayegh,' Barry said. 'I have to say, I didn't like her one bit. She came across as small-minded, and there was something nasty about her. She seemed suspicious of everything and everyone.

Apparently, she came to Britain with the family some years ago. I think she might see herself as a sort of guardian.'

'So she might also be involved with Mia's abduction, if she saw her as a threat to a family member?' Rae suggested.

Sophie held up her hand. 'It's all very well to speculate,' she said, 'but it's worthless without hard evidence to support it. Let's get busy.'

She took George aside as he was about to follow Rose to their desk. 'Sorry, George. I know you had plans for this weekend, but with Mia still missing, we can't afford to lose you.'

He smiled tiredly. 'I know. I warned Jade last night, and she's switched our plans to next weekend. She does understand.'

'I'll try and give everyone time off when we've got this wrapped up — whenever that is.'

She checked the time. The canteen staff should be in by now. She phoned through and ordered bacon sandwiches for everyone. After the first of the cling-filmed plates of food arrived, the mood in the room lifted enormously.

'Simple things like this help to make the world go round,' Barry commented.

'Don't I know it,' Sophie said. 'And, let's face it, most cops seem to be addicted to bacon sandwiches. Well, this lot are, anyway.'

Her phone rang and she moved aside to take the call. She turned to Barry. 'Theresa Jackson's back at the farmhouse. Amy's seen something. I'll go. You take over here. I'll phone when I've found out more.'

She grabbed her coat and ran for the exit.

* * *

Along with Theresa Jackson, the liaison officer allocated to the Birkbeck family, Sophie was sitting with the mother and daughter at their kitchen table. Amy's father was leaning against the sink, a mug of tea in his hand.

'You definitely saw someone, Amy? From your bedroom window?' Theresa asked.

Amy nodded. 'He was creeping around out in the yard, trying to keep to the shadows.'

'What woke you?' Theresa continued.

'Loopy, our dog. He sometimes sleeps on my bedroom floor. He jumped on my bed, then he started running to the window and barking, and he doesn't usually bark at night. Not like that. I went to the window to see what was up. Then he went quiet, but I stayed there for a bit. That's when I saw someone creep across the yard, back to the lane.'

'She's right,' her father said. 'The barking woke me as well, but by the time I came to, it was too late to see anything. But the light was still on. It's movement activated at night, and he must have tripped the sensor.'

'What did he look like, Amy? Can you remember anything about him?' Theresa asked.

'He wasn't one of the two men at the pool. He was tall and strong looking.' Amy looked down at the table and shivered.

'Did you catch sight of his face?' Theresa asked.

'No. He was wearing a hood up again, just like then.'

'Could it have been the man you saw in the woods last week?' Sophie said. 'The one you said looked like a hawk?'

Amy looked troubled. 'I don't think so. That man was a lot thinner.' She paused. 'Anyway, Mr Hawk moved different.'

'So the other man, the one you call Mr Hawk, wasn't one of the two at the pool? The ones who pushed the body in?' Sophie said.

Amy shivered again. 'No.'

'And last night's man wasn't one of them either?'

Amy looked miserable. 'It's hard to remember. There could've been someone else out in the lane. It was so dark. Someone might have been waiting in the part that was in shadow, someone smaller.'

Theresa reached across and felt Amy's fingers, which were cold, despite the warmth of the farmhouse kitchen. 'You've done really well, Amy.'

Sophie looked across at Andy Birkbeck and raised her eyebrows.

‘It was about one o’clock,’ he said. ‘And there are a couple of footprints in a patch of slurry by the outhouse. Just where Amy saw him.’

‘I’ll get forensics in right now. He must have had a vehicle nearby.’

* * *

The bank had sent some more information detailing the state of Janella Ramos’s finances, which had proved to be most interesting. The previous summary hadn’t shown an investment account she held, nor had it listed all the transactions from the year before she died, only the final month. Rae studied it closely. Money coming in regularly and irregularly, money going out in rather smaller amounts and a surprisingly large amount in the newly discovered savings account. There were regular transfers of hefty sums from the current account, but where had those deposits come from? Rae referred back to the current account details. Lots of cash deposits, each of different amounts and made at different times. That tied in with the suggestion from one or two of her neighbours that Janella had been working as a prostitute. Had her clientele been local? Moreover, had she been working alone, or had there been a pimp lurking in the background? From what Janella’s neighbours had said, it seemed to have been disorganised and low-key, so maybe she’d been working alone. Rae decided that it might be worth doing some online research once she’d got a bit further with Janella’s finances.

The bank statements showed that a regular amount was coming in each month from Sandline Developments. This must be her wages for the cleaning jobs she did. Outgoings included a regular amount to the same company — probably her rent, judging by the sum involved, plus energy and water bills. This was where the newly arrived statements from more than a year earlier were useful. They showed regular use of a bank card for groceries and other shopping. This had stopped some six months before her death, indicating that Janella had probably started using cash instead. Apart from that, and the cash deposited before being transferred to the savings account, there were no unusual transactions, nothing that Rae could get her teeth into. So why had Janella been killed? Somehow, she'd upset a person — or people — enough to warrant her murder. How had she become such a thorn in someone's side?

Rae wondered if the reason had been the same as for Mia, that Janella had discovered something unsavoury or criminal about Suleiman Hamdi or his business interests. What if, in her job as a cleaner, she'd been rather too nosey and had stumbled on the information that Hamdi was double-crossing his own government and acting as an arms dealer for the rebels? The problem was, as the boss had pointed out, that such speculation was a waste of time without any evidence. Was it likely that it existed? If Janella had been murdered for this reason, then Hamdi's people would have gone through the cleaner's accommodation, destroying anything that could be used to implicate them. Rae decided to pay another visit to the neighbours. But first an internet trawl. Rae collected the latest police list of sex contact sites, told Barry what she was about to do and sat down again at her desk. She steeled herself for the task in hand, entering the labyrinthine world of people's peccadillos and unorthodox desires. Places where people like Janella Ramos might exploit others' vices for their own gain and make the kind of money that had found its way into her bank account. Untaxed, of course.

That was when a sudden thought struck Rae with the force of a sledgehammer. Who did she know who may have had such a vice? Who had been over-secretive about his personal life? Who had behaved like a slimeball whenever he and Rae had been alone out of earshot, leering at her and making suggestive comments? Who had rented one of those flats and so would have had the opportunity to bump into Janella fairly frequently, get talking and spot a potential fellow conspirator? Stu bloody Blackman, of course. Now deceased, like Janella, his body thrown into the same dank pond, on top of hers. This was the problem with murder cases like this one. You couldn't help but wonder if some kind of rough justice was at work, using nasty, devious and immoral people to remove other nasty, devious, immoral people from the population. Rae purged the thought from her brain.

CHAPTER 32: WORRY

Mickie Rollins was beside himself. He was sitting in his office at the car showroom frowning, his elbows on the desktop and his chin resting in his hands. Why couldn't he seem to contact Vinny Foster? He wasn't answering his mobile, nor his office phone. He wasn't responding to emails. Where was the bastard and what was he up to?

Crustie came in, wiping his hands on an oily rag that was filthier than him. 'Wassup? You look as if someone just pooped in your coffee.'

Mickie didn't take the bait. This was too serious for light-hearted banter. 'Vinny's gone AWOL. I can't contact him.'

'Oh that. No need to worry. He's probably been lifted by the cops for that 'it and run. See the bodywork job I did on his Jeep? I told you it was a cyclist he'd hit. They'll be round to ask us about it, you can bet yer life on it. We'd better get our story straight, then we'll be in the clear.'

'Sure?'

'Oh yeah. We know nuthin', just did a repair job for 'im. It's the truth, innit? 'E didn't tell us what 'e did, did 'e?' He laughed. 'For the first time in years we can be truthful wiv the cops. Who'd a thought it, eh?'

Mickie didn't look reassured. 'What about the second lot of cops that came calling? The pair in plain clothes? They said they weren't here about the same thing as the traffic cops.'

Crustie snorted. 'What, 'er? She's not a detective, Mickie. She's just an ordinary cop who happened to be out of uniform that mornin'. Probably doing a favour for someone. She's got no more brains than me. I'm telling you, if she's made detective, they're really scrapin' the barrel. Even her young buddy looked wet behind the ears.'

'Well, I just hope you're right.'

'The other thing I 'eard was that this girl they've been lookin' for all week might be linked to Vinny. She was on his books. She might even have worked at Suleiman's 'ouse.'

Mickie frowned. 'Where'd you hear all this stuff?'

Crustie smirked. 'From Bren, Vinny's bit on the side. She's my stepsister. She phoned me earlier. Said Vinny'd spent the night in question at 'er place and overslept. That's why 'e was going like a blue-arsed fly — to get back 'ome before Maddie got in. She was on nights that week. That relationship'll be over when Maddie learns the truth. She was too good for 'im, anyway.'

'So you think the cops will be round here, asking us about it?'

Crustie shrugged. 'Bound to. Just take it easy, Mickie. Vinny didn't tell us nothin'. Stick to that.'

'D'you think I might be in with a chance with Maddie?'

Crustie nearly collapsed with laughter. 'Fuck no, you moron. If she's too good for Vinny, you stand no chance. She's got class and brains. What do you and me 'ave? Come on, be honest. Maddie. Ha, that's a good one.' He returned to the workshop, still chortling.

Barely an hour after this conversation, Mickie spotted a man and a woman getting out of their car and walking across the forecourt. Cops. They had that look about them. But not the same two who had called last week. The ginger-haired bloke had square shoulders and looked ominously determined. He also looked vaguely familiar. The woman was the same height and she too had a no-nonsense air. Obviously, the real detectives had come calling this time. He walked out onto the forecourt to meet them.

'Good morning.' He tried to sound cheery. 'How can I help you?'

Two warrant cards were flashed in front of his eyes.

'DS Gregson,' said the woman. 'This is DI Marsh. You must be Mickie Rollins. We want to ask you about a Jeep you repaired eight or nine days ago. It belonged to Vinny Foster. What kind of work did you carry out on it?'

Mickie felt his stomach muscles tighten. No beating about the bush with these two. Straight in without any cheery banter to relax the mood. They were the real deal.

'Come inside. It's a bit warmer. I'll call in my senior mechanic. He'll have done the repairs.'

Not a smile, just two hostile stares. The omens weren't good. Still, just as Crustie had pointed out, all they'd done was repair the damaged bodywork on a customer's car. No mud could be slung their way. They entered the showroom, which was only marginally warmer than the chill outside.

'Okay. Give me a mo.'

Mickie walked through to the back and found Crustie lurking behind the door. 'They're a hard-looking pair,' he said. 'Don't get them riled. And don't get riled yourself. You know you've got a short fuse.'

'As if I would,' Crustie whispered back. 'I'm not forgettin' the dodgy job we did for Suleiman. That could land us in really deep shit. No, I'll be as nice as pie. Do I stall them or admit to the repair from the off?'

'Didn't you say Vinny's place had been searched?'

'Yeah, that's what Bren said.'

'They could've seen the paperwork. Christ, why did he insist on a receipt? We'd have been fine with cash,' Mickie said.

'Probably some kind of tax dodge. He'll have put it through 'is company expenses.'

Mickie frowned. 'Let's be straight with them. Maybe it'll win us some brownie points. I don't want them digging around too much. You never know what they might find.'

Mickie could feel the detectives' eyes on them both as they walked into the showroom.

Crustie came straight to the point. 'You're in about that repair I did to the front wing of Vinny Foster's Jeep. I did it a week last Thursday and Vinny collected it the next day. Ain't that right, Mickie?'

Mickie nodded. 'Yeah, that's right.'

'What had caused the damage? Could you tell?' This was the tall woman detective, her tone aggressive. A good reason to be careful.

Crustie shook his head. 'Nope. He could have hit any number of things. A fence, a gate. It could've been some scrap metal falling on his front end. I didn't ask. I never do.'

'We think he hit a cyclist,' she said.

'Right. It's possible, I'll give you that. But I can't go no further.'

'Can't or won't?'

Crustie smiled thinly. 'Can't, of course. I've experience in bodywork repairs. I know these things.'

There was a short silence.

'Have you had the tyres on your Discovery changed recently, Mr Valentine?' the male detective said.

'Yeah, what of it?'

'Unusual to need all four changed at the same time, isn't it?'

'It happens. There was a cheap deal on from the suppliers, so I went for it. It's winter. I want good tyres under me in case the weather gets worse.'

'What did you do with the old ones?' the detective asked.

'We've got a contract with a place up in the north of the county. They all get recycled.'

'We know.'

Crustie was puzzled. 'You know what?'

'We know you took some tyres there last week. The staff were surprised because it was a much smaller load than your usual. Just your four and a couple of others. As if you needed to get rid of them for a reason.'

Crustie stared at him. 'What're you sayin'?'

'Why did you change them? The tyres were only partly worn and would have lasted another year at least.'

Crustie's blood was up. He ignored Mickie's warning hand on his forearm. 'I don't have to explain my reasons to you. It's a fucking free country. I can change my tyres when I like.'

Crustie and Mickie heard car doors slamming outside. A number of police vehicles were disgorging uniformed officers onto the forecourt and a forensic van pulled in behind them.

'Maybe we need to continue this conversation at the station,' the DI said.

'Yeah, maybe. I'm not sayin' any more without my lawyer, so it ain't gonna be a *conversation*, as you call it,' Mickie said.

The ginger-haired copper didn't seem fazed. 'We kind of expected that. Well, have it your own way.'

Mickie felt that things were starting to slip away from them, out of control. Why did these cops seem so confident? What did they know?

The woman detective said, 'That's your Range Rover out the back, isn't it? The one with the fresh mud and slurry stains on the wheels.'

Mickie suddenly felt faint. Those words weren't uttered casually, they carried real menace. Fuck. What was going on? Had they really checked those tyres Crustie had got rid of?

CHAPTER 33: HALLUCINATING?

Sophie spent much of the late afternoon tied up in an unproductive meeting with Special Branch officers, trying to ascertain whether the allegation about Suleiman Hamdi's double-dealing was fact or mere speculation. Maybe he just had highly placed enemies in government, people out looking for revenge for some perceived slight that had happened years before. Perhaps it was all down to resentment at the influence he seemed to wield. Possibly his government was uneasy at how well he and his family were adapting to life in Britain. Sophie listened to each of these suggestions with increasing frustration.

'He's an unscrupulous thug,' she finally said. 'I sat talking to him for nearly an hour and watched his reactions to the questions my DI and I threw at him, the way he responded. We then drew out his staff and acquaintances on how they felt about him. It was clear that they're all terrified of the man. So are his family. He's a very unpleasant individual.'

'That doesn't make him a traitor, does it? Someone who'd cheat his own government,' Karen Brody said.

Sophie sighed. Was it worth trying to convince these people to spend a bit of time carrying out some checks? Here she was, wasting a couple of hours while there were all these other things bearing down on her. And the problem with these two, particularly Karen, was that they tended to dismiss anything they perceived as a 'hunch.' To be honest, Sophie could understand their attitude, she too steered clear of hunches if she could. But sometimes there was little else to go on, and this was especially true in the case of Hamdi. He was up to something devious that his paid minions knew nothing about. Whatever this was had got Stu Blackman and Janella Ramos killed and put Mia Lockhart in deadly danger. All three of them had stumbled on some secret of his and had paid the price.

The meeting finally found its weary way to a conclusion, one that Sophie would have to accept. They'd take her concerns seriously and raise the matter with the higher echelons to take further.

'But I don't know how they'll find anything out,' Karen said, tidying her papers away. 'We're all so focussed on preventing potential terrorists coming into the country. This is something entirely different. We're not sure how it poses a threat to us.'

'We do have the Home Secretary with us on this,' Sophie reminded them.

Joel Kennedy grimaced. 'Yes, but she's not put any resources into it, has she? It's easy to talk.'

* * *

Sophie backed her car into her driveway. She felt desperately tired. Did she even have the energy to climb out? She glanced at the clock on the dashboard. Eight o'clock on a cold winter's night. Even in a spot as balmy as Wareham, tucked into a river valley close to Poole Harbour, that often meant a damp, chill wind. And so it was tonight, as she climbed out of the car, turned and closed the door. Martin would have something hot in the oven, maybe a casserole or a pasta bake.

She jumped. A dark, hooded figure slid out of the shadows in front of her. Startled, she glanced around, rapidly weighing up her options. The figure held a hand up, as if to calm her.

'Please. Just a message. Don't waste time looking for Mia. I have her safe. Spend your time on the others. The answer's at the flats. There's more there than meets the eye.' The voice was muffled, but Sophie could detect an accent. Middle eastern?

Her heart was racing. She stared at the person facing her. 'How do I know she's safe? This could be a trick,' she said.

There was a moment's silence. 'I will get her to call you. What is your number?'

Sophie pulled her card out of her pocket and handed it over. 'When?'

A shrug. 'Sometime this evening. Please. Keep it to yourself. The fewer that know, the safer we are.'

Sophie nodded. 'I'll have to tell my chief constable. I won't go out on a limb on this. It would be an unthinkable risk.'

Another silence. Then, 'Okay.'

The security light suddenly went off, its thirty-second illumination period having passed. Sophie stepped back and turned, forcing it back on. When she turned back, the figure had disappeared. She made her way to the front door, still trembling. Was this good news? It was impossible to know.

She opened the door and stepped into the warmth and safety of her house, and a faint aroma of herb-flavoured casserole. And the reassuring presence of Martin. He came out of the kitchen, smiling.

'Wine?'

She shook her head. 'Later. A cup of tea would go down a treat right now.'

'I wondered. The kettle's been on.'

It was bizarre. In an instant, she had gone from being in possibly mortal danger to peace and safety, the ordinary familiarity of home. Maybe the whole episode had been a hallucination. Was that possible?

She hung up her coat, followed her husband into the kitchen and sank onto a chair.

'You look done in,' he said.

'I feel it. I'm beginning to wonder if I'm getting too old for this lark.'

'What? You? Never!'

She took a sip of the proffered tea. 'Martin, did you see or hear anything outside just before I came in?'

He shook his head, looking bemused. 'No. What was it?'

'It's all right. Maybe it was nothing. Do I have time for a quick shower before we eat?'

'Of course. Fifteen minutes?'

She climbed the stairs, taking her mug with her, stripped off her clothes and stepped into a blissfully hot cascade of water. A warm towel, another mouthful of tea and on with a loose sweater and jeans. Back in the kitchen, she gulped the rest of her tea. Her phone rang.

'Hello. This is me, Mia Lockhart. I'm okay. I'm safe. Really, I am. Please give my love to Jacob. Tell him I'll see him soon.'

The voice didn't sound particularly stressed, but was it really Mia? How could she tell?

'Where are you?'

'I can't say. They smuggled me out because I was in danger.' With that the connection was cut. Sophie was given no time for more questions.

'I think I'm ready for that wine now.'

A glass of New Zealand Sauvignon Blanc in her hand, she phoned the chief constable.

'Do what you think best, Sophie,' she said. 'But be careful, for God's sake. We don't want everything going tits up.'

'I think it's genuine, ma'am,' Sophie said. She took another swig of wine.

'Food's ready,' Martin called.

Sophie felt she was in two places at once. It gave her the disconcerting feeling that she was still hallucinating.

An hour later, replete and more relaxed, she held a short teleconference with Barry, Rae and Lydia to fill them in on what had happened.

'It's a switch of emphasis, Lydia,' she said. 'Can you and Jimmy stay with us for a few more days? We'll quietly shelve the search for Mia without making it obvious.'

'Isn't that a bit of a gamble, ma'am?' Lydia said.

'Isn't everything?'

CHAPTER 34: CONFRONTATION

Sunday morning

What had they said? That there was more than met the eye at those pesky flats? Sophie stood in the small car park, looking up at the building. Was it just a general comment or was it coded in some way? She turned to Barry and Rae.

'What do you think, Barry?'

'We've already been through this place, every flat and cupboard. Jimmy even had a quick peek in the roof space. Nothing turned up.'

'So, in that case we're looking for something out of the ordinary,' Sophie said.

'If there's anything there at all. It could all be a hoax. You said so yourself last night.'

'I know. But I don't think it is. I think it really was Mia on the line, though we couldn't trace the call. Granted, I've never spoken to her before, but you get a feel for these things. And if that part was reliable, doesn't that give credence to the second bit of information?'

Barry clearly wasn't convinced. He merely shrugged. 'You've always told us to stick to the evidence. We're on very shaky ground here.'

They stopped talking when Lydia's small sports car came screeching to a halt in an empty bay. She climbed out, clutching a sheaf of papers, followed by Jimmy Melsom. They hurried towards them.

'I may have something,' she said. 'I've got plans from the land registry of what was here before the flats were built. It was an old workshop and warehouse. Look.'

She spread out a large sheet of paper across the bonnet of Barry's car. They drew in close to examine the diagrams. The plan showed the area some thirty years earlier, when it looked rather different from the domesticated scene of today, with its shrub-lined parking bays, greens and well-maintained apartment blocks. The diagram showed a workshop, storage building and several outhouses.

'What are we looking for, Lydia?' Sophie asked.

Lydia put a fingertip down near the workshop. 'Here. There was a basement. If I've got it right, the apartment at the end of the corridor is right above it.'

'Who owns it?' Sophie asked.

'It's flat one. You tell me.'

'That's the one Hamdi keeps for his own use,' Rae said. 'The search warrant is still valid, isn't it?'

'Yes. So let's go for a look-see. Rae, you wait here in the car park and warn us if anyone arrives. If it's Hamdi, follow him in. Jimmy, you stay in the entrance foyer. Vests on, everyone.'

She led Barry and Lydia inside the building. They hastened to flat one and knocked. There was no answer, so Sophie unlocked the door. They went in.

'It's the floor we're interested in. Agreed? If there's a hatch or something, it's likely to be hidden under a rug or furniture. Be creative.'

It was Barry who made the breakthrough, partly because he'd searched the flat above, the one Stu Blackman rented. The layout of Hamdi's own flat was identical, apart from a single feature. At the far end of the hallway, a huge built-in cupboard stretched from floor to ceiling and extended the full width of the area. He opened it and peered inside. It appeared to be just a walk-in storage unit, albeit rather large. It had an internal light, so Barry switched it on. Shelves with cleaning products, slide-out boxes of bed linen, towels, several cases containing a collection of vintage camera equipment. It all looked perfectly innocent. The floor was solid enough, with no signs of a hatch or removable boards. The cupboard would already have been checked thoroughly, of course, during the previous search of the building, and nothing unusual had been reported then. Barry came out of the cupboard and strolled through the rest of the flat, glancing at the layout while Sophie and Lydia tapped walls and examined floors.

He left the flat and climbed the stairs to the one above, unlocked the door and walked quickly around. Yes, he'd been right. The layout was identical to the one below, apart from that walk-in closet. Which wasn't really needed. There was more than enough cupboard space spread through each apartment, so why put such a large one in Hamdi's flat?

Barry went back downstairs and stood looking at the cupboard. This must hold the secret. He was aware of Sophie coming and standing behind him.

'Anything?' he asked.

'No. Nor Lydia.'

'This must be it. It's got to be something to do with this cupboard. It's in the exact spot.'

He stepped back inside, taking another careful look around him. Shelves, boxes, light switches. He looked again. Why were there two light switches? The first turned the internal light on and off, but the second appeared to do nothing.

'I need a measuring tape,' he said. 'I think I saw one in the cleaner's cupboard.'

He went out and returned with one, holding it up like a trophy. 'Okay, here we go.'

Lydia noted the measurements down as he made them. The depth of the cupboard. The length of the hallway as far as the cupboard door. The same dimensions on the other side of the internal walls, in the living room. He double checked the measurements.

'There's about a metre missing,' he said. 'The cupboard is shorter than it should be. There must be a gap behind it.'

He had another look at the shelves lining the back wall. They looked solid enough, although the supports were of timber and looked custom-built. But there was something else unusual about them. The shelves were only half width and were arranged stepwise on the two sides. It was as if they would fold into each other if one half could somehow be rotated away from the wall. Barry found a stepladder just inside the door and pushed it forward. He picked up a flashlight and clambered up, bending forward to examine the timber supports closely. He felt up the length to the very top. There was a sort of indentation close to the ceiling which turned out to be a latch, hidden from below. He unclipped it. Now the timber frame seemed less secure. Was there one at floor level? He climbed down, pulled the steps aside and felt the support. Yes. He unclipped that one, stepped back and tugged. The entire right side of the framework swung forward and rotated, the shelves interlacing perfectly with those on the left-hand side. Even the items on the shelves, the boxes and packets, had been carefully placed so that they didn't touch. Beyond was an opening, high as a door, lit by a bare bulb hanging from the small square ceiling area. Sophie operated the second switch, and the dark recess was suddenly illuminated. So this was what that other switch was for.

Barry could see a set of steep, narrow steps descending below the floor. He stepped inside the small enclosure and directed the flashlight downwards.

'Mia?' he called. 'Mia, are you there? It's the police.'

There was no answer. He started down the steps, followed by Sophie. A quick sweep with the flashlight showed a small basement area, containing a few stacked plastic boxes, each tightly lidded. There was another light switch on the wall at the bottom of the steps. The extra light merely confirmed what he'd already seen. An underground storage cellar, nothing more. No Mia. No chair. No furniture of any kind. So, what was in the boxes?

Both detectives slid latex gloves on and took a peek inside. The first contained documents. Sophie flicked through them.

'Details of arms orders and shipments,' she said. 'But it doesn't look as if they're to his government. Documents he wouldn't want seen, I guess.'

Meanwhile, Barry had been looking in a second box. Handguns, several of them, hidden among layers of towels. He glanced at Sophie.

'We have to take them,' she said. 'We can't leave them here.'

A third box contained ammunition for the guns and a collection of cheap mobile phones still in their wrappings.

Sophie called up to Lydia, who was at the top of the steps, peering down. 'We need a few evidence bags. Tell Rae and Jimmy to keep a sharp lookout and hold back anyone who turns up. Greg Buller's on standby with the armed unit. Get him here fast. Then call Dave Nash and send him across with his weapons forensic people. Quick as you can.'

'So, where the hell is Mia?' Barry asked.

Sophie shook her head wearily. 'I don't know. It depends on whether the person I spoke to last night was really her, and she wasn't being threatened.'

Barry slowly swept his phone around in a circle, taking a video of the small, enclosed area. Then they clambered out, back into the hallway of Hamdi's flat. Sophie's phone rang. It was Rae.

'Hamdi's just arrived,' she said. 'He's just getting out of his car. Maybe you've tripped an alarm of some kind. That other guy is with him, the one Amy called Mr Hawk.'

'Shariq,' Sophie answered. 'Just what we don't need right now. You and Jimmy keep them back. I don't want them in the building.'

She glanced at Lydia, who was still on the phone.

'Greg's just around the corner,' Lydia said. 'Do you want him to move in?'

'Yes, but tell him to keep it as low-key as possible.' Barry and Lydia were checking their firearms. 'Keep them holstered for now, but be ready.'

Sophie walked out of the flat and into the foyer. The group outside the doors seemed fairly calm. Ideally, Sophie would have liked to wait for the arrival of the fast-response unit, but Rae and Jimmy, neither of them armed, were outside with the two men who might well be carrying weapons.

She took a deep breath, opened the door and stepped into bright sunlight. The situation appeared calm, but she saw Hamdi's gaze sweep across her. He would have already noticed that Jimmy and Rae were in bullet-proof vests and he would see at once that Lydia and Barry were armed.

'Mr Hamdi. Mr Shariq.'

Hamdi looked coldly at her. 'This is victimisation.'

Sophie shook her head. 'No. Mia Lockhart is still missing. A search warrant remains active for three months and we can visit as often as is reasonable in that period.'

She watched the two men, weighing them up, trying to second guess their thoughts. Shariq was scowling but he had his arms folded across his chest. Any move would come from Hamdi himself. His eyes were darting around. He would know that he was almost surrounded, with Rae standing to one side and Jimmy edging slowly backwards to block any sudden dash by either man. Hamdi's eyes settled on Sophie. The air almost vibrated with tension.

'Whatever you're thinking of doing, Mr Hamdi, think again. There are five of us here. There's a fast-response unit waiting just around the corner. Think of your family. Think of your daughters and their future.'

Suddenly Hamdi's hand slid towards the pocket of his coat. Barry and Lydia did the same. But Shariq intervened, gripping the arm so that it froze in position. He muttered something to his employer in Arabic, and said, 'That would be madness, Suleiman.'

Jimmy took the opportunity to jump forward and grab him from behind, forcing his arms behind his back while Rae cuffed him. Barry spun Shariq around and did the same to him.

Greg Buller appeared around the corner with three colleagues. He laughed and shook his head when he saw the two men in cuffs. 'Spoilsports. Looks like we've missed the fun.'

Sophie said nothing, surprised at how much the tension of the last few minutes had affected her. It was all she could do to stop herself from trembling. She walked away from the group and stood beside a small green space, taking deep breaths. Maybe what she'd said to Martin had been right. She was getting too old for this.

She turned back to the small cluster of people. Hamdi was being patted down for concealed weapons. Barry drew a handgun out of his coat pocket. Jimmy searched Shariq but found nothing. Hamdi was led away towards the waiting van. Shariq hesitated and turned. Sophie caught his eye.

'Where?' she asked, almost under her breath.

His lips barely moving, he said, 'Bath. Shazia's flat.'

When the two were safely stowed in the van, Sophie turned to Greg. 'Go easy on Shariq. He's an undercover cop, but keep it to yourself for now.'

She beckoned to Lydia. 'Fancy going to Bath with me? It's a bright sunny morning and I'm feeling optimistic. I thought you might like to visit a couple of young ladies. I just need to get the address of Shazia Hamdi's flat from Rae. We'll take my car. I'm expecting to bring someone back with us, and your little racer doesn't have room.'

CHAPTER 35: RESCUE

Sophie didn't much like the drive to Bath. The route was one she had been forced to use frequently, either to her mother's home in Bristol or that of her grandparents in Gloucester. The road wound north, full of twists and turns, and the section between Blandford and Shaftesbury, skirting the edge of Cranborne Chase, was particularly bad. This meant, of course, that the countryside around it was particularly pretty, but Sophie had to concentrate on the road, so she always missed most of it. At least the road was relatively quiet today.

They'd made a brief stop at police headquarters so that Lydia could check her gun back in and Sophie could brief the ACC on the morning's events. Now, ninety minutes later, they were finally there, looking down upon the famous Georgian city from the high ground to the south, and then winding their way through the narrow streets towards the centre. The satnav indicated that their destination was just ahead, on the left. Sophie drew into a convenient parking slot, and they looked up at the building. It was an old house, tastefully converted into flats for the wealthy, and beyond the means of most students. They saw Gamila's red Mercedes parked in one of the slots for visitors. A silver BMW sports car was sitting in Shazia's bay. Sophie felt the bonnet. It was still warm. She phoned Rae and asked her to check on the owner. Sure enough, it belonged to Shazia, who wasn't due to return to university for the spring term until the following day. Her presence would complicate matters. And if Mia was still hiding out here, it might have led to friction. Sophie rang the bell at Shazia's flat. A tentative 'Hello?' crackled from the small loudspeaker.

'Detective Superintendent Allen from Dorset police,' she said.

There was a short pause, then the door release buzzed, and they entered. The two detectives climbed the stairs to the first floor. They found the door ajar, with Shazia's angry face peering out.

'What do you want?' she said.

'Can we come in, please? We have news.'

Shazia opened the door wider and stepped aside. She nodded towards a door on the left. Sophie and Lydia entered a spacious sitting room with a high ceiling. Gamila was standing in front of an armchair, her hands clenched together in front of her. She looked tense. Shazia followed them into the room. She didn't invite them to sit. Judging from Gamila's tearful expression, Sophie wondered if they'd interrupted a row.

'We've come to collect Mia. We know she's here. We assume it's for her own safety. You both should know that we arrested your father earlier this morning for a series of criminal offences, with more in the pipeline. Can we see Mia now, please?'

The two sisters glanced at each other. Both looked as wound up as coil springs.

'Is he all right, our father?' Gamila asked.

'Yes, of course. We have him in custody, but he's safe.'

'What is he being charged with?' Shazia snapped.

'We still have to consider the exact charges, but they will be serious ones.'

With a glance at her older sister, Gamila left the room. They heard a muttered exchange out in the hall.

Shazia walked to the window and looked out, making it obvious that she had nothing to say to the detectives.

'When did you get here, Shazia?' Sophie asked.

'This morning.' She kept her back turned to them.

'You must have set off early. Why was that?'

'It's not against the law, is it? Or do you plan to arrest me on some trumped-up charge as well?'

'We don't arrest people on trumped-up charges, Shazia. We always wait until we have evidence to support our actions.'

The room fell silent. Shazia radiated hostility. Sophie wondered why she had hotfooted it up to Bath in such a rush today of all days. Did she want to be here when they came for Mia? Was she keeping an eye on her younger sister? Had she been tipped off about the arrests? Or had she just found out that Mia was hiding in her flat?

Gamila returned with another young woman. Mia Lockhart. The two detectives had looked at enough photos to recognise her immediately. She hesitated in the doorway looking nervous and glanced at the glowering Shazia. Clearly, she was uncomfortable with her presence.

Sophie moved towards her. 'Mia, I'm Detective Superintendent Sophie Allen. I've been leading the investigation into a series of murders and abductions in Dorset. My colleague is Detective Sergeant Lydia Pillay, who's been heading up the investigation into your disappearance. We don't want any information from you right now, but we do want to move you away to somewhere safe. We'll keep all our questions until then.'

'I'm sorry if I've caused trouble for you,' Mia said. 'I was told my life was in danger.'

'Were you taken against your will?' Sophie asked.

Mia looked unsure. 'Not really. I didn't want to listen at first, but Gamila convinced me. She said I needed to be well away from Poole. I wanted to tell the police, but I was told they had bribed someone in the police. So, Gamila brought me here to Shazia's flat because it was going to be empty until the start of term. I wanted to get a message out, but it was too risky. Was it you I spoke to on the phone last night?'

'Yes. We have several people in custody who we suspect are a threat to you. And we know who the corrupt officer was. He's no longer a danger.'

'So I'm safe now? I can go home?'

'We'll talk about that on the way back. Did you bring much with you?'

Mia shook her head. 'No. I've been borrowing Gamila's clothes.' She turned to her friend. 'Gamila, I can't thank you enough for what you've done. Can we stay in touch?'

Gamila nodded. 'Of course.'

It was obvious to the two detectives that neither of the two young women wanted to say much in the presence of Shazia. Sophie could still sense the tension, the distrust between her and them.

She turned to Gamila. 'We'll need a statement from you as soon as possible. This afternoon, if you can. Is that doable?'

She really didn't want to leave the two sisters together. She suspected that Shazia might browbeat her younger sibling into sharing too much information, particularly about the events surrounding Mia's supposed abduction and the role played by Abdal Shariq.

Gamila jumped at the chance. 'I'll follow you back if you like, but I really need to check on my mother.'

'That's fine. Do that first and give us your statement this evening. We'll come to the house.' Sophie wondered about the relationship between the sisters. The younger had been so eager to leave with them rather than stay behind with Shazia, who still seemed to be bristling with hostility. Was that because she objected to her flat being borrowed, possibly without her permission or knowledge, or was it something deeper?

They left the flat and Sophie waited until they were at the cars before turning to speak to Gamila.

'I must ask you not to tell anyone how you persuaded Mia to go into hiding, not until I give you clearance. This is still an active investigation. No talking until we've spoken at length. Do you understand?'

'Of course.' Gamila looked up at the apartment window. Shazia was watching them. Gamila turned towards her car.

Sophie waited until the red Mercedes had driven out onto the road before setting off herself. It seemed important that she keep the sisters apart, although she wasn't entirely sure why.

* * *

Lydia turned round in her seat to speak to Mia. 'Those two Hamdi girls are very different, aren't they?'

'Yes, but it's not surprising, is it?' Mia said.

'What do you mean?'

'Didn't you know? They're half-sisters. Shazia's mother died just after her birth. I heard that she was an important person back where they come from, the daughter of a sheik or something.'

Sophie was annoyed with herself. Why hadn't they managed to find out more about the Hamdi family? Maybe it had been deliberately kept secret. 'No, we didn't know. They did well to keep that little fact hidden.'

'There was no way we could know, ma'am,' Lydia said. 'The family obviously kept quiet about it.' She turned back to Mia. 'Are you sure?'

'It was something the housekeeper said once. She's been with the family for yonks.'

'Has there always been that level of animosity between Shazia and Gamila?' Sophie asked.

Mia shook her head. 'Not as bad as it was today. They're very different, but I think they used to get on okay, as long as Gamila didn't do anything Shazia disapproved of. It was just this morning when Shazia arrived a short while before you. When she saw me, she hit the roof. Gamila wasn't really prepared for it and she burst into tears. Then you rang the bell.'

'Let's go back to Monday night, Mia. What happened?'

'Gamila was waiting for me at the park entrance. She said she feared for my safety and someone else was too. We walked a bit further into the park and Abdal Shariq appeared. Well, when I saw him, I started to run, but he grabbed my wrist. They both calmed me down and convinced me that my life was in danger. I was really surprised. I'd always thought of him as a real hard man. I mean, everyone seemed so scared of him. Anyway, they kept saying I was in danger. Gamila said she'd overheard her father talking about me on the phone.'

'Did she know who he was talking to?' Sophie asked. 'Could it have been Abdal Shariq himself?'

She shook her head. 'Gamila didn't think so. We already knew Abdal wasn't what he seemed. We got drunk in Bournemouth one night back in the autumn, and some guys were threatening us. Gamila phoned Abdal and he came and got us out. He kept quiet about it afterwards, and even joked about it with us. He became a sort of ally. We asked him about the phone call, but he said it wasn't him.'

'Did Gamila think it was someone local?'

'She didn't know.'

'We may decide to keep you in a safe house for a few days, until we're sure no one's still out there looking for you. It's too risky to just leave you,' Sophie said.

Mia looked thoughtful. 'I guess I owe them my life.'

Sophie nodded gently. 'It's possible.'

'So, where are you taking me?'

'You're staying with my detective sergeant for a few days. She lives in Wool and has offered to let you stay in her spare room. But we'll take you to your own place first to collect whatever you might need. Shall we go via Jacob's?'

'I don't know how he'll feel about me now,' Mia said. 'He might be really angry.'

Lydia shook her head. 'No, he isn't. He's been as chirpy as a budgie since you messaged him a couple of days ago. He told me yesterday.'

'Oh, God. I've caused everyone so much trouble, haven't I? I know I have.'

'As it turned out, Mia, you did exactly the right thing. Gamila deserves our thanks. So does Abdal Shariq.'

'I don't understand him. He always seemed such a threatening presence when I worked in the house. I was still sort of scared of him, even after that time in Bournemouth. So was Gamila.'

Back in Poole, the two detectives waited in the car while Mia rang Jacob's doorbell. They watched him open the door. He looked shocked for a second and then threw himself forward, his arms wide, and they hugged each other. There was little doubt about his feelings for her, or hers for him.

* * *

Sophie and Barry returned to the incident room, ready to interview Abdal Shariq. They would need to be cautious in their approach, but some facts would have to be established. Who was he, exactly? Who did he work for? How had he wormed himself into such a position of confidence in the Hamdi set-up? And, most importantly, what could he tell them about the events of the last few weeks?

Rae was waiting for them, looking exasperated. 'You're too late.'

'What?' It took Sophie a few seconds to understand what she meant.

'They left five minutes ago. A Special Branch team came down from London and took him away. They had the security chief from the embassy with them. There was nothing we could do. I nearly got arrested myself.'

CHAPTER 36: BLUDGEON

Monday morning

Barry looked around at the assembled officers at the early-morning briefing. They all looked tired and jaded, as if they needed a good dose of vitamins and energy boosters, but all they had to hand was tea or coffee. Maybe the case would be wrapped up soon. There were only one or two loose ends remaining, weren't there? He glanced at Sophie, then at his notes, and cleared his throat. The group fell silent.

'We've got some initial forensic reports. There were several sets of fingerprints in that cellar that proved interesting, Stu Blackman's for one. At least one other set that they can't yet identify, but they're working on it. It's possible they might belong to Janella Ramos, but a lot more checking needs to be done.'

'Did Hamdi find out Blackman had been in the cellar, sir? Is that why he was killed?' George asked.

'Possibly. It would provide a motive because he'd have seen what we did — the guns. The documents that showed Hamdi was running weapons to the rebels back in his own country. That information would have been dynamite.'

'How would Hamdi know Stu had seen it, though?' George said.

'He had a simple webcam rigged up inside the cellar, along with an alarm. That's why he was there so quickly yesterday morning. When I opened that cupboard and found the hidden steps, he was alerted. He must have grabbed Shariq and gone there right away.'

Rose was puzzled. 'Why would Hamdi get involved with shady gun running in the first place? He had loads of dosh from his proper, legit dealings. Why bother with this rebel stuff?'

'People don't always support rebels for profit, Rose,' Sophie said. 'There's often an ideological motive, a belief in a cause. Rae discovered something interesting yesterday. Do you want to go ahead and explain, Rae?'

Rae rubbed her forehead wearily. 'His first wife, Shazia's mother, came from the rebel-held area. She was the daughter of a tribal chief. Soon after she had Shazia, she returned to visit her family and was killed in a rocket attack. Within a year, Hamdi had married again, but it looks like it was more a marriage of convenience. Press reports at the time described his first wife as a real firebrand.'

'A bit like Shazia herself,' Sophie added. 'And it helps to explain Shazia's constant belligerence. I wonder if she's been the driving force behind his help to the rebels. The shipments were going to that region of the country, and if she's got family links there — well, that says it all.'

'Do we need to bring her in?' Lydia asked.

Barry shook his head. 'Not unless we think she's involved with our local murders. Special Branch will investigate her for the international dealings, we've got enough on our plate. The search team are still working their way through the cellar, though we don't expect them to find much else. Remember, we'd already been through the rest of the building last week. All the juicy stuff came to light yesterday. At least it tied up the connection between our two bodies. We found a heavy bludgeon, wrapped up in a cloth and stowed in a dark corner. It's been cleaned, but forensics are confident they'll get something from it. Its shape fits the wound on Stu Blackman's head pretty closely, and quite possibly Janella Ramos's too. If they get some DNA from the grip, it'll be case closed.'

'So, what's left?' Rose asked.

'Vinny Foster. He's still on the loose. Somehow, he seems to be linked to everything. We want to find out more about his background and how much he was involved in Hamdi's operations. Then there's the incident that left Tommy in hospital. He's probably the last loose end.'

Rose frowned. 'What about this other Arab guy, Shariq? Isn't he the hard man here? What's he been saying since you lifted him?'

Barry glanced at Sophie, who said, 'He's been working undercover, Rose. He's a cop back in his own country. It causes a few problems because they didn't tell anyone here, which is what the accepted protocol says should happen. Special Branch have him at the moment, and they're keeping him well away from us, which suits me fine. He's taken up a lot of our time needlessly and scared young Amy Birkbeck half to death. On the plus side, he may have helped save Mia Lockhart's life, along with the younger Hamdi daughter, Gamila. Hamdi knew what she was up to. Shariq could have stayed back and done nothing and kept his cover intact. Thank God he didn't, because Mia and Gamila would probably be dead by now.

'So, as Barry said, that leaves us with Vinny Foster. Where's he hiding? Has he changed his car? What's he planning? Our guess is that he was closer to Hamdi than we first thought. He may have been involved directly with the two murders and then used Crustie Valentine and Mickie Rollins to dispose of the bodies. He's smarter than them. He's kept himself largely out of the limelight. If it hadn't been for that accident with Tommy, we might never have suspected him of anything. So, that's who we concentrate on now. We find him and bring him in. But we need to be careful. If he had access to

Hamdi's arms cache, he might have a gun. No going after him alone, anyone. Is that understood? We need to work with the armed-response unit. Anything to add, Rae? You interviewed him.'

Rae frowned. She was disappointed in herself for not spotting Vinny's central importance when she'd seen him a few days earlier. Yet how could she have known? She quickly put her thoughts in order.

'He's not stupid, so don't underestimate him. I also got the feeling that he could easily resort to violence. He's got the height and the weight to be able to look after himself in a scuffle. I wonder if he might also go to self-defence classes. He had a certificate on his office wall, but I couldn't make out the exact wording. I guess the key thing is not to let yourself be taken in by him. He'll try to come across as an engaging sort of guy, but in reality, he's a hardman. Remember that and you'll be okay.'

* * *

After the briefing was over, Lydia and Jimmy went to visit Mia, now safely ensconced in a secure location. They chatted while Mia put the kettle on and made them all a cup of tea.

'In a way, I'm a bit surprised you didn't make contact earlier,' Lydia said. 'Even with Jacob, just to set his mind at rest.'

'I wanted to, I really did, but Abdal explained how dangerous that could be. If Jacob let anything slip, it would have been easy to trace me. They all knew how friendly I was with Gamila, and she came up to visit several times — in secret of course. We were worried about what would happen to her if the news got out. Shazia would have started wondering, and she knows a lot about mobile phones and how to trace calls.'

'When did you find out that Abdal Shariq was working undercover?' Lydia asked.

'I didn't, not for sure. Gamila and I just realised there was more to him than we'd first thought. He hinted at it when he helped us out back in the autumn. But I trusted Gamila. It was only when Shazia arrived yesterday, much earlier than we expected, that it got difficult. I don't like her at all. She can be really nasty.' She changed the subject. 'When can I get back home, and start work again?'

'Don't be impatient, Mia. We're all working as hard as we can, but we have to be sure that everyone's accounted for.'

'Did they really kill a policeman? That's what made Abdal so cautious, I think.'

'It looks very much like it,' Lydia said, 'but we can't comment any further, not on an ongoing case. Look, as soon as we're sure you're safe we'll get you back to your home. We're all working flat out on this.'

* * *

Barry marched into Sophie's office, looking triumphant. 'Know what? Those forensic guys are wonderful, plain and simple.'

Sophie looked up. 'Something positive, then?'

He nodded, smiling. 'Just like we hoped, they got a minute speck of blood from a shoulder seam on that dress. It had somehow survived the cleaning process. And the DNA is fascinating. It nearly matches Suleiman Hamdi, but not quite.'

'Really? Let me guess. Fifty per cent?'

'Yup. It's probably one of his daughters. Gamila's already offered to give a DNA sample, so Rae's on her way there to take it now. That leaves Shazia.'

'Well, it fits, doesn't it? There could have been the same type of flare-up that happened with Mia at New Year, but Janella Ramos hit back even harder. Maybe we need to bring Shazia in after all. It looks as though she wasn't entirely honest with us last week. What do you think?'

Barry was about to answer when his phone started ringing. He glanced irritably at the caller display. 'Sorry. It's Dave Nash. I'd better take it.'

Sophie watched the various expressions flicker across Barry's face — surprise, satisfaction, puzzlement, incredulity. He slipped the phone back into his pocket, his mouth still open. 'Unbelievable.'

'Come on, Barry. Stop teasing me. Spill the beans, as the copper said to the allotment thief.'

Barry raised his eyebrows. He hadn't heard that one before. 'Dave fast-tracked a DNA check on the grip of that bludgeon. You'll never guess what the results showed.'

She sighed. 'No. I never will. Out with it.'

'A fifty per cent match with Hamdi. It wasn't him.'

Sophie was already out of her seat. 'Shazia. Let's go. You drive. I hate that road.'

* * *

They rang and rang the doorbell at Shazia's flat. There was no answer, no sound of movement. Should they break in or try to find her at the university? Sophie opted for the latter, so they drove back out of the city and up the steep incline of Bathwick Hill to the campus.

'It's lovely here,' she said to Barry as they approached the hilltop and its sprawl of modern buildings. 'A bit windswept in winter, mind you. I had a couple of friends who were students here. They really liked it. Great social life, but then that's true of most universities.'

Barry kept his mouth firmly closed, hoping she'd take the hint. For once, she did. Maybe one day she might register his annoyance with this middle-class obsession with universities, their campuses and their obscure hierarchies. Or was it just a weak point in his makeup, resentment because of his relatively poor farming background? He deliberately switched his attention back to the here and now. They drove into the campus, where he found a convenient parking bay close to the administration block. They hurried to the main door. It took them only minutes to identify themselves and find the information they were looking for. A member of staff took them across to the northern edge of the sprawl of buildings where the Politics Department was located. Shazia couldn't be found. She was meant to be attending a tutorial but hadn't turned up, a rare occurrence for her. None of the other students had seen her.

Sophie turned to Barry. 'She's done a runner. We'll need to get into her flat after all.'

* * *

It was afternoon before the frustrated pair got back to the incident room at Wareham. Shazia's flat had yielded no clues as to her whereabouts. A simultaneous search of all the known Hamdi properties in the Poole area, carried out by the rest of the squad, had also failed to find her. Had there been an escape plan in place all along? One triggered by an incident such as her father's arrest the previous day? It certainly looked like it. Could she even have fled the country? Sophie wondered if she had been guilty of a lack of foresight. Should she have anticipated this and planned for it? She sighed and turned to Barry.

'It's going pear-shaped after all. Despite all our best efforts. Those unmentionables from Special Branch have really mucked things up for us by whisking Shariq away with them. We're left in the dark when we could be using him to pin this all down.' She shook her head wearily. 'I'll tell you what the problem is. They know I've got a direct link with Yauvani Anand, so they've jumped the gun to prevent me using it. Bastards.'

'You can't contact her now and ask for her help?' Barry said.

Sophie shook her head. 'No. That would put her in a difficult position. A Home Secretary can't act outside of normal protocols, not without ruffling too many feathers. It might cost her the job. I wouldn't want to put her in that position. It wouldn't surprise me if Shariq, or whoever he really is, has already been whisked out of the country, back to the Gulf, with Whitehall approval. They'd want to get their tracks covered quickly. You've got to hand it to them. We didn't realise it, but someone in Whitehall's been watching us like hawks and knew when it was time to act.'

'Maybe Shariq got a message back to his handler.'

'Yes. The strange thing is, I was convinced he wanted to help us. Maybe having given us the clues, he decided he'd done enough.' She looked at her watch. 'Well, there's nothing we can do about it now. Let's get on with wrapping things up.'

CHAPTER 37: REVERSE AMBUSH

Amy Birkbeck was in her element. It was almost two o'clock on a cool but dry January afternoon, and as usual, she was way out in front. She was feeling particularly pleased with herself. This wasn't the weekly routine cross-country run. This was the end-of-month area competition, open to all the schools in East Dorset and, on this occasion, held on home turf. Of course, this gave her an advantage, since she knew the terrain. She could anticipate the inclines and bends in the track, knowing when to hold back a little in order to build up extra strength to power up the next slope. She was so far ahead that a quick backward glance showed only two of the other competitors within sight, and they weren't cutting into her lead. She just kept running, moving smoothly and efficiently, trying to remain on the drier side of the path where the footholds were rather firmer, resulting in a slightly lower expenditure of energy. She was now on the third lap of five and approaching the most remote part of the circuit, a turn into a lightly wooded area that edged up against one of the other local farms. She could see some sheep ahead, in the field that lay to the right of the route she was following, but they disappeared from view as she entered a scrawny copse.

What was that woman doing there, standing beside the path? She hadn't been there on the previous laps. She was fairly young, with olive skin and dark hair peeping out from under a headscarf. Maybe she knew someone in the race and had decided to cheer them on from further back than the finish line. Amy ran past, then down the slope to a bend by a clump of bushes. There was someone there too, a man this time, tall and thickset. He had a phone in his hand, which he was just putting back into his pocket. He looked up as she approached. Instinctively, Amy accelerated and shot past. This was the most remote part of the circuit, the most difficult for spectators to reach. What were they doing there? Who were they? She felt uneasy. Had she seen that man somewhere before? She turned various questions over in her mind as she turned and ran along the home straight, passing the lap marker. Should she stop and tell someone about the two spectators in the furthest part of the circuit? Maybe she was just being paranoid. She decided to see if they were still there on the next lap. This was the most important race of this half-term, with selection for the county championship at stake. She couldn't afford to slow down now and risk losing her place.

Amy kept up her steady pace, still moving smoothly and showing no sign of fatigue. She was on her fourth lap and the path was getting increasingly chewed up, with the muddy areas expanding. It was becoming increasingly hard to find a good grip in some spots. She was forced to run a bit more slowly than before on the uphill section, but she knew the same problem would face the other competitors, so she wasn't worried. She regained her momentum on the long section along the ridgetop. She was happy with the way the race was going but a little apprehensive about those two spectators. Maybe they'd have gone by the time she reached the copse. She turned the corner and saw no one there. Phew. Amy ran extra fast as she went down the slope, then slowed slightly as she turned the bottom corner and started to accelerate. There he was. And the woman was there too, on the other side of the track. They were waiting for her. They'd left only a couple of feet between them for her to run through. It was a trap. Their eyes were fixed on her and their bodies were poised, as if to make a grab when she ran past. And now she knew who he was — the man who'd been lurking in the farmyard late the other night.

She lurched right, just avoiding crashing into a bush and jumped over a small ditch. This route took her behind him. He was already turning, and the woman stepped across the muddy running path to cut off any chance Amy had of regaining the track. Amy didn't hesitate. She veered off further to the right, heading deeper into the woods. It wasn't a race against the other competitors anymore. It was a race for her life.

* * *

Rae was feeling frustrated, but there was no one to vent her anger to. She'd wanted to catch the whole of Amy's important race, joining the young girl's family in wishing her good luck and watching the start. It was not to be. In an investigation like this one, work took priority. She glanced at the clock on the dashboard as she drove into the car park and swung into a vacant spot. Maybe she'd be in time to catch the closing stages of the race. Even though she was in a hurry, she still glanced around as she stepped away from her own car, a habit ingrained into her detective's brain. She stood still. Across in the far corner was a dark-coloured Jeep. She could see the pink furry dice dangling from the rear-view mirror. And next to it, a silver BMW sports car. Vinny Foster and Shazia Hamdi. Here, at Amy's cross-country event.

Rae grabbed her phone and put through an urgent call to her boss as she ran to the start point and the small cluster of onlookers. She stopped short and looked at the spectators spread out in front of her. She spotted Amy's parents and the family liaison officer, Theresa Jackson, standing some ten yards further on. She recognised a few faces from the previous week's race, probably staff and a few hardy parents. But no Vinny Foster and no Shazia Hamdi. So where were they? If they were up to no good, they'd probably be at a remote part of the track. But why? Rae managed to catch Theresa's eye and beckoned to her. Then she ran, with Theresa following, across the track, jumped the rope at the other side and hurried across the open heathland towards where she expected the circuit to lead. There was a thin area of woodland across there, the ideal spot for an ambush. But what could be the reason for such a drastic course of action? Unless, of course, Foster had been the shadowy third figure near the pool that Sunday night and the person Amy spotted lurking in the farmyard a few nights earlier. Was Shazia the second figure? What if they'd seen her face at the window? Rae hurried on, hoping desperately that she wasn't too late.

She slowed slightly to allow Theresa to catch up and, gasping, told her of her suspicions. They hurried towards the far corner of the route and found the rest of the runners bunched together in a group, with the two who'd been in second and third place gesticulating furiously. They'd seen two strangers attempt to seize Amy and wanted the other runners to join them in a chase.

Rae and Theresa told them all to return to the start and wait, then set off in the direction described by the two runners. They were joined by Amy's father, who had spotted them crossing the field. Rae decided not to refuse his help. The presence of the strong, fit farmer would be a bonus once they tracked down the missing Amy and her pursuers. The witnesses had said they'd only seen two people confront Amy, and the descriptions corresponded to Vinny Foster and Shazia Hamdi, but what if there were others?

* * *

Amy quickly calmed down once she realised she had several clear advantages over her two pursuers. She was faster, quieter and knew the terrain. She had a clearer idea of where she was and where she wanted to go. She also knew the truth of the matter — that she and her pursuers were trapped inside a large, semi-circular loop of the River Frome with nowhere to cross. Added to which, following the heavy rainstorms earlier in the month, the river had partly burst its banks, causing big pools of shallow flood water to collect in the lower-lying areas, although these had started to recede in the past week or two. She'd seen enough of her pursuers to spot that the man was wearing heavy boots, but not the woman. She was in flat ankle boots that looked fashionable and comfortable but were probably not best suited to running across wet, slippery ground.

Amy soon realised that it would be easy to lose her two pursuers, certainly in this scrubby area. So, which way should she lead them? She was at one disadvantage, of course. She knew that she could run in near silence but, even with her hearing implants turned to maximum, she could only just make out the occasional sound of heavy footfalls behind her. She would need to be very careful. She ran north, towards the river. To the east lay the village of Stoborough. She'd been at Stoborough Primary for six years — it was where she'd first taken up cross-country running. She knew where she was, and she knew these narrow paths. She broke out into the open, ran twenty yards, turned and stood facing back, hands on hips, getting her breath back. She saw three figures in pursuit, further back on the slope, not yet descended to flood-plain level. Yes, that was her father. The other two were the police officers, Rae and Theresa. She waved and was rewarded with a return wave from her dad.

This was quickly followed by the muffled sound of someone breaking through undergrowth. The man appeared, already mud-spattered and gasping heavily. He was soon joined by the woman, equally out of breath, her trousers covered with streaks of dirt and her face grimy. She looked as if she'd fallen into one of the ditches that Amy had leapt across. The young girl watched them carefully. What would they do?

Rapidly, the two separated and advanced on her, trying to come at her from the sides in a sort of pincer movement. She turned and ran, this time more slowly. She kept to a path a couple of inches above the surrounding field. Amy knew it from her running sessions at the primary school, under the watchful eye of one of the teachers. She was luring them, bit by bit, into a damp, soggy area. Moreover, they were no longer close together.

She stopped and turned. They had both slowed, their feet sticking in deep mud. Amy took a breath and ran as fast as she could back the way she had come. She shot between them before they could move more than a couple of yards. They slithered towards the path she was on and finally made it onto the firmer surface. At the same time, the three pursuers appeared, having broken free of the bushes. Amy ran towards them and threw herself into her father's arms.

Vinny Foster sank to his knees, clearly exhausted. Shazia Hamdi stood panting, glaring at the approaching group. In the distance, the flashing blue lights of squad cars could be seen drawing to a halt at the end of the track.

'I've lost the race,' Amy gasped.

'No, you haven't,' her father said. 'The other runners saw what happened and decided to abandon it. If I could write tomorrow's headlines, guess what they'd say? "Amy Birkbeck Wins Through!"' He hugged her.

'In every sense,' Rae added. She watched the two would-be abductors, looking furious, trudge in their direction. A police Land Rover appeared ahead, blue lights flashing. Another came up behind them, having found a way into the field from a farm track.

'Looks like the cavalry has arrived,' she added, a wry smile on her face.

CHAPTER 38: INVITATIONS

Friday evening

'How's Amy?' Barry asked. He was standing at the bar of the Halfway Inn, ordering a round of drinks. Andy Birkbeck was beside him.

'She's fine. She's basking in the glory of not only winning a place on the county cross-country team but also helping to capture two criminals. Apparently, she's become her school's number-one celebrity. That's a big step up from her previous position as "that odd deaf girl who keeps bat boxes." Geraldine heard it from some of the other mothers. Apparently, Amy's friends can't stop talking about it.'

'Well, she did show tremendous maturity in how she coped on Monday afternoon. I can't think of many adults who'd have been so cool-headed.'

'It could have turned out very differently, though, couldn't it?' Andy said. 'The thought keeps me awake at night.'

'Life is full of what-ifs,' Barry said. 'Don't let yourself get obsessed with them.' He picked up the tray of drinks and carried it towards their cluster of tables, Andy following. He handed a glass of orange juice and a packet of crisps to the young girl. 'Any idea what you might want to be when you grow up, Amy?'

Amy shrugged, and started to pop crisps into her mouth.

'I think she sees herself as the next David Attenborough,' Geraldine said, smiling. 'That, or Britain's answer to Greta Thunberg.' She looked at her watch. 'We can only stay twenty minutes. It's already way past Alex's bed-time.'

Amy finished her mouthful. 'I'm just gonna stay on the farm,' she said. 'I want to take over when Dad's too old.'

Andy ruffled her hair. 'That's my girl. It's the best answer you could have given.'

* * *

Mia and Jacob were back in the La Scala Italian restaurant, the scene of their first date two weeks earlier.

'Could we go clubbing afterwards?' Mia suggested. 'I feel like celebrating.'

'Is that why you're wearing that dress?' Jacob replied, smiling. 'I thought it was a bit racy for a casual meal.'

Mia frowned. 'Is it too conspicuous? I only bought it yesterday. It's a bit, er, flimsier than the stuff I normally wear. I thought it might be too revealing.'

'I'm not complaining,' Jacob said. 'It really suits you. That shade of green really goes with your skin tone.'

'Thanks. Some of the others from the office said they'd be in Red Zone tonight. It's that newish club that's opened up down by the harbourside. It's meant to be really good. Shall we try it?'

'Fine by me. Don't expect too much of me though, I'm not much of a dancer.'

Mia laughed. 'Don't worry. You make up for it in other ways.'

She wrapped some more spaghetti inexpertly around her fork and shoved it into her mouth, trailing ends and slurping them up. 'I'm useless at this. I need a bib, not a serviette.'

'What's happened to the Hamdi family? Do you know?' Jacob asked, serious now.

'I was really worried about Gamila,' Mia said, 'but she phoned me earlier and we had a long chat. She and her mum are still in the house, so I may call round sometime over the weekend so I can collect my laptop. She was keeping it hidden for me. She said her mum was actually rather relieved. She'd grown more distant from Hamdi once she realised how many secrets he was keeping from her. She comes from quite a wealthy family, so she'll be looked after, I expect.'

'Well, that's good. Will they be able to stay in Britain?'

Mia shrugged. 'I think they'll have to wait and see. But they can't have much hope, can they? Not after what he was up to. And as for Shazia — well, I'd never imagined her to be quite that bad. I knew she wasn't very nice, but a murderer? God, I'd have been more careful if I'd known.'

'Best forget it, Mia,' Jacob said.

'Only I can't, can I? I'll be a witness in the trial.' She looked glum.

'You'll be looked after. And I'll be around — that's if you'd like me to be.'

She gave him that lovely, heart-warming smile. It lit up her face.

* * *

Empty and near-empty plates littered the tabletop, along with wine and beer glasses. Sophie leaned back and glanced around at her colleagues. Rae had obviously caught up on her lost sleep and was her usual bubbly self. Rose was on the phone to her teenage son, asking him to switch her electric blanket on so she could fall straight into bed when she arrived home. George was glancing at his watch, obviously judging when it would be safe for him to leave. He'd been on soft drinks all evening because he had to drive to Oxford later, where he was spending the weekend with Jade. Tommy was still looking tired but less so than before. He was well on the road to recovery. Lydia and Jimmy seemed ready to leave, making sure they'd made enough of a contribution to the kitty, a pile of banknotes in the middle of the table. They all looked reasonably relaxed and seemed to have enjoyed the evening. Except for Barry. Sophie looked at him again. What was wrong with him? He'd been unable to settle since the departure of the Birkbeck family more than an hour earlier. He looked jittery and nervous.

This needed pursuing, Sophie decided. 'Barry, what on earth's wrong? You look as though the world's about to end.'

He sighed, reached inside his jacket pocket and pulled out a bundle of envelopes. 'I've been putting it off,' he said. 'Waiting for the right time. I'm not sure this is it, but Gwen won't be happy if I put it off any longer.'

Suddenly everyone was looking at him. He pushed an envelope towards each of them.

'Is this what I think it is?' Sophie asked, recognising the handwriting on her envelope.

He shrugged. 'Probably.'

Looking at each other and murmuring, they opened their envelopes and extracted some cards. Written in Gwen's neat hand, each one invited the recipient to attend her wedding to Detective Inspector Barry Marsh.

'About time, Barry,' Sophie said. She spread her arms wide, wrapped them around him and gave him a loud kiss. 'About bloody time.'

THE END

ACKNOWLEDGEMENTS & NOTES

This is the tenth Sophie Allen novel and won't be the last. Producing a set of novels such as this is very much a team effort. I'd like to thank all the staff at Joffe Books for their support and help since the first novel, *Dark Crimes*, was published. Emma Grundy Haigh for her enthusiasm and help, plus Rudi, Nina, Jill and the others. But there are two people I need to thank especially: Jasper Joffe (the boss) is due extra gratitude for showing faith in me back when I was a rookie novelist, and Anne Derges, my main editor throughout the series, has helped so much. I can't thank Jasper and Anne enough.

Thanks are also due to my fellow Joffe authors. They're a great bunch and they use social media much more proficiently than me. I sometimes feel ashamed of my half-hearted attempts to use Facebook. I loathe the bloody thing! I'd like to reassure readers, though, that if they email me direct, they will always get a response. I do like email. Visit my website (www.michaelhambling.co.uk) to make use of my contact form.

I'm very grateful to my sister-in-law, Liz Mason. Liz, who lives in Paisley, is a retired teacher of the deaf and was very helpful in answering my questions about deafness in children. This allowed me to have confidence that I was getting the details of Amy's hearing problems correct. Any errors are mine.

Norden

The fictional farm where Amy's family live is near Norden. This small hamlet, close to Corfe Castle, lies at the northwest end of the Swanage Steam Railway, so visitors can park their cars and hop on a historic train in order to steam down the line to Swanage. It's a beautiful journey. The area is criss-crossed by miles of public footpaths — through woods, heath, farmland and across the Purbeck Hills.

Food and Drink

A few explanatory points about the food and drink mentioned in this novel. Blue Vinny is a famous Dorset cheese. We love it. It's comparable to Stilton but has a slightly softer, more mellow flavour. Why not try it with some crackers? I suppose the popular biscuit for this cheese is the somewhat saucily named Dorset Knob, but it's good on any wheaten crackers. You can buy them both at the Purbeck Deli shop in Swanage, along with a whole range of other goodies, including the lovely beers from Hattie Brown's Brewery. These beers are fine in bottled form, but to get the real taste visit the famous Square and Compass Inn in the nearby village of Worth Matravers, where you can sit in the garden, drinking the draught versions of Hattie Brown's ales, eating the pub's famous pasties and gazing across the hummocky grazing land to the sea beyond. Sophie and Martin Allen are regulars there (in my imagination, anyway). If the four-mile walk from Swanage along Priests' Way or the slightly longer trek along the coast path puts you off, the number 40 bus drops you a mile from the pub. Or you can remain in Swanage and visit two of my other favourite pubs, the Black Swan and the Red Lion. Both pubs include Blue Vinny on their cheeseboards.

Norden is close to a cluster of good pubs in Corfe Castle. In the other direction, towards Wareham, there's a beautiful thatched pub called the Halfway Inn (mentioned in the final chapter) only a mile or two away. The nearby town of Wareham has some great pubs, and its ancient Saxon walls are worth a look, as is the picturesque riverside quay.

GLOSSARY

A & E: Accident and Emergency Unit in a hospital.

Home Office: a ministerial department in the UK government, responsible for immigration, security and law and order.

PPS: Parliamentary Private Secretary; an MP who functions as the eyes and ears of a government minister, often seen as the first stepping-stone to a future ministerial career.

Special Branch: an arm of the UK police service that deals with terrorism.

UK Police Ranks (in descending order of seniority)
Chief Constable (or Commissioner in London's Metropolitan Police Service)
Deputy CC (Deputy Commissioner in London)
Assistant CC (Assistant Commissioner in London)
Chief Superintendent
Superintendent
Chief Inspector
Inspector
Sergeant
Constable

Detectives hold the same ranks but with a prefix before the name (DC, DS, etc.) There is sometimes career movement back and forth between detectives and uniformed ranks.

THE JOFFE BOOKS STORY

We began in 2014 when Jasper agreed to publish his mum's much-rejected romance novel and it became a bestseller.

Since then we've grown into the largest independent publisher in the UK. We're extremely proud to publish some of the very best writers in the world, including Joy Ellis, Faith Martin, Caro Ramsay, Helen Forrester, Simon Brett and Robert Goddard. Everyone at Joffe Books loves reading and we never forget that it all begins with the magic of an author telling a story.

We are proud to publish talented first-time authors, as well as established writers whose books we love introducing to a new generation of readers.

We won Trade Publisher of the Year at the Independent Publishing Awards in 2023 and Best Publisher Award in 2024 at the People's Book Prize. We have been shortlisted for Independent Publisher of the Year at the British Book Awards for the last five years, and were shortlisted for the Diversity and Inclusivity Award at the 2022 Independent Publishing Awards. In 2023 we were shortlisted for Publisher of the Year at the RNA Industry Awards, and in 2024 we were shortlisted at the CWA Daggers for the Best Crime and Mystery Publisher.

We built this company with your help, and we love to hear from you, so please email us about absolutely anything bookish at feedback@joffebooks.com.

If you want to receive free books every Friday and hear about all our new releases, join our mailing list: www.joffebooks.com/free-books

And when you tell your friends about us, just remember: it's pronounced Joffe as in coffee or toffee!

Printed in Dunstable, United Kingdom

64628527R00160